"Strong and vivid."

— *The New York Times Book Review*

"Not to be missed."

— *The Sunday Times*

"Detailed, realistic, and with excellent character development and motivation, this is as good as . . . Scott Turow's *Presumed Innocent.*"

— *Library Journal*

"Forceful, vibrant, highly-charged."

— *Booklist*

"Intriguing . . . action-filled . . . An entertaining intelligent look at police work and the law."

— *The News Journal* (Wilmington)

"Brandt writes with energy and an insider's knowledge of the criminal justice system."

— *The Birmingham* (AL) *News*

"Unique insights . . . blending a fast pace with realistic detail."

— *Richmond Times-Dispatch*

"A winner! . . . Lots of action, a crazed vigilante, a couple of murders, a little romance…fascinating."

— *Knight Ridder Newspapers*

"Just when you think all the angles have been written and the stories told, along comes someone like Brandt . . ."

— *Star-Banner* (FL)

"An excellent, wonderfully entertaining crime story. From beginning to end, a superb page-turner with an expert's eye throughout."

—**Robert K. Tanenbaum**

STEERFORTH

The Right to Remain Silent

The Right to Remain Silent

a novel

Charles Brandt

STEERFORTH PRESS
LEBANON, NEW HAMPSHIRE

Steerforth Press L.L.C., 31 Hanover Street, Suite 1
Lebanon, New Hampshire 03766

Cataloging-in-Publication Data is available from the Library of Congress

Printed in the United States of America

ISBN 978-1-58642-263-9

1 3 5 7 9 10 8 6 4 2

For Tripp, Mimi, and Jenny Rose; Laura and Denis

PREFACE

A street crime wave hit the major cities of the US starting roughly in 1961. At first those of us living in New York were told it was an illusion created by new methods of recording crime. There weren't more crimes, just more crimes being reported.

Across the country, chiefs of police, on the other hand, said that the increase in street crime was real and had been created by new US Supreme Court rulings that, it was felt, diminished the rights of policemen to search and to interrogate, each a major tool of police work. The rules increased the rights of criminals to be free from searches and questioning, rights my pals and I never had as teens.

Women found tighter and safer ways to carry their pocketbooks. Soon there were fewer and fewer pocketbooks being seen on the streets.

As a welfare investigator in East Harlem, I watched my territory's streets become more dangerous due to the crimes related to the 1960s epidemic of drugs that were sold on the top floors of the apartment buildings I entered to make home visits. By the time I left East Harlem to go to Brooklyn Law School in 1966, it was no longer possible to blame the crime wave on better methods of crime reporting.

My goal was to be a prosecutor in the Brooklyn District Attorney's office. Then a month prior to graduation during a speech on the importance of ethics to lawyers by the Brooklyn DA Eugene Gold,[1] a classmate with whom I was very close leaned over and said, "Listen to this bullshit; my husband delivered a bag of cash to him on Atlantic Avenue. He split it with Aaron Koota," the prior DA who'd become a trial court judge.

I called friends in Delaware — where I had gone to college — who had been urging me to become a prosecutor there. Overnight I moved to Delaware to do just that. Delaware was and is a state judged to have the highest ethical standards at the bench and bar.

Unexpectedly, I found that the Delaware I had known in college, ten years earlier, had become riot-torn and with a high murder rate, no longer a safe place, not even close to the relative safety of Brooklyn.

In Delaware the Office of the Attorney General has jurisdiction over every single crime, from speeding tickets to first-degree murders. On May 1, 1971, Attorney General W. Laird Stabler, Jr., swore me in as a deputy attorney general. The chief of police of New Castle County stood beside Stabler as he explained to me that he expected his deputies to provide assistance to the police in the field, especially in murder cases. The police were to have our unlisted phone numbers. We could expect to be called as soon as a body was found. This was necessary because of new rulings that were coming down from the bench with regularity restricting police. We prosecutors were to ensure that a rule violation did not cause a good murder case to be thrown out of court. We were to carry guns when appropriate.

Then Stabler had the chief swear me in with the powers of a policeman. After three years in the office, thanks to the

1 In 1983, Gold would would confess to molesting a child.

detective work I did in the field and the jury trial work I did in the courtroom, Laird swore me in as his chief deputy attorney general. I was to carry Badge Number Two as the second-highest law enforcement officer in the state. Laird's successor as attorney general, the experienced and talented Dick Wier, kept me on in that capacity for two more years. We worked eighty-hour weeks in the AG's office, and for more than five years I participated by my count in more than fifty homicide and attempted homicide investigations. I had a knack for interrogation and for working my way around the new rules governing murder cases, staying within the law. I had expert tutoring by outstanding detectives such as Stan Friedman, the supervisor of the Wilmington Robbery Squad, whose jurisdiction included homicide. Stan's badge adorns the front cover of this book.

Recently, talking old times on the phone, Stan said to me: "I can't believe you were in the office only five years. If I had to guess I would have said twenty, all the shit you did."

The book in your hands is fiction, but it's based on some of the actual "shit" I did, including interrogations and confessions that convicted the shooters of a policeman in the head and the near strangulation of a child by a young drug user who, on release from jail, shot both of his own parents to death.

When I left the AG's office in 1976 to start my own law practice, I continued to work murder cases, now as a defense attorney, while I concentrated on medical law. I represented Frank "The Irishman" Sheeran, a Mafia hit man chronicled in my book *I Heard You Paint Houses*,[2] and got him released from prison many years early on medical grounds.

The Right to Remain Silent is a novel written and to be read for entertainment, but it also encourages study of the art of

---

2 Steerforth Press, 2004

interrogation and contains the line that "confession is one of the necessities of life, like food and shelter." To quote my interrogation mentor, the late Wilmington detective Charlie Burke, "They want to tell you, Choll."

Though the big Irishman, Frank Sheeran, had been indicted along the way for the murders of Robert "Lonnie" DeGeorge, Fred Gawronski, and Francis "Big Bobby" Marino, he was never convicted, and he had never talked about his life of violence to an outsider. Whenever he was hauled before a grand jury as a suspect in the murder of Teamster president Jimmy Hoffa, he asserted his Fifth Amendment rights. He read this book while serving a long sentence for convictions on lesser crimes, and its major theme triggered his own sense of remorse, a remorse I would prey on to obtain confession upon confession to his participation in twenty-five to thirty murders, including those of Hoffa and Joey Gallo, and to his guilty knowledge of the Mafia's role in the assassination of President Kennedy, all portrayed in *I Heard You Paint Houses*. His decision to hire me to pursue his early medical release from prison was made with the knowledge that, like the fictional hero of *The Right to Remain Silent*, Lou Razzi, I had cracked cases through interrogation and confession. The five-year process during which I would handle the Irishman like a hostile witness had its genesis in 1988 with this novel.

Charles Brandt
Ketchum, Idaho
January 2020

The Right to Remain Silent

1

January 9, 1961 7:40 P.M.

"Figaro, Figaro, Figaro," I said to myself and took my foot off the gas. "That's no way to make a friend." I lowered Elvis's latest hit record on the car radio and had to pump my brakes to keep from sliding. The City of Wilmington snowplows hadn't yet reached the bottom of French Street. Had I kept inching my way home and ignored Figaro, the next fifteen years would have been different, but facts are facts.

John Figaro in plain view under a streetlight — white male, age twenty-two, apprentice number writer — had just kicked a lone little girl's sled out of his path on the sidewalk. It made the child cry. She leaped past Figaro after her runaway sled. He paid no attention to her crying or to her sled, even when it bumped into the white concrete stoop of an old brick row house. Figaro had a look on his face that said that nothing was going to stand in the way of this badass tonight. He was content. One kick was good. A man of purpose, he strutted down the block toward Janasek's Hotel.

I adjusted my rearview mirror a little at a time to keep his back in sight while I steered to the curb and parked by a hydrant. Figaro had been had for many crimes in his brief life. And now sled-kicking. They're writing grand opera,

John, but not about you, and from the looks of things they never will.

I clicked the radio all the way off. Elvis would have to wonder if she was still lonesome some other night.

Figaro passed into the yellow glare coming from the glass door of Janasek's melancholy excuse for a hotel. In the lighting, his camel's-hair topcoat looked new. And it fit poorly, like a stolen coat bought off the back of a truck. I noticed a bulge inside the coat under his left arm. Bearing goodies larger than number sheets, I'd say, John. With a skip he lightfooted up the steps and disappeared into the hotel.

"Figaro, Figaro, Figaro," I said again and stared at the hotel entrance. Have you been naughtier than usual?

To begin with, I asked myself, what is John Figaro doing with a camel's-hair anything? What the hell, Figaro. You look collegiate. That's the word, *collegiate*. Sis, boom, bah. And right then I decided to follow him. I got out and quietly closed the door of my '56 red-and-black Ford convertible.

The little girl, no more than eight and snowsuited, lay across her old rusty sled, shielding it from the Figaros of the world the way the Secret Service protects the president from gunfire. Her big brown eyes looked up in wonder at my blue uniform. She appeared to be a Gypsy, probably from one of the families that used to move in and out of the flats around the corner on Front Street.

"Sled okay, honey?" I asked as I squatted to her.

"Curse him," she whimpered defiantly, tears still filling her eyes.

"Let me take this one, partner." I touched her light-brown cheek and straightened up. "I'm good at sled-kickers."

There, now I felt like a detective again. I'd spent this day off of mine working a private-pay job, directing traffic for society wedding guests. My uniform smelled of mothballs. I hadn't worn it in three years, and I'd never worked a private-pay job before. Rent a real cop in a real uniform with a real gun, for those times democracy doesn't provide enough privilege. You see, my wife, Marian, was unplanned-pregnant and going around the house singing songs with the word *money* in them. So at the age of twenty-eight, at the dawn of the New Frontier, I signed the duty roster for private-pay jobs. Now, on my way home, I figured I had the right to stop off for a little real-cop nightcap.

By walking to Janasek's four-story reddish-brown brick hotel instead of backing up my car, I'd be giving Figaro enough time to get settled into whatever he had in mind. Figaro always had a sly way of looking up to no good, but on this blustery night he looked to be overachieving. Even so, I didn't figure him for a stickup of one of Janasek's marathon crap games, or anything as sis, boom, bah as that. You don't kick sleds on your way to a robbery.

Janasek's Hotel, long since demolished, was near the southern border of the city, a half block up from the Pennsy Station. A nice convenience for high rollers from New York City. They'd take the two-hour train ride south to roll the dice at Janasek's Hotel in Delaware, then indulge their lower torsos in a little salt-and-pepper lust at Janasek's other joint, the appropriately named Body & Soul Lounge across the state line in Chester, Pennsylvania. It was a regular package deal. Rumor on the job had it that old-time actors like George Raft and Lawrence Tierney still came down for the tour. No, the little raisin might be up to something big, but he couldn't get into the crapshoot at Janasek's, much less stick it up. Figaro was a Lincoln Street Little Italy cool guy who up until tonight had always given the impression of knowing his place and keeping it.

He'll leave the New York gamblers alone, I thought, and so will I unless I can't avoid them. Actually, I felt a little sorry for them. The New Yorkers had had enough trouble last October with Mazeroski's World Series home run. Besides, gambling's belonged to Vice since the beginning of time, and detectives have always stayed out of it with pleasure. And, too, Janasek supplied Vice with so-called valuable information, and he kept his prostitutes across the border at the Body & Soul. He'd earned the right to be left alone in Wilmington, or so they claimed.

I opened the glass door, and the smell of a century or more's accumulation of tobacco attacked my nostrils. I moved into the hazy, overheated lobby and patted snow from my dress blues. It melted when it hit the green floral-design linoleum.

A trail of probably Figaro's melted snow led to a flamingo-pink Formica reception counter. On a stool behind it, next to an antique brass cash register painted high-gloss pink, sat Janasek himself. His shiny red face was full of smooth, rounded fat and topped by fluffy white hair. It made him look like Santa Claus without the beard. He had on an orange flannel shirt buttoned at the neck. His double chin hung over it. He wore black suspenders. He grunted through the gray hairs coming out of his nose, put down his dog-eared copy of *Peyton Place*, and peered at me from wire granny glasses.

"Where's your fuckin' luggage, rook'?" He snarled like a pit bull at a cocker spaniel. "You gotta have luggage to register here. You better go check with Vice before you go hangin' out in my joint. Scarin' my guests. You gotta be new. You don't like walkin' around the snow, you shoulda been a bartender. This ain't the little town of Bethlehem, and I ain't runnin' no fuckin' manger."

I took off my patrolman's hat, raised my head and displayed my full face, and said, "Jingle bells, Janasek."

He took off his glasses and cleared his throat, but didn't say anything.

"You wired tight with Vice?" I asked. "My new partner just moved in out of Vice. I'm going to make a point of asking him all about your luggage requirement. Do you know Detective Rocco DiGiacomo?"

He opened his mouth, about to answer, but inhaled through it instead.

"Don't ever hold back with me, Janasek. Know my partner, or don't you?"

"I don't know," he said. "I don't know if I know him."

"I'm going to ask you a different question. Point blank. Janasek, are you a godless communist?"

I waited with my mouth open, kind of dopey, adenoidal. He folded his granny glasses and put them in his shirt pocket.

"They're for readin'," he said casually, leaning on the counter, cozy, as if it didn't matter whether it was me or some rookie cop. "These glasses fuck up my straight-ahead vision. I couldn't tell it was you. How come you're wearin' a uniform?" He hadn't responded to my communist question, and he didn't wait for me to answer his uniform question. He steadied his voice and his gaze, and then said, "You want something from me, Detective Razzi? Seriously, what do you want?"

"Your mouth sounds dry, Janasek. Getting the heebie-jeebies?"

"No. You don't worry me. Why should I be worried? It's just funny we never met before. In a small city like this. Seriously, what are you actually here for? You ain't in Vice now or nothin', are you? Ah, what am I talking about? I know you ain't in Vice." He chuckled softly. "The uniform."

"Are you a communist? It's a simple question. Let me put it another way; do you support Mao Tse-tung or Chiang Kai-shek? Or do you not give a shit?"

Once again he ignored my nonsense. He ground his teeth audibly. He barely heard me, a sign of a man more interested in protecting whatever is on his own mind.

"Look, I ain't got nothin' to hide," he said. "I'm just sayin', you know. I seen your picture in the paper all the time. Always solvin' some murder. 'S funny we never met or been introduced or nothin'. Let's forget about before. Put that totally behind us." He paused to chuckle. "All them smart remarks about luggage and Vice and all. That's me. I'm just sittin' here by myself. Then the next thing you know I start gettin' grouchy."

"You keep getting grouchy and you won't go to heaven."

"Yeah." He chuckled for the third time. "You know, seriously, by the time I was raggin' you about bartendin' I could already tell it was you. I was just layin' it on. Now let's get down to brass tacks. Let's start gettin' frank with each other. What can I do for you, I mean personally. Not the whole Detective Division, y'mean?"

"I think you're getting to the good part."

He cleared his throat, wiped his hair, and said, "Maybe you need a little information? Is that it? I ain't a stoolie, but however, I hear things. I like to do whatever I can for the dicks. Youse got it toughest of everybody. Believe me I know."

"Outstanding." I pulled my four-inch .38 from my holster and held it in my right hand pointing toward the floor. Sweat formed on his forehead, the way it quickly forms on some people when they first walk into a steam bath at the Y. "Don't your guests ever put their shooting irons on the poker table?" I asked. "I think I'll set off your fire alarm and see what tumbles down the stairs."

"Aw c'mon," he said quickly.

"Then give me Figaro's room key."

"Figaro," he said with relief. "Jesus Christ. Is that all you want? I ain't got nothin' to do with him, the little shit."

"The little shit's key, please."

"He took both of them, I swear." He pointed a chubby finger at 208 on the key rack.

"Give me your master."

"We don't keep no master. My hand to God. That's common knowledge. And that you really could check with Vice. There's lots of people like it we don't keep no master key. It's what you call a selling point. Y'mean? A guy wants good privacy he takes both keys off the rack. You know, a married man with his secretary." He winked.

I winked back. "Is he alone?"

"Not unless somebody come from another room, which is possible, but ain't likely, or flew in the window, which ain't possible and ain't likely." He winked again.

"Is he expecting anybody?" I winked again. "You know, to sit on his lap for dictation and talk about the first thing that comes up."

"I don't know. . . . Ah, well. What the hell." He leaned closer and glanced over each shoulder before continuing. "He didn't say who she was. Look, this ain't none of my business. Seriously. I wish I knew more. He walks in and pays cash in advance for one night for him and some snatch that's gonna come later. I ain't no rat, but however, if I knew he was up to somethin' more than knockin' off a little poontang, I'd tell you."

Now it was my turn to glance over each shoulder and lean closer, wide-eyed. "Deep down I know you're keeping something from me." I smiled. "And I resent that."

"I already talked too much. If it was anybody but you, they'd've gotten the bum's rush. Eighty-sixed right outta here.

That's a tribute to your reputation. You know what I mean, Lou. Can I call you Lou?"

"First you have to tell me what you're thinking about telling me. Does your fire alarm work? You're not violating the city fire code, are you?" I tapped the gun against the side of the counter. "I can read faces, Janasek. You're the cat that swallowed the canary. I'll give you one last chance to tell me what you're keeping from me."

"Oh yeah." He laughed out loud. "You mean the new hundred. I was gonna tell you about that. He was lookin' real good for him, you know, and then he pays me with a crisp hundred-dollar bill, which I gotta wonder where a guy like that gets his hands on."

"Did he get his hands on it from a package under his coat?"

"I did see a little bulge, but he had that hundred in his hand when he walked in. It even felt cold."

"Then he must have carried it near his heart."

"Hey, I like that. That's pretty good."

"Stay put and wipe the sweat off your face."

"My pleasure."

I opened the stairway door. The landing on the second floor had a single red lightbulb that glowed above a fire extinguisher, but not much beyond that. I holstered my weapon. The old wooden stairway looked as if it would break from the weight of a pregnant cat. I untied my black Corfam shoes, slipped out of them, and tiptoed carefully to the top, creaking all the way. I opened the door to the second-floor hallway. It was empty. Smack in front of me was 208. I put my ear to the wooden door and heard the nasal high-pitched tones of Figaro wondering why fools fall in love. I stepped back into the red stairwell, doo-wop, doo-wop, and lifted the copper-plated fire extinguisher from the wall. I opened the second-floor door again, cradled the extinguisher in my arms, and heaved; but when I saw the Fox lock plate on Figaro's door, I didn't ho. I went back and put the fire extinguisher on its hook, tiptoed down the stairs, put on my shoes, and walked out to the lobby. Janasek gave the impression that he'd remained in place next to the pink cash register.

"What gives?" he asked, turning to me, yawning. "Checking up on me? I ain't gettin' involved. You can have the little shit. He ain't nothin' to me."

"We're all God's children," I said. "I'm thirsty. Before the peasants come and nationalize your water supply, would you mind getting me a very big glass of it?"

"You want a little something in it? Four Roses to warm you up?"

"Make it warm water."

"Tea? I make good tea."

"Warm water is all I want, Gunga Din, but I want it now."

He went to an office behind the counter and returned with the water in a sixteen-ounce glass with Daisy Mae chasing Li'l Abner on it. "I heard you was really different," he said. "You take the cake. Warm water. What next?"

I climbed to the second floor, this time with my shoes on. When I got outside of 208, I called out in a downstate Delaware drawl: "Hey you, drunken nigra. Get away from that door. What you think you're doin' pissin' against that door. You common nigra. I'm 'onna wipe that piss up with your pickaninny ass."

I poured the water at the foot of 208 so that most of it went under the door on the hardwood floor.

"Niggers!" groaned an outraged Figaro through his nose. "What kind of dive is this anyhow?" When his door opened a tentative crack, I did my ho. His body swung in hard with the moving door. It pinned him flat to the wall like a Tom and Jerry cartoon. I walked in and shut the door behind us, freeing Figaro from the wall. He hunched over, coughing.

"Exquisite taste," I said, staring wide-eyed at a bed covered with new hundred-dollar bills. "Don't tell me. Let me guess. You won all this on the 'G.E. College Bowl.' Come over here, you little Ivy Leaguer, you."

He stumbled over to me. "I found it in the closet," he whined. "I figure some hooker musta left it there and forgot about it. I was just gonna call yez. You read minds. I think we better stay here and nab the hooker when she comes back for her bread. I think I know who she is even. She's pro'ly comin' later. I bet. I mean I figure. I mean whatta we got to lose by waitin'?"

Despite the nervous chatter, he instinctively put his wrists behind his back, like a dog that knows only one trick and does it all the time. I cuffed him and patted him down. I pushed him to face the wall with his back to the bed and me. I picked up the telephone receiver and dialed the front desk. "Conrad Hilton, report to two-oh-eight, and bring Figaro's hundred with you. It's part of a matching set. The little shit's up here trying to put the blame on his secretary for leaving something behind. Isn't that just like a boss?"

"Aw, please," said Janasek. "I can't get involved in nothin'. Seriously, you don't need me gettin' involved against one of my own guests. Aw c'mon, please. Don't do this."

"Do I have to teach you social responsibility, or what?"

"I'm comin'."

In a minute Janasek knocked on the door and I let him in.

"Cheez," he huffed, exhaling hard as his eyes took in the incomparable beauty of a bed full of money. He inhaled and shook his head. "To tell you the truth, Detective Razzi, the man did not give me no hundred. I musta made a mistake. He give me a new twenty. Here, you could have it. Take it. Seriously, you know I wouldn't try to bullshit you."

"You've been picking on me since the second I walked in tonight. Trying to keep out of this by hiding that hundred is not good business. It just gets you in deeper, and here you were trying to stay neutral, like Nehru. Get over near Figaro and face the wall."

He did so. I took one cuff off Figaro's wrist and snapped it on Janasek's. At the time I never thought a thing about it.

"This cop's nuts," muttered Figaro.

"What about my nuts?" I asked quietly.

"Tell him, Janasek. Stick to your guns. Like you said, I didn't pay with no hundred. How could I? Some hooker left all 'a them hundreds in the closet. I think she's comin' back to get them. I bet you know her even. Tuh! Where'm I gonna get a hundred? He ain't got no call bustin' in on me."

"Piss on you," growled Janasek.

"He already done that," pleaded Figaro. "He'll do anything, this bull. He already killed two guys. Remember Joey Termini? Blam. We gotta stick together. He put that bread on the bed. He took it right out the closet. I didn't even know it was in the room. He's gonna frame us both together if he don't shoot us first. Everybody knows he's a sick fuckin' weirdo."

"Now don't tell me you're going to start picking on me, too," I said. "You keep that up, and you'll hear from my lawyer." I picked up the telephone.

"You must be crazy," Figaro blurted out over his shoulder, gaining courage. "You must be crazy. What makes you think you can get away with this?"

"You must be crazy. What makes you think you can get away with this?" I repeated enthusiastically. "Déjà vu." I held the telephone without dialing. "Figaro, I just heard that line on the late show last night from the old movie *Body and Soul*. It's the next to the last line in the movie. The villain says it to John Garfield. You know, after Garfield double-crosses the mob and wins the fight. I bet you can't remember what John Garfield answers. C'mon, take a shot. If you guess it, I won't charge you with sled-kicking. I mean it. The racketeer says, 'You must be crazy. What makes you think you can get away with this?'. . . Can you picture them all at ringside with Lilli Palmer on Garfield's arm . . . remember the music? *Body and Soul*? Last chance. Garfield stares him in the eye and says: 'What are you going to do, kill me? Everybody dies.'"

"Listen to him. 'Everybody dies,'" said Figaro, his voice up an octave. "Listen to what he's sayin'. 'Body and Soul'! Get it? He's going after your Body & Soul Lounge in Chester. We gotta stick together. Some hooker musta left that bread in the closet. Ain't that right, Janasek? You pro'ly know who she is. I bet."

"Shut up!" boomed Janasek. Figaro jumped two inches straight up and shut up. "What if I could locate that hundred? Maybe I didn't look hard enough. Maybe I got a little nervous."

"Maybe you did. When I look I promise not to get nervous." I dialed the dicks.

"Detectives," said Tony Landis.

"Louis John Razzi here, remote from the beautiful downtown Janasek. Listen, Tony, I got a bust for you and your Caucasian partner."

"A crumb for us?" asked Tony. "How thoughtful. What're you doin' workin'?"

"I'm not working, I'm playing. I'm going to make the city pay me a little overtime tonight. Do me a favor, Tony, you and Judson sit in Janasek's lobby and find me the girl that's looking for John Figaro. I'll be up in two-oh-eight with Janasek and our favorite member of the House of Figaro. He's under arrest for trying to make an impression on his fiancée. She might be a Body & Soul girl from up Chester."

I hung up and the three of us waited. I sat in the only chair in the room and my prisoners stood facing the wall, shifting their feet. I whistled Coleman Hawkins licks on "Body and Soul." Next I did my rendition of a white male Billie Holiday singing it. Then I switched to some irregular Thelonious Monk rhythms on my song of the day, again not thinking.

In twenty minutes Tony Landis and his partner, John Judson, the tall white bowling pin to Tony's squat ebony ball, walked in bearing a wiry loudmouthed olive-skinned girl I'd seen around the bars at night. On her elongated lips she wore bright pink lipstick and on her nails shiny polish to match. Her black hair was teased and sprayed into a glossy beehive. At the sight of the money on the bed, her eyes popped and she bellowed, "What?" poking the air with a long pink fingernail. "You got nothin' on me. I'm here to meet a personal acquaintance. This is a free country." She surveyed the room and froze when she saw Figaro's back. "What the fuck you gettin' me into, you moron?" He jumped, and Janasek snapped him back to attention with the cuff. "I ain't got nothin' to do with that little creep. I swear. I don't even know who the fat fuck is. Who's the fat fuck, anyway?"

I said to Janasek: "She doesn't mean to hurt your feelings."

"Oh yeah," she screamed, looking from cop to cop, her eyes burning. "Don't tell me about feelings."

2

At the end of a row of army-green metal lockers, our personal lockers in the hallway outside the Detective Division, stood an old oak bench. We cuffed our prisoners to the bench. Lieutenant Elmo Covaletzki of Vice was acting captain while our regular captain of dicks was in traction with a slipped disc. I told Covaletzki what we had.

"Tell you what," Covaletzki said through thin lips that revealed his bottom yellow teeth and released a monotone that rookies mimicked when he wasn't around. "Let's save you some time, Razzi, and get you back home to Marian on your day off. I'll start the questioning with Janasek here while you start filling out your reports."

"I'd like to question Janasek."

"Why's that?" He squinted.

"To see if he gets the right answers."

"Razzi, you're a card, you are. I can handle this. You start your reports." He gave me his one-eye-larger-than-the-other look, then winked the large one at me.

"It's my arrest, Lieutenant," I said.

"Captain," he corrected. "Tonight I'm your acting captain. You understand? I've been in Vice a long time, Razzi. I know how to talk to guys like Janasek. Maybe you don't think I can handle it?"

"That's not the point," I said.

"You're right that's not the point," he said. "The point's these bars on my shoulder."

"Man, I hate that," I said, and turned to my desk and began reporting the incident in longhand. I had spent no more than three minutes on the report when Covaletzki came out of the interrogation room and said, "Janasek ain't seen Figaro in over a year and he don't know squat about the money. It's a waste of department time to try to hold him even if he did stiff us out of evidence on that hundred-dollar bill. I got his word he'll turn it in to us. There's no reason to bust his balls for personal vengeance. I'm lettin' him go. He's never lied to me and he's given us plenty of good intelligence over the years, a lot of which we forked over to dicks. Go on. Get out of here," he called back into the captain's office, and Janasek made straight for the doorway. He avoided me as he went by, and in no time his footsteps faded past our green personal lockers. Covaletzki then told Tony Landis to interrogate the loud-mouthed girl, Tina Darvi, while, "to save time," he'd "work on" Figaro in the captain's office. Each went his way and shut the door behind him.

"Can you beat all this time saving?" said my first partner, Shy Whitney, from his desk in front of mine, his fat cigar in his mouth and his Tennessee down-home grin wrapped around it while he talked. "Looks from my perch like Covaletzki wants to part you from your work product. You just going to sit there and let him fuck up your bust? Which he will."

"Well, Holmes," I said. "Sooner or later you get enough credit on this job, somebody'll shoot you. At least according to Mrs. Whitney's little boy."

"Shh, don't tell 'em where you got it. Every sum'bitch'll want me to break 'em in."

John Judson knocked on the Captain's door, and when Covaletzki came out Judson said he'd finished counting the money — there was $9,400 and, guess what, it was counterfeit.

"You mean you didn't see that?" Covaletzki leered at me.

"I gathered the evidence," said Judson, "and I didn't notice it. Lou never touched the money."

"He must be part of a counterfeit ring," said Coveletzki, nodding his head, all-knowing.

I said, "Nobody with brains enough to use green ink would be in any kind of a ring with Figaro, but any con man could sell bad paper to a chooch like him. Ask him how much real money he paid for it."

"I'll be back out," Coveletzki said and went back in.

"Shoot, boy," said Shy. "Don't tell me I ever taught you anything. You don't know damn thing one 'bout police politics. You just handed that particularly dumb sum'bitch from Vice the whole case. He could no more figure out sum'in like 'at than a shithouse rat. Don't tell him no more, you hear." He blew a big puff of smoke from his Muriel cigar. "Fuck 'im."

"And the horse he rode in on," I said and walked out the door and down the empty hallway past our green lockers to the soda machine and brought back a Bubble-Up to drink while I fine-tuned my reports.

Ten minutes later Covaletzki strolled out of the captain's office and over to the interrogation room. I could hear Tony Landis tell him that all the Darvi girl knew was that Figaro told her there'd be a big surprise and a hundred in it for her if she came right over. "I swear on a stack of Bibles," she said, coming out of the interrogation room. "You could ask anybody, I don't lie for nobody. Especially for that moron." Covaletzki pushed her pink leatherette purse toward her, told her she could go home, and told Tony Landis and his partner, Judson, to get started on their reports. Tina Darvi strutted out the door like a wronged lady, and Covaletzki went back in with Figaro.

We all wrote in silence. A few minutes later a set of footsteps approached from far down the hall. Deputy Chief Francis X. Hanrahan walked into the division wearing a mackinaw jacket of red and black squares with snow on the hood and shoulders. He said "howdy" to no one in particular, went into the captain's office, and crisply shut the door. In less than three minutes Covaletzki came back out, shutting the door behind him.

Shy Whitney asked Covaletzki: "What's the drill on counterfeit hun'erds you get a deputy chief in on a night like 'is?"

"Routine," said Covaletzki. "Fig says he trusts Hanrahan. He won't talk to nobody but him. No big deal."

"You callin' 'im 'Fig'?" said Shy, smiling. "Sounds like you're winnin' 'im over. The acting captain here is usin' psychology, Lou."

Covaletzki twisted his lips and said, "Keep it up, cracker," as he walked into the hallway with a smug look on his face. I heard him pass our green lockers and get to the machine, and I heard a soda can clunk out.

Then Hanrahan jerked open the captain's door and rushed past us with his eyes fixed on the floor. He disappeared into the hallway, walked to the soda machine, and said in a calm but very loud and dramatic voice: "Lieutenant Covaletzki, return with me, please, if you will, to the captain's office. This Figaro fellow is making very inappropriate remarks that cause me concern, and I want you to listen to them."

We listened to their steps as they walked back together. They entered the division and went straight into the captain's office and shut the door without looking at us. Shy looked at me with raised eyebrows.

I said to Shy: "They must be onto something bigger than counterfeit hundreds. What do you think, Saint Valentine's Day Massacre?"

"He's leadin' the Great White Hunter into quicksand, that's what I think. Walk in on 'em. What're they goin' do, throw you out? You talk to ole Figgie baby. Those boys'll be in there all night 'fore he tells them how old he was when he got laid."

"I'll wait until he tells them he'll only talk to the mayor."

The door to the captain's office opened again and Covaletzki walked out, staring at me while he shut the door behind him.

"Make 'em beg," muttered Shy.

"Razzi," said Covaletzki, "don't take any offense, but I gotta ast you to stand up and empty your pockets."

"Ah, no," said Shy. "What's 'at li'l pus-sucker tellin' you? With all due respect, this is the Detective Division. 'Is ain't Vice. We been lettin' you handle 'is little scumbag long enough. 'S time to turn 'im over to us. You don't do sum'in like 'is based on sum'in Sergeant Bilko in 'ere would say. Get my point?"

"I'm on orders from the deputy chief," said Covaletzki.

"Make 'im come out and give the order," said Shy.

"Empty your pockets," said Covaletzki. "I gotta 'ast' you."

I stood up. "You empty them," I said.

He had been a light heavy in the navy during the war. He stepped toward me, crouching slightly and watching me all the way. He reached for my pants pocket. I slapped his hand away when it got close.

"I meant for you to empty your own goddamn pockets," I said. "Not mine. It's bad enough you took my arrest."

"All right," he said in his monotone. "Let's everybody empty his own pockets. Shy Whitney. Me. And you. Now that's a direct order, and you're both subject to getting fired if you violate it. You got that, Whitney? You want to lose your pension, well you'll lose it. That's a direct order that comes from the deputy chief. He wants to see empty pockets right now. Both of you."

Shy stood motionless, glared at Covaletzki defiantly, and then folded his arms.

"Empty your pockets, Whitney, or you're on charges."

Shy and I had both played the same trick and trap that Covaletzki was playing on me now. The brown leather chair. Put the toughest kid from the gang of suspected car thieves in the brown leather chair behind the glass door and beat the hell out of the chair with a stick and warn the kid to scream with each whack so that his friends in the hall can hear him, otherwise you'll hit him for real. And he screams and the other kids confess in tears to save him. Not to save themselves, of course. I looked at Shy. I didn't want to cause him problems, even if it was a bluff. I emptied my pockets, and when Shy saw me, he emptied his, all the while humming "Dancing in the Dark" in that tenor of his.

"You and Hanrahan right proud of yo'selves?" Shy asked when he'd finished. "Lou Razzi should interrogate Figaro. Whyn't you two stick to whatever it is you do and leave interrogating to Lou. All you brass're jealous of 'im. Ever' damn one of you. I'm sick of 'is fuckin' department."

"No harm done," I said to Shy. "It's better than a stick in the eye."

"I'm only doin' what I was ordered," said Covaletzki. "I was ordered to have you empty your pockets. I could have had Shy search you, but I only went as far as I was ordered to go. Now there's one more thing. What's the combination to your locker, Razzi?"

"Lowlife," said Shy as he very deliberately placed his cigar into his brown glass ashtray. "I'm 'bout to hit you just one time. And you know what you can do with your pension. And you know what you can do with your Marquess of Queensberry. 'Is ain't goin' be no aircraft carrier match, boy. I'm goin' hurt you."

Covaletzki took a step back and hollered, "Chief Hanrahan!"

Hanrahan came out. He had on his Irish priest expression. A faint odor of rye whiskey hit the air as he spoke. "What seems to be the trouble? I merely asked Lieutenant Covaletzki here to quickly disprove certain malicious allegations that that little greasy Figaro . . . now Razzi, nothing personal is meant by any of this. You're a credit to our city and to all the Italians in it. I see deputy chief for you some day. Mark my words. The first Italian deputy chief. Now kindly cooperate with Lieutenant Covaletzki and we'll be turning your prisoner back to you. They tell me you're the best interrogator in the whole Detective Division, with your college degree and everything. Imagine the blarney that Figaro won't talk to you. The gall that he'll only talk to me on a miserable night like this. Look now, you've got Detective Whitney all worked up and getting himself insubordinate. I beg of you that we get this night's work over with and get you home to your beautiful wife. Been working a private-pay job, have you? Lieutenant Covaletzki here works a private-pay job every chance he gets. It's a sign of ambition. I worked 'em all the time when I was young. Give us the combination or we'll break your lock."

"Break it," said Shy.

"Eighteen–twenty-four–two," I said.

Hanrahan backed into the captain's office, shaking his head, and closed the door. Covaletzki led the way out the Detective Division, past the oak bench where I'd first cuffed Figaro,

Janasek, and Tina Darvi, and along the dark-green narrow lockers just short of the soda machine. Mine was the twelfth. RAZZI, L. was printed on a cardboard label stuck in a frame for it. Shy Whitney, Tony Landis, John Judson, and I watched Covaletzki painstakingly twirl 18-24-2, with his tongue peeking out from a corner of his mouth. He opened the metal door wide and pointed to new counterfeit hundreds on the floor of my locker. And even Shy Whitney took a step back from me.

3

April 17, 1976

"Telefonica. Telefonica."

"Who is it?" I yelled in Portuguese at the sweaty office boy. I cut off the engine on the bulldozer and jumped down to the freshly sheared earth.

"Interurbano, America." He shrugged his shoulders as a fly landed on his nose. It was a very hot day for April, even in the dry Nordeste of Brazil, and he looked anxious to get back under the electric fan in the shanty. He didn't do much, but then he really didn't work for me. His father, Lopes, was my foreman and the kid just showed up every day. If I gave him a job, tomorrow his cousin or his brother would take his place under the fan, and so on.

Long distance. America. I wondered what it meant. The last interurbano, America, had been from Marian, calling from Delaware. That was ten long years ago in 1966 and five years after they'd arrested me. When I had heard the sound of her voice say "Lou," I wondered whether my support check had gotten lost in the mail. But she fooled me. She said, "I'd like you to hear something, and she put Sally on and a preschool voice said, "I want Daddy Carlton to 'dopt me." Marian wanted me to sign a termination of parental rights form. She was going to marry Professor Carlton Cruset. The professor "agreed" to adopt Sally, give her the gift of his locally powerful name and inherited fortune, and I was to terminate my parental rights when the papers reached me in Brazil. "Marrying a Cruset is marrying with real skill," I said. She said that because of Cruset's trusts set up by a grandfather who'd patented something or other for the DuPont Company, she no longer had any "practical need" for the monthly money I was sending. That "voluntarily" signing the form was the "easy way." The hard way was to "drag Sally through a court battle. Besides, you heard her. That's what she wants. She doesn't even know you."

I said, "That's not my fault," and she said, "Lou, let's not talk about fault. Things are what they are. I hope you're still content mining for opal in Brazil, making a new life for yourself. Let Sally and I make one for ourselves. God, I hope you're not still torturing yourself. I told you in prison —"

"I remember what you told me in prison. You said I had lost my sense of humor. You know, I've only got eighteen days left on the probationary part of my sentence. Maybe I'll get my sense of humor back on day nineteen. Not one of these past five years since the jury said 'guilty' has been a corker."

"Lou, admit it. Those two years you spent in prison did terrible things to you. It made your mind so little. I hated visiting you in prison. I dreaded it. The only thing you ever talked about was your case. Who could blame me for getting tired of hearing about that hallway, and those green lockers and that ridiculous soda machine, and that the only reason you got two years in jail was because you were a cop. Oh brother, I hope and pray, for your sake, you're still not going over it in your mind at night."

With the use of my little mind and for Sally's sake, I signed the papers when they arrived. Daddy Carlton could "'dopt" Sally. I had made my choices a long time ago, for better or for worse. Whatever plague had struck me down and caused me to lose my sense of humor should not infect my daughter.

I had seen Sally once. Marian didn't want to bring her into the prison, and the older cons had warned me not to see her because it would make the time harder, but I insisted. Marian held her up to the glass in the visitor's room. She was barely six months old, in a pink snowsuit, and I had been in the workhouse seven months. The old cons were right as rain. It hurt like crazy. Marian never brought her back. Five months later she visited and said she was divorcing me and that if I had any grip left on reality I wouldn't try to see Sally when I got out, and she'd prevent me if I tried. It was going to be "hard enough" on Sally in a small town like Wilmington without me "cropping up" and exposing Sally to the shame of the whole "sordid" affair.

I walked into the shanty, turned off the noisy fan, and picked up the telephone, bracing myself for Marian's voice again, a decade later.

"Razzi Enterprises, Lou Razzi."

"Sounds prosperous," said a gruff voice.

"Who is this?"

"You fart in a windstorm," said a second, more familiar voice.

"Shy Whitney," I said, "and Rocco DiGiacomo."

"Very good," said DiGiacomo. "You gonna quit now and take the Cadillac or move on to the next plateau? Hah?"

"Where are you calling from?"

"Delafuckinware," said DiGiacomo. "Now listen up, Razzi. This is long distance and we didn't call collect. Now am I right, you had the knack for knowing if a guy was lying better than anybody? Hah?"

"What are you getting at?"

"*Stati zitto*, Luigi," he said. "I'm doing the talking. You're doing the listening. Now, remember the way you used to brag you could read a lie from a sucker's eyes, the corner of his mouth, his words, and the sound of his belch, and all the rest of that hocus-pocus. Hah? What? Well, my friend, you finally showed us all."

"Out with it."

"Patience, hoss," said Shy. "You been waiting fifteen years for this. You'll wait a little longer while the Rock gets to it."

"Did something break on my case?" I asked sharply.

"I think he's got it," said Rocco. "By George he's got it."

"Tell him," said Shy. "I hate to see a grown man squirm over the telephone."

"Figaro went for it," said Rocco. "He confessed. He admits you were framed by him and, get this, Deputy Chief Francis X. Hanrahan himself, Friar Drunk."

When you're the human target of a false accusation, it can be enough to kill you. At the least, it rips the supports from a lifetime of foundations. It devastates you by its profound injustice. During the frame, you can't even look at people you know and love and feel any comfort. Nothing makes you feel good. Not even rebuilding your life into something new. Being unframed by a telephone call doesn't begin to repair the destruction. Being unframed fifteen years later gives the comfort that licking with your tongue gives to a badly infected tooth. It takes time and patience before it does the slightest good, but Rocco and Shy deserved some kind of reaction.

"That's great news," I said.

"Yeah. You remember Figaro disappeared while you was doing time in the old workhouse?" asked Rock. "Well, he resurfaces here and there over the years and he builds himself a rap sheet you could brag about. Finally he gets busted in New Orleans on third-offense federal drug charges. It was either become a government informer or spend every night for the rest of his life in the federal joint in Atlanta with a different dick up his ass. Well, as part of the deal he had to tell the government prosecutor every damn thing he ever done, and that's where you fit in. They passed the information to the FBI in the Wilmington office. Them guys interviewed him and sent a report to the State Attorney General. I read it. The governor's gonna sign your pardon next week, and I got the union lawyer right now trying to get you reinstated with back pay. Not that you want to come back. I don't know. That's up to you, but you ought to get some money out of it. Only thing is, the lawyer says it ain't gonna be that easy 'cause of the statute of limitations. But I don't know. This is an election year, and the boys in city hall need the Italian vote. They'll do the right thing by you."

"Thanks, Rocco. Thanks, Shy," I said. "It's starting to sink in. What else did Figaro say?"

"He didn't say much," DiGiacomo continued. "But what he said was solid gold. He lied on the stand when he said he seen you grab some bills off the bed and pocket them. He said he slipped Hanrahan some bills that he had in his crotch in his underpants to surprise that little loudmouth twat, Tina Darvi. She's an old junky now. Burned out on PCP. He figures Hanrahan slipped the hundreds in the air slits in your locker when he went down the hall to get Covaletzki. He said he don't know why the old bastard done you, which nobody believes, and he don't know whether anybody else was involved. It looked like to him to be a spur-of-the-moment idea that Hanrahan got just to fuck you 'cause he had a hard-on for you. Anyway, the scumbag goes along with Hanrahan so he can get immunity from prosecution for possession of the counterfeit zoot in exchange for testifying against you."

"Where is he now? If I do come to the States, can I question him?"

"He's in a new thing called the Witness Protection Program. Not even the FBI can get to him. They gave him a new identity in a small town. Forget about it. I already tried. I tell you, Lou, if there's a hell I pray that Hanrahan's in it, and Janasek, too. Your old lawyer, Barnesie, was on the right track blaming Figaro and Janasek. It made sense at trial. Figaro and Janasek sitting on the oak bench cooking it up, stashing the bills behind the bench, and then Figaro sayin' he'll only talk to Hanrahan, stalling so Janasek could get let go, grab the bills, and drop them in your locker. That ain't the way Figaro tells it now, but somehow that Janasek was involved in this thing. It's just we'll never know how. It's one of them unsolvables. But at least Janasek and Hanrahan got theirs while you were still in jail. The bastards worried themselves into heart attacks that you were gonna come back on the noon train and shoot it out. You know, Lou, I don't care what anybody said, I said you was smart to go to Brazil day one when you got out of the joint. I said, and I still say, it was that three years' probation hanging over your head that was the motherfucker after you got out. That was the worst part. That part about you couldn't go near Figaro or anybody who testified. It tied your hands, Luigi. Don't worry, I know. Even if you combed the country back then and got your hands on Figaro, all it would've meant to you is another three years in. Figaro could've grabbed you for another three years just by saying you called him up on the phone. Yeah, I said to everybody, that was a smart move leaving the country, what with Hanrahan and Janasek dead anyway. I even told you at the time. You had nothing to stay for. We kinda halfway thought you'd come back after the three years' probation was up, but the way Marian treated you and all about the baby. Hah, sometimes you bide your time and it all works out. Hah? What?"

"What about Covaletzki?" I asked.

"He's chief, Lou, and like I said, Figaro don't say nobody else was involved. Covaletzki was supposed to be getting a bottle of Nehi grape out of the soda machine when it went down. Figaro wouldn't have no reason to cover for Covaletzki now. I know the way you always felt about him, Luig, with your instincts and all. You got a knack all right for reading people, and you could be right about him, but there just ain't nothing there and there's never gonna be. Not without Figaro saying something or Covaletzki, if he even knows anything. The whole thing is one of them unsolvable things. Like trying to find out what's on those eighteen minutes of tape of Richard Nixon."

"It's funny. I was arrested January ninth, 1961, Nixon's last birthday as vice president, and now I don't even know who the vice president is."

"It's Rockefeller, but he ain't runnin'," said Rocco. "It's gettin' hard to keep track."

"This call is bringing a lot of things out of me again," I said. "All at once. They must not have been buried very deep. I want to know why they framed me, Rock. I read something in the Bible when I was in jail that I haven't thought about in a long time. 'And ye shall know the truth, and the truth shall make you free.'"

"Yeah, but where you gonna hear it from?"

4

In the next two months there were many long-distance calls, "interurbano, America," but they were all from the Fraternal Order of Police lawyer. It got so that I started paying the Lopes boy, and sure enough his cousin showed up. It was just as well because before I left I put Lopes in charge of everything. And with me gone he'd need both boys, and the cousin's father. And now it was June 28, 1976. The crash of lightning that struck in the hallway outside of dicks in 1961 was 5,649 days ago, but who was counting.

On the journey from Belém to Miami, I imagined I was a lot like one of those wild-eyed Japanese soldiers they'd find on jungle islands years after the war. The guys they used to show on Movietone News. The malnourished buggers had no idea the war was over and couldn't believe at first that Japan had been defeated. With lights glaring and cameras rolling they'd be introduced to the industrial wonders that postwar prosperity had brought to mankind, and they'd be told that the American newsmen were now brothers under the sun to the Japanese soldier as if the Death March at Bataan had never happened. But this soldier wasn't buying it.

When I got off the plane at Miami International Airport, the changes that immediately hit my eyes in the bright fluorescent lighting were not industrial wonders.

Everybody looked tired and somehow insecure. The young people sitting around me in the waiting room didn't look nearly as cool as I remembered. Neither did the adults, except maybe for one or two, like the sparkling red-haired woman sitting alone across from me. Make that except maybe for one. Her. I took a close look at the others. They made me think of a description of French peasants that stuck in my mind from a teacher at the University of Delaware. He said that French peasants didn't trust banks and buried their money in their backyards and lived in fear that their neighbors knew their spot.

Whatever caused Americans to look mistrustful was at that time none of my business. It had all happened without me and could go on happening for all I cared. I was probably what Sigmund Freud's pet cat would call alienated. My business was sifting dirt in Brazil, and while I intended to sift a little dirt in America, I didn't intend to make a career out of it. I didn't intend to be away from my real business longer than a month, whether or not I found anything in the dirt in America.

I tried vainly to get comfortable in my short-backed, gray plastic waiting room seat. I thought of going for a walk, but I liked sitting across from the redhead. I closed my eyes and focused on Wilmington and how it had looked when I got out of jail in the summer of 1963. First, I remembered that it was a hot day and that Kennedy was still president. I remembered that men's ties were skinny, and olive green suits were popular, and so were Ruby and the Romantics. I remembered that the murder of famous people almost never happened. That was a funny thing to remember. The last one I could think of before Kennedy was Huey Long in the thirties when I was in short pants.

I opened my eyes, and tiny things around me, no matter how trivial, began to hold my attention. I couldn't stop reading the grafitti on the walls. I read every word compulsively. It was dumb stuff, nothing clever, and probably there had been some when I left, but I didn't remember it. At least I didn't remember that so many public walls and plastic seats were assaulted by so many streaks of swirling black paint.

Was the paint made in Delaware? Land of the DuPont Company. Gunpowder mill on the Brandywine. The chemical capital of the world. Nylonville. Corfamburg. Teflon-Del. Cruset country. Maybe I should get some swirling black paint and scrawl on the first wall I see in downtown Wilmington: "Louis John Razzi, Jr., lived here from April 4, 1932, to June 11, 1963, and returned one day in the year of our Lord nineteen hundred and seventy-six."

Would I get a thrill being back on the department?

I doubted that I'd work much longer than that one day. Under the deal the F.O.P. lawyer negotiated with city hall all I had to do was send a medical report from Brazil saying that I was physically fit and fly north and work one full day on the job. Thanks to a pension-bridging clause of the city charter for rehired employees, the mayor was going to exercise his power to bridge my pension over the years, and I'd pension out on half pay at a sergeant's rate. More than enough to hire every Lopes in the Nordeste. Plus the city paid my legal fee for the union lawyer, the cost of my round-trip flight, and $5,000 in spending money. The city also agreed to issue a public apology. It was something I think the lawyer wanted so he'd get his name in the paper and the mayor wanted for his reelection campaign.

I also had a demand. I knew that Covaletzki would never answer any of my questions, but I asked that the feds let me talk to Figaro in person. And I didn't have to be alone with him. A roomful of FBI agents and the American Red Cross was hunky-dory.

In the end, they wouldn't let me talk to Figaro even if I waived my pension, my expense money, and my apology. Even if I paid them.

That Figaro went unpunished and that I still didn't know why I was framed or whether Covaletzki was part of it were, according to the union lawyer, "hard facts of life" that I would have to live with. "Additionally," he pointed out to me during our last long-distance argument, "if you were so cocksure of who was really guilty and you wanted to see them all punished, you could have gotten some torpedo to put a snatch on them and build a nest of rats around them. Don't tell me you were so sure." Taking the law into your own hands had obviously become a fashionable topic over the years. Vigilante chic. Anyway, I think this tough guy's point was that my first lawyer and I never had any more than a hunch about who actually did it and no way to ever prove anything, and I was lucky to get this break.

I pressed my back into the plastic seat and closed my eyes. The old white-haired shanty Irish bastard, I thought, it was himself all along, but not himself alone, dear Rocco. They were all involved, including your new chief, our new chief.

I decided to focus on the redhead. You don't see many in Brazil and you don't see a person like her every day. I watched her close her magazine promptly and efficiently and put it into her maroon travel bag when the flight was announced. She looked taller than I. She got up; she was. Her forest-green suit clung nicely to her wonderfully proportioned body, and I glanced at her large, round hazel eyes, made perhaps greener by the suit, her red eyebrows, sparse freckles, and red hair. It was nice, light-red hair. Soft and long and wavy. Flowing on her shoulders. It made me feel good to look at her. Like a pretty watercolor. She was definitely my type, the kind of girl who exercises, eats a balanced diet with plenty of fiber, and wears no wedding band on the road. I followed her.

I was beginning to feel better with each step. I wanted to samba. That's all it takes. When you've got a bitter taste in your mouth, eat something that tastes good.

As we boarded I stood right behind her and inhaled her fragrance. She wasn't that much taller, an inch in heels. There were no assigned seats on the small jet, so it was easy for me to sit beside her. And I felt myself starting to get a little color in my cheeks. She smiled at me. I could tell that she smiled a lot, the kind of smiling that got Robert Browning's Last Duchess into trouble every year in freshman English. Now this could be something, I thought. At the very least we'd have made a good commercial for the airlines. My short, curly, jet-black hair; my dark brown eyes; and my olive complexion made darker by the sun of Brazil. Her long, light-red hair; her hazel eyes; and her pink skin with freckles. Such a handsome couple, who wouldn't fly the friendly skies —

"Excuse me, are you a lawyer?" I asked, trying to match her smile for smile.

"As a matter of fact, I am. I'm a prosecuting attorney in Wilmington."

She buckled her seat belt, removed her magazine as promptly and efficiently as she had put it away, and began to turn pages and read at a rapid rate. Not at all willing to enhance the airline's image by making small talk with me.

I'll remember my holdover in Miami as a series of openings and closings of my eyes. I closed them again. This time I wondered what Marian looked like, whether there was any gray in her hair and whether Sally still looked Italian like me. During that great big exploding phone call DiGiacomo had told me that he knew exactly where the Crusets lived. I toyed with the idea of watching from across the street like the little match girl in the fairy tale. Only the way the Rock described it, it sounded too exclusive an area to have an across-the-street. Still, there were probably other ways to get to see them. Like going up to the front door and knocking.

When it caused a knot in my stomach, I decided to change the subject. I used my newly acquired subject-changing technique. I simply reopened my eyes. Next, I turned to face and win over a red-haired French peasant who obviously thought I was after her buried money.

"Excuse me," I said to her. "I don't mean to be forward, but I've been in Brazil for thirteen years. I haven't talked to an American girl in a long time, and I noticed that you were reading about Kandinsky. I just feel like talking to you."

"That's an honest approach. Do you like abstract painting?"

"No, but I'll pretend I do if it'll keep you talking to me."

She laughed. I beamed.

"Haven't I seen you somewhere before?" she asked, then suddenly laughed again. "Talk about cornball lines, oh boy, but you really do look familiar. How could you tell that I'm a lawyer?"

"I heard you talking to the check-in lady. I was behind you when you told her that you had 'indicated' a preference for a dinner flight, and she told you none were available. 'Indicate' is a lawyer's word." I was talking fast.

"Why do you say that?" She looked intrigued.

"I don't mean to offend your profession, but lawyers do a lot of 'indicating.'"

"Indicating?"

"In my previous line of work, when I was a Wilmington detective, I used to deal with lawyers all the time. They never 'said' anything to anybody or 'told' anybody anything, and nobody ever 'said' anything or 'told' anything back to them. People always 'indicated' things. 'Indicate' has a lot of 'imply' in it. 'Indicating' leaves plenty of room for wishy-washy maneuvering. You know, you 'indicate' by sort of, more or less, pointing in the general direction, and when somebody 'indicates' something to you, you're never pinned down to his exact words. Precision and neatness don't count. Like abstract painting. You don't have to color inside the lines. 'Your Honor, my client indicates an inability to raise that amount of bail.' Now that doesn't exactly mean he said he can't raise the bail if he borrows five for six on the street, which he'd rather not do if he can get the bail lower. See what I mean?" I illustrated my point by sort of, more or less, pointing toward the wing of the plane with a zigzagging forefinger.

"So you've got lawyers figured out, do you?"

"Well . . . some lawyers."

"I know you," she said. "I recognize you from your picture in the paper. It's an old picture, but it's you all right. Isn't it?"

"Yeah, I'm me all right."

"I read the transcript of your trial. It was lying around the office. It looked like a pretty tight frame against you. They never found out why they framed you, did they? Do you have any ideas?"

"Do you? I started talking to you to get my mind off it."

"Look, this conversation isn't working, and don't burn your brown eyes at me in that way," she said huskily and with deliberation. "I like Kandinsky, and I happen to like the way lawyers talk."

The smile was gone, and her hazel eyes darkened as the pupils dilated. She reopened her magazine and returned to the read.

I thought to myself that I was more famous than I realized and that I was at my best with strangers when they were criminals and that I was only good with them because I had rehearsed all the time as a kid in the forties preparing for the day I'd go on the job. I decided that the best time I'd had in Miami was when my eyes were shut. I shut them and kept them shut the rest of the way to Wilmington.

I dreamed that my teeth fell out in big clumps and that the clumps were held together by a hard, shiny black plastic that looked a lot like the black opal I'd been finding in the jungle. When the plane landed, my jaw hurt from pressing my teeth together.

5

"Jeez, you look good," he said as he smothered my five feet ten inches with a tight bear hug. The .38 in his clip-on holster dug into my side.

Rocco Cosmo DiGiacomo is a big, fitting name for a very big man. He released his grip and held my shoulders in his spreading hands. He'd been a pitcher in Triple A ball, a step below the bigs, and a baseball could get lost in those meaty fingers. His gut was stretching to the limit the fabric of a copper-brown double-knit suit. His shirt was a faded green iridescent. His soiled yellow knit tie was tacked with miniature pewter handcuffs. He was hatless and had lost most of his hair in the fifteen years since my arrest.

"Jeez, you look good," he said again, still squeezing my shoulders. "There ain't no fat on you, Luigi. What you been doing in Brazil, digging opal with your bare hands?"

"Hey, Rock, it's good to see you."

"Jeez, you look good . . . Don't worry about how I look," he said, reading my mind. "Say something."

"What's there to say, Rock. It's good to see you, but it's hard to feel good. You know what I mean?"

"Ah, what are you gonna do?" he said, which is East Coast Italian American for many things. I'd disappointed him. He let go of me, shrugged, and lumbered away in the direction of the luggage return and the guillotine-shaped metal detector, a device for which there was no need when I left the country.

"Hey, goombah," I called out. "I don't have any luggage, except what I'm carrying. Let's get me home. It's been too long."

"All right, Luigi, all right. That's more like it. You never was one to complain. Talk? Absolutely. You were the best talker around, bar none. To this day. But you never complained. Come on, let's go. Talk to me."

He put his arm around me. We walked through the magic-eye self-opening doors and into the humid night air. He was parked the wrong way in a one-way lane and partly on the sidewalk.

"I forgot how to park on a sidewalk," I said, pointing to the OFFICIAL POLICE sign in his window. "Maybe I'll rent a car in the morning so I can have a little fun tomorrow before I put in my retirement papers."

He laughed and said, "That's more like it. You scared the piss out of me back there for a second. Like we did something wrong bringing you back. Hah?"

We got in his faded blue 1970 Plymouth for what turned out to be a thirty-minute expressway drive to downtown Wilmington and the Hotel DuPont. It used to take a lot longer.

My imprisonment had left an open sergeant's slot, and Rock had filled it, but he'd never made lieutenant and had quit trying. He and Angie had just celebrated their twentieth together. His oldest, Theresa, was working nights in the post office, and the other five were still in school. The next oldest, Dominick, was about to graduate from St. Thomas's High School and go into the marines. After his hitch he'd go to college courtesy of the corps. Rocco, Jr., the next oldest, was a sophomore at Shelton High School. He was born about a month before my Sally, and while I'd seen Theresa and Dominick as babies, I'd never seen Rocco, Jr., and the young ones.

"I hate to complain myself," said Rocco, Sr., "but my Junior's turning into a wrong guy. He got in with some dopers at public school. The dope's not as bad in Catholic school, but since Angie stopped working on account of her back, we don't have the money to send the four young ones. Next year they're gonna put in school busing, too, you know, from the federal court, and they're gonna raise tuition. It's a mess, that public school. One of the girls in his class got knocked up and named the kid Crystal Meth after the drug. Can you imagine? Crystal Meth McGraw. Poor little kid. Ah, what are you gonna do? That goddamn kid of mine can pitch. Smoke. Wicked curve. I taught him a change, then the next thing he goes and gets himself thrown off the team. He wouldn't cut off his hair. I could never get my curve over. He throws his for strikes. What a waste."

"Is he running with a gang? Fighting a lot?"

"Gang? What gang? There ain't no corner gangs no more. I wouldn't mind so much if he was fightin' and raisin' hell. He's just a wart on my ass. I can't sit down to a meal without feelin' that little cocksucker trying to irritate me. Shit. Gangs. Lou, I wish he'd run with a gang and get his ass kicked once in a while. It's good for a kid, but kids don't do that shit no more like we used to. Nobody has it out. Everything's to the death. Like the moolonyons used to be with razors. I blame all this karate from the Japs. No more fair fights where the worst you get is a broken nose or maybe a broken jaw once in a while or maybe a broken hand. Today it's double-oh-seven all the way. Everything is for blood."

When I didn't say anything, he lit up a Chesterfield.

I had trouble looking at Rock, and so I looked out the window. The way I remembered old-time detectives, they got more self-confident as they got older. They aged like hickory wood. Maybe old-time detectives were now supposed to age like wood-grain plastic.

By the time we reached the hotel I was looking forward to bed. After parking next to a hydrant, Rocco told me he was going to see me to my room, which he then began to do without asking my permission.

The hotel lobby was as elegant as I remembered. Shiny beige marble floors and walls. Carved mahogany paneling high up framing a ceiling of gold-, red-, and green-painted ornamental plaster.

"It's funny," said Rock as he reached the desk clerk. "What annoys me about this place is the men's room. You can't flush the urinal."

"I never used it."

"Try it sometime. There's no flusher. The thing flushes by itself. The first time I used it I looked all over the place for the flusher, but there is none, and by the time I'm drying my hands on a paper towel, the damn flusher goes off and scares the piss out of me."

"The piss out of you?" I said. "You go again. It flushes again. It sounds like a vicious cycle, Rock."

The desk clerk told me my room was unavailable. The guest in it had decided to hold over. After a pause and after getting no comment from me, she told me that at no extra charge they'd put me in the presidential suite. She wasn't very good. Neither was Rocco. If they'd really had no room for me, Rocco would have jumped right in during the pause and offered to put me up at his place.

We got in the elevator. The presidential suite was on the eleventh floor. I held the key. We rode up in silence. My nostrils widened a little bit and my heart got just a touch racier.

Rocco moved too casually, too nonchalantly. You got to know a partner when you rode with him even for a little while, and nothing could make you forget him. In the eleventh floor hallway he began to cough loudly.

"Sounds like you're getting a cold. Maybe you could use a rock and rye," I said and stopped. "Let's go down to the Brandywine Room and have a drink. There's no point in your seeing me to my room."

"Get settled first, then we'll go down," he answered, looking directly into my eyes without blinking. The first sign of deception by a cop. He controlled his eyelids to prevent the subtle but rapid flutter of your garden-variety civilian liar.

I put the key in the door, pushed it open, and the lights went on. I turned to Rock with a look of mock anger and he gave me a sheepish look. Shy Whitney was the first one to me. I grabbed his hand and shook it and then shook hands with Tony Landis, John Judson, and Clem Augrine. These five men, and these men alone, stopped by the trial at various times to wish me luck. "Is this my welcome-home party or my retirement party?" I asked as they gathered around me, shaking their heads and smiling.

"This is welcome home," laughed Judson. "You don't retire 'til tomorrow night. Then we'll throw you another party."

"Any you other guys retired?" I asked.

"Only Judson, only White Trash," said Tony Landis. "He's right here in hotel security. That's how we got this great big room. Nobody's hiring retired cops anymore. Judson got out just in time. The rest of us stayed on past twenty. It pisses off the young guys. They want us to put in our papers so they can get our rank, but they can fight over my rank during my autopsy. How 'bout it, Lou, you hiring broken-down cops down there in Brah-seal? Damn, you look good. What they got down there, the fountain of youth?"

"You make 'ese boys look old," said Shy Whitney.

"What do you mean 'these boys'?" asked Clem Augrine. "What's he mean? About twenty years ago they stopped making rocks as old as Whitney."

"Speaking of rocks." I went over to the bar they'd set up, poured a Rolling Rock beer into a water glass, raised the glass in toast, and drank. Its cold flavor was like a splash. It was the first sensation that felt familiar about being back. Here I was the Japanese soldier, adjusting slowly. Doesn't anyone know there's a war going on?

It turned out that Judson had retired as a lieutenant. All the rest were sergeants and still pretty much worked together in dicks. Shy Whitney still smoked cigar after cigar and still sang "Believe Me If All Those Endearing Young Charms" at every cop's wedding. He was a limited edition of one, an irreplaceable, with snow-white hair and a ruddy face, and he was the strongest man I ever saw. One time he punched a car thief through a closed and moving Mercury window and broke the guy's jaw. I was there. Clem Augrine, a short, pudgy "dude" with glasses and brown mustache, still repeated himself when he talked and still wore three-piece suits. Shy, the oldest, and Clem, the youngest, had been partners when I left, and Shy had broken him in just the way he broke me in. Tony Landis was no longer Negro. He was now a black man, and he missed his old partner, Judson, and seemed to resent the DuPont Company for hiring him away.

The more we talked, the more I sensed that something was missing with all of them, not just Rocco. There was no aging hickory wood in this pile either. Shy had gotten more round-shouldered. Augrine was balding like Rocco, and Tony Landis and Judson were gray, but that wasn't it. There wasn't any energy to their voices when we talked about the job, except a trace when we talked about things we'd done together back in detectives, cases we'd worked in the late fifties, that sort of thing.

They were like a baseball team that was sitting on a lead in the seventh game of the World Series and watching it dwindle inning by inning as the opposition got stronger. It was as if they were concentrating on not making errors in life.

"You wouldn't believe all the new rules and procedures we got now for working cases," said Tony Landis.

"Rules? Fools. You would not believe the young fools we got now," said Clem Augrine. "We got fools now that could not find their ass with both hands."

"The young guys ain't so bad, Clem," said Rocco. It's the rules. You seen that cartoon in the F.O.P. magazine? The cop's got a blindfold over his eyes, a piece of tape across his mouth, big puffs of cotton in his ears. His gun is chained to his holster, and his hands and feet are tied together. On the bottom it says, 'Now do your job.' Hah? What are these young guys supposed to do? What do you think, Lou? You was never big on rules."

"Maybe not," I said, "but I learned how to follow rules in the workhouse, and on probation."

"Yeah, that's a good point," said Rocco. "What hurt Lou was that probation over his head. Nowadays we all got like a probation over our heads slowin' us down. He couldn't even work his own fuckin' case when he got out, and now it's too fuckin' late. It's harder on the young cops."

"Old cops, young cops," said John Judson. "When we were young the old cops said we'd never be any good."

"Yep," said Shy Whitney as the attention focused on him the way it usually did when he had something to say, "but those old cops were jealous of us. We had it down good back then." He looked at me and put his cigar back in his mouth. "Nothin's too fuckin' late."

"I hope," I said.

"Yeah, well," said Rocco, "that's a horse of a different color. Some of the old cops were jealous of us, sure. They were jealous of Lou mostly. But that's history, right? Water on the dam, hah? What?"

"That's right," said Clem Augrine. "No sense in stirring up a lot of old memories. Old memories, who needs them, right Lou?"

"And ye shall know the truth, Clem," I said, "and the truth shall make you free."

"He's chief now," said Tony Landis, staring in my eyes, getting to it.

"He knows," said Rocco.

"He's a good chief," said Tony. "He's fair and he leaves us be. He's not trying to force anybody to retire who don't want to. He locked you up, but don't forget he was on orders from Hanrahan. The real devil was Hanrahan. We all knew he was no fuckin' good."

"That's right," said Augrine. "Friar Drunk. But there's nothing on Covaletzki. Nobody said nothing about him."

"I appreciate your thoughts," I said.

"Hey, this is a party," said Rocco. "Let's keep it light. Any you guys seen that rookie pitchin' for Detroit, Mark 'The Bird.' He puts me in mind of my youngest boy. What a nut."

There was silence and then Landis said, "I heard about him, but I've not seen him."

There was more silence and then Augrine asked, "Anybody want to play liar's poker?"

Nobody did. We drank some more cold Rolling Rock and in a little while they left, but they weren't any livelier.

6

I groped for the receiver to nail the 6:30 A.M. wake-up call. I didn t want to be late for my day on the job, even though my body wanted more horizontal time.

I walked over to my Hotel DuPont room window. I was a tourist surveying the city. A new city in many ways. There were a couple more fifteen- to twenty-story office buildings on Market Street, and still more new buildings east of Market on King. New office construction was under way another block east on French. The next north–south block was Walnut, the black-populated border street of the all-black neighborhood of the East Side, a neighborhood with its nose up against the glass of the business district. Although the *favellas* of Brazil are worse slums, to be sure, there's no such thing in Brazil as a neighborhood with darker-skinned Brazilians than the next neighborhood. It seemed curious to me as I stood in the window, but when I grew up I never gave it a thought.

It was light outside. A young cop on a brown horse scratched his horse's neck and yawned in the grayness of a Wilmington morning. We'd had no horses, but then we didn't have a pedestrian mall running south clear down the heart of Market Street from Tenth to Fourth. When you have pedestrians you really need horses. You sit up high above the lunch-hour crowd and get a better view of purse snatchers.

Beyond the slums of the East Side and partially hidden by fog, the Delaware River slipped its way north past the oil refineries and chemical plants of Claymont, Delaware, and Chester, Pennsylvania, all the way to the ports of Philadelphia and Trenton, then farther north to the green of upstate New York. A rainspout compared to the Amazon, I thought.

After showering and shaving, I put on a starched-white cotton shirt, a white linen suit, and a red silk tie with gray cherries printed on it. The rest of my uniform consisted of a burgundy belt, burgundy Italian loafers, and burgundy socks. I topped it with a yellow narrow-brimmed Panama hat with a navy blue band. Very un-Wilmington. Dressed to kill, if the need or occasion arose. Come on back, red-haired prosecutor. Give me another chance. In the lobby I rented a silver Ford Granada with red interior, just for the day, a Ford in honor of our first appointed president. I parked it across from the hotel entrance in the Eleventh Street outdoor lot and walked the one block across the grass of Rodney Square Park to the Public Building. The all-purpose gray granite building with large pillars in front and what the bureaucrats would call wasted space inside had been my place of business from 1954 to 1961. I'd spent a lot of time in the city-side police station and a lot of time in the county-side courtrooms, including my own trial. The majestic turn-of-the-century Public Building, three stories high, faced and looked out over the grass and park benches of Rodney Square. It was impressive, especially in the summer. All that green of the square right smack up against all that gray of the building, with the thin black line of King Street separating them. As instructed, I reported to something called Youth Diversion, not to be confused with Youth Division, in the basement of the city side of the Public Building.

"Hello, I'm Lou Razzi," I said to the small, thin, toothy, blond-haired young man with a tan shoulder holster and a blue four-inch Colt .38 dangling upside down in it under his armpit. He was the only person in the youth diversion room. He was leering, not something you see much of in modern times, what with laws against inbreeding. One look at him and the Youth Diversion room, and any chance at nostalgia was squashed like a bug.

"I'm Tim Gronk," he said but didn't hold out his hand for a shake. "This is your desk. This is your weapon, your shield, and your ID." He opened a drawer and showed me. "Sign here."

I picked up the items and stuffed them all in my right-side suit pocket. I signed the receipt.

"Is it loaded?" I asked.

"Yeah, it's loaded," he said as he stared at the clumsy bulge. "You want a clip-on holster?"

"That would be nice."

He left, and I looked around the room, which didn't take much doing. It was no more than ten-by-twelve, with two small gray desks, each with a telephone and a beat-up manual typewriter. The walls were cream-painted cinderblock and were crowded with posters about an Officer Friendly and how much help he could be in life to little boys and girls. There were boxes of multicolored Officer Friendly pencils and rulers stacked all around the room.

I sat down, dialed Information, got the number, and called Marian.

"Cruset residence," an elderly black female voice answered. She sounded fat and formal.

"Marian Cruset, please."

"Who's calling, sir?"

"Detective Sergeant Louis John Razzi, Junior."

"Please hold the wire." Her voice stiffened.

I grinned, reached down, and grabbed hold of the wire. My little mind again. Marian had come a long way for a townie.

"Lou, is that you?" asked Marian.

"Nobody else would claim to be."

"It's so dear of you to call. I read in the newspaper that you were returning. Isn't that something about Deputy Chief Hanrahan? You were always suspicious of him. I remember how you used to talk about him. Tell me, Lou, how are things with you?"

"I work hard. I make money and I'm used to the life."

"Oh that's super. That is super."

"And how've you been?"

"Just fine. Perfectly fine. Aged a tad, but I keep my spirit young with my five o'clock 'tini." She laughed.

"And Sally, how is she?"

"Yes, of course. We don't call her Sally anymore. I'm sure you remember her given name is Sarah. We've sort of agreed on Sarah, Carlton and I. As I indicated to you he would, Carlton has adopted her."

I sidestepped the "indicated" very nicely. "Well?" I asked.

"Well what?"

"Well, how is she?"

"She's just perfectly fine. And you know, I think with all this publicity she'd love to meet you, to get to know you before you go back."

"Are you sure?"

"I think it might be a good idea," she said. "Her therapist feels it might be important for her."

"Therapist? Is she all right?"

"Yes, certainly. Her therapist." She sounded offended. "Sarah has no overt problems as such if that's what you're thinking, but in this troubled day and age Carlton and I feel strongly that a young girl — after all, she's almost fifteen — needs a little push to pull through and compete successfully. She's in a very competitive school and her therapist is affiliated with the school. She's a success, really, academically. It's true she doesn't make friends easily, but I think that's good. She's a selective child, very serious about life. Perhaps too intense. Well, you'll see for yourself, won't you? She's a lot like you. She loves old movies on the late show just like you."

Tim Gronk walked back in with the promised clip-on holster and put it on my desk in front of me.

"Sure," I said. "I'll see her. I want to. You're making it easy. I had you figured wrong. I'll call you tonight."

"Don't call me at night," she said quickly. "We have a family rule about personal calls in the evening. I'll call you first thing tomorrow morning."

"Do you know where I'll be?"

"At the police station?"

"Not necessarily. Today's my last day. I'm staying at the hotel."

"I'll find you," she said. "My God, Lou, I really need to talk to you. It's strange after all these years, but I feel as if you're the one person in the world I can talk to."

She hung up quickly. Her last words sounded like the Marian I knew. She must have paid an imposter to do her talking for her until those last words, when it counted. From the time my mother died of cancer in a Philadelphia hospital, when Marian and I were seniors at Wilmington High, I never once needed anything from her until prison. She needed me constantly to help her "pull through."

"Sarah," I said aloud with contempt.

"Excuse me," said Tim Gronk.

"Nothing," I said. "What the hell is Youth Diversion?" "It's a federal grant. Don't you know what it is?"

"Do you?"

"Yeah, I know."

"Then what the hell is it? What do you do for a living?"

"What do I do for a living?"

"Sonny, if I kissed my wife and kids good-bye every morning, strapped a badass .38 under my arm, and showed up at a concrete room like this with a sign on the door that said YOUTH DIVERSION, I would spend every waking second planning my escape. What do you do besides keep an eye on me? Count Officer Friendly rulers? Come on, tell me the truth. You're a civilian volunteer. Nobody pays you a cop's salary to divert youth."

"You're worse than they said you would be." He shook his head in disgust.

"Don't worry, sonny, you've only got another seven hours of me."

I took out the phone book and found the number for the local FBI office and dialed.

"Mendez here," a male voice answered.

"I'm Lou Razzi, ever hear of me?"

"Sure, I was wondering if you'd call."

"Excuse me," I said into the phone, and then to Gronk, "Junior, you better write down that I'm calling the Federal Bureau of Investigation." When he didn't respond I said to him: "If you and Covaletzki think I'm stupid enough to walk into this room at 8:00 A.M. and not know that part of your job is to spy on me, neither one of you is bright enough for the Officer Friendly team."

Gronk said nothing. He narrowed his eyes on purpose to look mean and lean. Then I heard the voice on the phone. "He's Covaletzki's son-in-law," said Mendez.

"Bingo," I said. "You know, Agent Mendez, I like you. We've never met, but I think you know something about what I've been through and what I'm after. I'm entitled to talk to Figaro. I don't want to know where you've got him. Bring him to Delaware. I'll talk to him in your office with me wearing a straitjacket. I just want to see his face and hear his voice when he answers my questions."

"I'm not saying I would anyway, but I can't. It's a physical impossibility. The Witness Protection Program is run by the marshals. We have no jurisdiction over them."

"Agent Mendez, in Brazil everything comes from the central government. You can't get your electricity turned on without practically going to Brasilia, but sometimes if you get liked by the right person you can get anything done. How can I get you to like me?"

"If you want to be liked, go back to Brazil."

"Agent Mendez, I was put in a coma for fifteen years. Don't tell me to leave empty-handed. I had every single thing that means anything in this world taken from me, and I don't even know why. Let me tell you a story. Please hear me out. You, too, sonny. When I was in high school I worked in old man Fisher's drugstore."

"Shot in a robbery," interrupted Mendez. "Unsolved."

"That's terrible. He was a fine man. Anyway, we kept rubbers in the drawer behind the counter. In less than a month I could tell a hundred percent of the time whenever a man was going to ask to buy rubbers. It got so I could tell the second a man walked through the door fifty feet from my counter. When I told old man Fisher he said, 'What's the big deal; so could I. Just be nice to them.' And so could the other clerks. Mendez, you can tell a lot by looking at people. Covaletzki was involved in my frame. I could see it in his face. Do you know what I mean?"

"Not really."

"Well, all right, you feds operated under tight-ass rules and you worked on cleaner crimes, and damn few of them. You never had to spot a junkie from a block away and try to tell if he was holding drugs. But you must have heard of what I'm talking about. You must've seen it in the movies."

"What's the point?"

"I was standing in the hallway with Covaletzki when he walked up to my locker. When he opened that locker he was like a junkie holding drugs. Like a man buying rubbers. He knew that money was in there."

"You can't prove that. You don't know that. Figaro never told us that. And believe me we asked him. He said he handed the money to Hanrahan when Covaletzki was out getting a soda."

"And Hanrahan took that kind of chance in that hallway with Covaletzki right there?" I shouted into the phone. "I appreciate what you've done for me, but you're wrong. I'm not asking for much. All I want to do, as the victim of a crime, is to talk to Figaro face-to-face."

"Sorry, no can do."

"Do unto others as you would have others do unto you."

"Sorry, I can't."

"Let me talk to you, then. Just you. Face-to-face."

"Maybe tomorrow."

We hung up. Gronk stared at me. I sat there. The frustration reminded me of doing time.

My mood was interrupted when Chief Elmo Covaletzki appeared in the doorway with two lieutenants whom I thought I recognized. They were probably cadets in recruit class when I was arrested.

Covaletzki walked up to my desk. He had changed even more than my friends. He'd kept his body in shape, and he was probably still one of the best boxers in the department; but his face was now a mass of lines and deep ravines, and he was practically bald except for a tiny bit of gray hair at the sides. The lines in his forehead and at the corners of his eyes and lips reminded me of shrunken Jivaro Indian heads I'd seen in São Paolo. His nose was on the red and puffy side, and he now wore tortoiseshell glasses over his gray eyes.

We looked at each other. He must have rehearsed this entrance. He spoke in that deep monotone, carefully pronouncing each syllable:

"I know all about the noise you been making and so does my legal counsel . . . in case you cross over the line slander-wise. You see, I got my own little theory on all of this, and you'll hear me out without any interruption. That's a direct order from your chief to you. Everybody knows that when a punk like Figaro tries out for the Witness Program he always exaggerates his prior crimes so he can look like a real important witness to the government prosecutor. Some crimes he makes up altogether, especially the juicy ones that nobody can disprove. If he told the truth he'd be just another small-time punk who doesn't know anything worth paying for, which is what Figaro is, always was, and always will be. If everybody in this administration is quick to insult the memory of a dead man who gave his career to this department, so be it. I know you called the FBI," he said, his lips in a thin curl of contempt. "I was in the hallway. I hope they let you talk to Figaro. If you find him, give me a holler. I want to talk to him, too."

"I'd like to talk to you, too," I said.

He looked away. "C'mon, Tim, we're going over to Rodney Square to watch Mondale's speech," he said.

"I already heard my speech today." I said. "I guess that leaves me in command of the Officer Friendly project. Hey, Tim, where'd you leave off on the ruler count?"

The two lieutenants made a great facial show of ignoring me and at the same time expressing their amused pity for the bitterness inside me that could only destroy me. I felt like hitting them.

A tall, distinguished-looking man appeared in the doorway wearing gray slacks, white shirt, blue-and-red-striped tie, and a blue blazer with shotgun-shell insignia buttons. He nodded hello as if he knew me. He was maybe a dozen years older than I. He had a precise black-and-gray mustache, 1930s' matinee idol, and wore large metal-framed aviator eyeglasses with a yellow tint that would have looked good on a state trooper.

"Sergeant Razzi," Covaletzki said, relishing each syllable, "I'd like you to meet a good friend of mine, Professor Carlton Cruset. Professor, meet Sergeant Razzi."

"I hope I'm not interrupting anything," Cruset said in a well-modulated and well-controlled voice. "I was told I'd find the chief here. We'd planned on watching the campaign speech together."

"Oh no," said Covaletzki, "you're not interrupting anything. We were just leaving, and Razzi has a lot of work to do."

"It'll get done," I said. "Every bit of it before I go back to Brazil."

The entourage walked out, with Cruset nodding at me and me at him, and my adrenaline scoring a 9.5 even with the Russian judge.

I settled down all alone with Officer Friendly to divert youth. Shy Whitney peeked in to say hello, but he couldn't stay because he had to work the Mondale speech. "Nobody wants the son of a bitch killed in Delaware," he said as he left, puffing on his Muriel. "Although I could use the overtime . . ."

At 11:03 the phone rang. I picked it up and said, "Youth Diversion."

"Tim," said a woman's voice.

"Tim won't be back for a while."

"Oh no, I don't know what to do." The woman was crying. "My husband said to call Timmy."

"What's the problem?"

"My little Stevie got hurt something terrible. I'm at the hospital, and they're asking us questions. I don't know what to say. I know it's my fault. Dear God, my little Stevie's such a nice boy. He walked off from the backyard, and somebody musta tried to kill him. They choked him half to death. I know it's my fault. I feel terrible. I don't know what to say to them questions she got. Timmy knows us. That's why Ralph said to call Timmy."

"Ralph what?"

"Morris."

"What hospital?"

"Delaware Division."

"I'll send someone right over," I said and hung up. "After all, I am a sergeant," I muttered. However, when I went up a flight to the mezzanine to detectives, there was nobody to send. I checked Traffic and Patrol and they were all out, too. Everybody was watching Mondale.

Then it started coming back to me, like riding a bicycle, the scent of the old familiar hunt. I figured I'd go myself. There was really no decision to it. It flowed naturally from the bulge in my side pocket.

7

It was easy to spot Mrs. Morris and Ralph at the emergency room. They were sitting in cold-looking pink plastic seats and they were holding each other tightly. They were in their late forties. Little Stevie had apparently come late in life. Mrs. Morris was small, pudgy, and round, with an orange kerchief surrounding her dark hair. Her tight powder-blue slacks bulged, as did her rose-colored pullover. She was crying very loudly, drowning out a soap opera on the waiting-room TV. Mr. Morris was a short, skinny man with long, hairy arms that were full of muscle and were wrapped around his wife. He wore faded dark-green work clothes.

"I'm Sergeant Razzi from Wilmington, the one you spoke to."

"The doctor's got little Stevie now," said Ralph Morris, letting go of his wife as her crying got softer.

"Is he walking and talking normally?"

"Yes," they both said at the same time.

"How old is Stevie?" I asked, changing the subject and relieved that he probably wouldn't be left paralyzed from the choking as long as he was moving around well.

"Almost four," sobbed Mrs. Morris through her tears. "It's all my fault. Everything is always my fault. There's no use talkin', Ralph, the whole thing is my fault. This never woulda happened if I watched him better."

"You have no right to think of yourself at a time like this," I said sharply. "Now what happened? Every detail."

"I was puttin' in the laundry," she said while she sniffled. "Down the cellar, you know. I was only down a couple minutes. I finished maybe half a can a beer from upstairs. Then I put the laundry in. What's it take to put the laundry in? And Stevie was out in the yard. Our yard don't have no fence. We shoulda made the landlord put up a fence, dear Jesus. We're only four houses up from the hill where the B and O tracks is. You know where that is. Anyways, when I come up from the laundry I couldn't find Stevie. I thought I would die. I never been so scared in my life the more I looked. So, I went all over the alley and then I knocked on the neighbor that's home days. Right? She ain't seen him. So, I went down the hill to the B and O over by the tin shack, you know the one in the woods. There he was all beat up, thank God, and almost dead, oh dear Jesus. He was terrified — like he seen a monster." She started crying again. "I'll never open another can of beer as long as I live. Am I telling it right?"

"You're doing fine," I said. "What did Stevie say?"

"He ain't said nothin' yet. He ain't talked really. He just keeps sayin' 'bad boy' and crying. I told him he's a good boy. He most probably thinks he's a bad boy for going down to the tracks."

"He musta been in shock," said Ralph Morris as he lit a Pall Mall and exhaled through brown teeth. "He talks pretty good for his age, I think."

"Precisely where did you find him?" I asked.

"Like I told you, in the teenage boys' tin shack in the woods there on the other side of the B and O," she said. "Right inside the shack on a dirty mattress."

"Describe Stevie's appearance when you found him."

"Oh," she wailed, and put both chubby hands over her face and cried. A sopping wet handkerchief fell to the floor from between her moist fingers. "Oh," she wailed again and shook her head no.

"She can't talk about it," said Ralph. "I seen the poor kid. He got little red dots covering his whole face like measles, but they ain't measles. And he got choke marks like on his throat. So far they ain't found nothin' on the X-rays. They're doin' lab work, too. We're just waitin'."

"How about his clothes?" I asked of Ralph as Mrs. Morris sobbed into her hands.

"All he had on was a shirt when she found him. His dungarees and underpants is most probably gone, I guess. She put his red blanket around him and we drove right here. I'm home on disability. I was sleeping. I get tired easy with my back. He ain't even four years old yet. The poor little thing. What a sight. We kept him from lookin' at himself in any mirrors. I don't blame her for carryin' on so. This wasn't her fault."

Ralph fought back his own tears by biting on his lower lip. He took me aside and said softly: "It's hard on her, you know. We never thought we could have kids at our age, so we stopped usin' protection. But we got married soon's she got pregnant. It's been rough on her bringing him along this far. He's got a crooked foot, you see, and he never goes down by those B and O tracks. I think he was took down there. It's a good steep drop down there. He's a good boy. He wouldn't go down there by himself. Not to that teenage hideout."

"How was his breathing?"

"Okay. I guess. He was just screaming a lot and we was both trying to keep calm in front of him. They musta just kept pokin' his face with a stick to make all them bloody dots."

"Have you talked to the doctor yet?"

"No. Just some Spanish woman which wasn't no nurse or nothin'. Kept asking my wife stuff is all, and so I said to call youse. She's gonna come back after Mildred calms down and ask all her questions again."

We walked back to Mrs. Morris and I said, "The red dots on his face are hopefully nothing to worry about. They're petechial hemorrhages. Tiny blood vessels in his face must have ruptured from cutting off the air supply in his throat. They're bad to look at for a few days, but they'll clear up. He's probably still a little shocky like your husband says. Where is Stevie now?"

"Back through those doors," said Mr. Morris.

"What's your address?"

"Twenty-two-twelve Clifton Avenue," he said.

"Just answer all the lady's questions. First thing the hospital has to make sure of is that you or your wife didn't do this."

"Jesus, Mary, and Joseph," cried Mrs. Morris as she sobbed more loudly.

"Don't take it personally, Mrs. Morris. Meanwhile, I'll find out what I can about who really did this. I know you didn't."

I walked through the double doors. He was in an examination room sitting on the edge of a stetcher, with a gray-haired heavily made-up nurse of about sixty standing next to him. Stevie was very skinny. His hair was over his ears, stringy and blond. His eyes were light blue and the pupils somewhat dilated. He looked cold. His red blanket was around him. You would not want him to look in a mirror.

"Stevie," I said.

He didn't answer or look up but stared straight ahead uncomfortably.

I stuck my hand in my jacket pocket and pulled out my gold WPD badge. "I'm the police," I said as I put the badge on his knee.

He reached out very slowly and kept it from falling. He held it tightly in his hand.

"We've got to work fast to catch the bad boys and spank them. I need your help, Stevie."

"We're waiting for the psychologist," said the nurse. "Do you really have to question him now?"

"Best thing for him," I said and looked intently at her eyes. "Get his mind active. Get him fighting back."

Stevie looked from me to her and back again, and his expression showed that he sided with me.

"Tell me all about the bad boys," I said. "What did they look like?"

"Bad boy," he said "Bad boy choked me."

"Only one."

"Uh-huh."

"Was he younger than me?"

"Umm . . . yeah."

"Was he older than you?"

"Y-yeah."

"A teenager?"

"Yeah." He answered with less hesitation.

"This big?" I said and held my hand to the top of my head.

"Yeah."

"Was he bigger than me?"

"No."

"Skinny like your daddy or heavy like Mommy?" I puffed air into my cheeks and held my arms out in front of my body like a fat belly.

"Like Daddy."

"Was the bad boy a white person?"

"Yeah."

"Was his hair dark like my color?"

"No."

"Light color hair like yours? Blond?"

"Yeah."

"My color eyes?"

"Don't know."

"Long hair like hers?" I pointed to the nurse.

"No."

"Short like mine?"

"Yeah."

"What else, Stevie?"

"Shiny teeth."

"Oh, that's wonderful, Stevie. That's very good. What else about the bad boy, Stevie?"

"He laughed like a monster."

"What else, Stevie? Can you tell me anything else about the bad boy?"

"The bad boy is a shit. The bad boy is a fuck of a shit. I hate the bad boy."

"Good boy. You're a good boy. We'll punish the bad boy."

I tugged at my badge in his fingers, but it only made him hold it tighter. I gave up and tugged the blanket around Stevie, checked his chart, saw no signs of rectal tearing or penetration of the anus, and went out to his parents. The description I had of a tall, thin, white male teenager with short blond hair and "shiny teeth" — braces or a lot of fillings — meant nothing to them. Ralph took me aside and told me that there was semen on Stevie's dungaree pants and that his wife had found them on the mattress but hadn't left them where she'd found them. "She took them and she threw them out the car window on the way to the hospital," he said. "She don't want it to come out in the papers as a sex thing. She don't want the boy to live with that when he gets older."

I nodded, and then I asked both Morrises to promise they'd get my badge from Stevie and put it in a safe place.

I went straight to the twenty-two hundred block of Clifton Avenue and walked around back of the Morrises' house.

No one was out back. A scattered chorus of watchdogs barked from fenced-in red-brick row homes on either side of me. A gray-haired woman with glasses watched me from a second-story window as my eyes scanned the dirt and grass. I wasn't dressed like a cop, so I thought I'd better act like one before she called the police on me. I squatted and studied the dirt intently as if looking for clues. Actually, I was trying to listen and could hear youthful voices and a rock-and-roll beat through the gaps in the barking.

I walked over to a driveway and beyond that to a dirt path through wild growth.

Once at the path, I looked down and saw a steep seven-foot drop to railroad tracks. Sloping down from the tracks there was a wooded area that, judging from the sound of the music, contained the shack.

I removed my .38 and checked the cylinder to see if it was loaded, put it back in my holster, and climbed down the slope. White linen pants turned spotted brown from the dust. It was obvious that Stevie would have had an impossible time making it down to the tracks by himself. The almost-killer would have had to carry Stevie, and a struggling Stevie would have been a problem and an embarrassment. The almost-killer must have befriended Stevie and carried him down the slope in his arms to be killed.

I headed over the tracks and through the woods.

At 12:07, I confronted seven of what cops call "subjects," all white male youths ranging in age from roughly twelve to sixteen. None of them had braces or obvious silver fillings. When I approached I could smell a sweet pungent odor that I recognized from police training to be marijuana.

I was back in police work. Pure and simple. I was talking to myself in the language of a cop. It was almost as though I'd never stopped being a cop. The feelings and the routine reactions, the instincts, came back to me as if I'd been doing it yesterday.

The subjects were sitting on top of, inside of, and leaning against what appeared to be an abandoned sheet-metal chicken coop situated in a grove of tall oak trees. The trees had little puncture wounds, some fresh and some probably old. The scars appeared to have been produced by steel-tipped arrows, as pieces of broken arrows were noted on the ground.

The rock music was coming from a large boxlike black-and-chrome portable radio on top of the shack.

Two of the subjects leaning against the shack appeared to put out and then swallow hand-rolled marijuana-type cigarettes when they saw me.

Nobody said anything as I strode to the shack. The youth closest to the radio, a muscular pimple-faced boy with his head shaved, smiled insolently, reached over, and put up the volume full blast. It was one of the loudest experiences I'd ever had. I smiled back at him, walked up to the radio, snatched it by the chrome handle, and swung it overhand into the thick trunk of an oak tree growing next to the shack. The music stopped, and chips of shiny black-and-chrome plastic rained from overhead.

"What the fuck, you can't do that, pig motherfucker. That's my fuckin' radio, you asshole," said a dark boy of about fifteen who had been leaning against the tree. He was five nine, about one hundred forty pounds, with a dark-brown shoulder-length hairdo parted in the middle and fluffed out at the ends. He wore faded dungarees and black engineer boots and a faded dungaree jacket with the name ROCK embroidered on the left breast pocket.

With my left hand I picked him up by the front of the jacket near his neck and pinned him to the same oak tree, dangling him a foot off the ground. Leaning my body weight into my left hand and into him so that my arm didn't have to do all the work, I pointed the chrome handle of the radio "box" at his eyes.

"You can't search me," he squeaked through a tight throat. "You ain't got probable cause. I ain't holdin' nothin' anyway."

The other subjects scrambled and ran. Three of them stopped to watch from what was a safe distance in their minds, about fifteen feet.

"Where's the torpedo with the braces?" I said softly and leaned harder into him. "And don't waste my time talking any more bullshit."

"I can't talk. You're choking me." He squirmed.

I held him and looked in his brown eyes. He looked from my eyes to the handle of the radio. I tried to look bored.

"Well," I said. "I'd sincerely like your cooperation."

"Let him down," yelled Baldy from behind me. "You're killing my best friend, man. You hurt him, you're gonna pay for it. Let him down I said. The creep you want went to school today." The good old brown leather chair worked again.

"Police brutality," yelled another. "Kick him in the nuts, Rocco. You're in the right."

"He ain't no cop," said the third. "Your old man don't do shit like that. Cops can't do that shit. Kick him, Rocco."

So this was the "little cocksucker," Rocco DiGiacomo, Jr. A bullshitter, too. Coincidences like this happened in a small town like Wilmington, a city not much larger than the population of Yankee Stadium on opening day, a city and a friendly small town at the same time. I continued to hold Junior with his brown hair spread out against the tree. He was turning red.

"What school?" I said and leaned harder when I felt him slip.

"Shelton," said the baldheaded best friend from behind me as he picked up a big stick and pounded his palm with it. "Let him down. He can't take no more."

"Tell me the name of the creep with the braces," I said slowly.

"John Gandry," Rocco, Jr., squeaked through his constricted larynx.

I let go and he fell a foot to the ground, collapsing into his chest and coughing. His face slowly began to get some natural color back. I could have held him against that tree all day and he'd never have developed petechial hemorrhages.

"You don't know what strangling is, you leech. Where's Shelton High School?" I demanded, and kicked him in the sole of his boot.

"Over there." He pointed to a yellow brick building that was barely visible through the woods about a quarter of a mile away on a little hill in the opposite direction from Stevie Morris's home.

"Why don't you leave me alone?" he said, crying. "I ain't done nothing. My father's a real cop. I know my rights."

"I don't know what kind of bullshit they're teaching you in school these days, but, kid, you shouldn't talk bullshit to me. Now I'm going to put you on my probation. For the next year I'm going to be your probation officer. Whenever I see you again, anywhere, anytime, I'm going to hit you. If I see you in these woods I'm going to hit you five times. That's a lot of times to be hit by me. Go to school, kid. It's safer than hanging around, with me on the prowl." I started walking uphill.

"He's stone fucking crazy," said Rocky's bald friend with the stick. As I passed him, he made a wide circle around me to get to young Rocky.

At Shelton High I went to the principal's office on the first floor — a Darwin Hearn — and asked his middle-aged thin-lipped secretary in a purple dress if I could see him on official police business about a male student. While I stood over her desk, the secretary talked to Hearn on the phone and then kept me waiting five minutes, and enjoyed it. She finally showed me in. Two other men were already in the room. Hearn was sitting, and they were standing on either side of him. They must have come in through a door on the other side of what in private business would be considered a very large office. The principal looked to be less than thirty and the other two over forty, more my age.

"Sergeant, my secretary says you'd like to speak with us about one of our students," said the principal through his blond beard and red lips.

I looked at the other two, waved at them with each hand, and said, "Sure, why not?"

"They're my assistant principals, Mr. Scharff and Mr. Govados," said Darwin Hearn.

"Sergeant Lou Razzi," I said and shook everyone's hand.

"John Gandry," I said when we finished the handshaking.

"I kind of knew it," said Govados, a good four inches shorter than me, wearing a five o'clock shadow and a pepper-and-salt crew cut, and sporting a brand-new gray University of Delaware sweatshirt. "The real bad ones only come to class when they're hiding from the law, or the family court makes them. The term has two days left, and John Gandry shows up in gym today. Late, but he shows up. He hasn't been to school in a month. I knew he was in trouble. He had that look, you know."

"Believe me, I know. What time did he show up?" I asked.

"Gym started at eleven and he was about ten minutes late. What's he done?"

"He's suspected of attempting to kill a three-and-a-half-year-old boy sometime before eleven this morning at a shack a quarter of a mile due east of school. Does it sound like something he'd do?"

"It doesn't surprise me," said Govados.

"I know the spot," said the principal.

"That's another thing," I said. "There were seven boys lounging around the shack. They should have been in school, and even though it's been a long time, I recognized the odor of marijuana. Two boys swallowed their reefers when I got there or I'd have brought them with me. Somebody better tear the shack down, and you ought to be aware of what's going on so near the school. Marijuana leads to heroin."

Govados and Scharff looked at Hearn. The three men looked confused.

"Yes, of course," said Hearn. "We do our best to keep it out of the school, Officer. There is absolutely no marijuana smoking permitted on school property. The smoking lounge is for cigarettes only. The shack, of course, is not on school property."

Now I was confused, but I'd been away a long time.

"Where is Gandry now?" I asked.

"What section's he in?" asked Scharff.

"Nine-two," said Govados.

Scharff stepped over to a big white cardboard chart on one wall of the principal's office. It was full of neat rows of black lines and letters. He extended the pinky and thumb on each hand and ran them down the chart, keeping a straight line. That must be his job, I thought. Chart reading.

"He's in Sociology," said Scharff.

"Is that an advanced class?" I asked. "Is he bright?"

"God no," said Hearn. "Sociology and Social Problems is a required part of the curriculum here at Shelton."

"He's a dumb shit," said Govados.

"Yeah," said Scharff.

"My height, long blond hair, skinny, about sixteen," I said.

"That's him," said Govados.

"Can I look through a window of his classroom," I asked, "and see him without him seeing me?"

"Sure. Take him up," said Hearn to Govados. "I see no violation."

"Violation?" I asked.

"School Board rules, the *Student Rights Handbook*, due process. I take it you must work with adult crime. Not too much experience with juveniles, eh, Officer?"

"I guess I'm a little rusty," I said.

Govados took me up a flight of stairs to room 213. We looked through the window pane in the rear door. The students' backs were to us, and most of the kids were more or less facing the front of the room. A young black-bearded and very skinny male teacher in a green corduroy jacket and tan corduroy pants was sitting on top of his desk at the front, with his feet on the desk and his arms wrapped around his bent knees and skinny legs. The students were doing many different things, but only a small group in front of him was looking directly at the teacher and paying attention to him.

"It's the end of the term," said Govados. "I guess it's hard to keep their attention."

"I'll bet you could," I said. "Gandry?" I pointed to a desk in the far corner by the window. I had his profile.

Govados nodded.

I studied Gandry. Blue jogging shoes. No socks. Dungarees held up by a wide black leather belt. Yellow cowboy shirt with mother-of-pearl buttons. No books on his desk or anywhere near him. His head was bowed and he stared at the top of his desk. He looked like he was doing time, or had done some and knew how to do it. Tall for his age. Very thin. And very guilty of something. He was sitting there practicing a look of innocence and waiting for someone to find the body.

I told Govados that I'd be back and to keep John Gandry in school any way he could think of.

I walked back though the now empty woods to the Morrises'. They were pulling up behind my rented car. Good timing. There's plenty of good luck around when things are going right. When a case breaks, it's like an avalanche if you move quickly enough. Speed counts for everything.

I waved them to my car and opened the passenger door. "Let's take a little ride," I said.

"Did you find the bad boy?" Stevie asked when they all got in. "Did you spank him?"

"We'll see," I said and gave him a hug with my right arm as we drove away.

"Is that the bad boy?" I removed my arm and pointed to Rocco, Jr. He was standing on a corner. When he saw me point he ran away down the street.

"No," said Stevie.

"When you see him you tell me, okay?"

From the back seat the Morrises stared intently out each side window.

"I hope we're doing the right thing," said Mrs. Morris nervously. "They said he was okay but he should get plenty of rest." When no one answered she made a sucking sound with her teeth clenched, as if she had been stung by iodine on an open wound. Finally, she sighed loudly. "I hope we're doing the right thing, letting Stevie get mixed up in a thing like this. He shouldn't be sittin' in the front seat of a car neither."

A block from the school a black-and-white Wilmington

patrol car with its red top lights flashing passed by me in the opposite direction. A young cop was behind the wheel, and he didn't seem to be in too much of a hurry despite the emergency signal.

"Is that cop gonna catch the bad boy?" pleaded Stevie. He turned and looked back at his mother. "I don't wanna catch the bad boy." He started sniveling and cried softly the rest of the way, with his father saying, "There, kid," and with me trying to comfort him with my right hand.

A bell sounded inside the school when we pulled up. Govados was outside waiting. I got out of the car and went straight up to Govados as the Morrises got Stevie and lagged nervously behind.

"It's a change of class," said Govados, "but it doesn't affect Gandry. He's still inside. He won't be —"

"Stop it, Stevie!" yelled Mrs. Morris from behind me.

I turned to see Stevie furiously trying to pull his hand loose from his mother's grip and get back in the car. Stevie started to scream and to breathe in an unnatural pattern. He inhaled short, quick, audible gasps and exhaled loud crying screams. "I don't wanna catch the bad boy," he begged.

"He seen himself in the mirror," Ralph said.

"I'll take care of him," Govados said to me and bounded toward Stevie. The screaming continued as Govados carried Stevie into the backseat of the car and put him down flat.

"I'm not puttin' him through no more, and he ain't goin' through no trial neither," Mrs. Morris yelled at me with her face pushed up to mine the way a short baseball manager might argue with a taller umpire. She then pushed Govados aside to scoop up Stevie in her chunky arms and hold him outside the car. Stevie's breathing got more normal as she engulfed him and rocked him back and forth.

"When she says somethin' she means it," said Ralph. "You're gonna hafta find 'is guy without Stevie."

"Stevie," I said. "You're scared because you're little. Your mom's scared because you're scared. Your dad's not scared because he's a brave man. Are you scared, Mr. Govados?"

"No, not at all," he said.

"I'm not scared either, and I'm very strong and I have a gun." I pulled it out and held it up. "And your daddy and Mr. Govados and I won't let anything happen to you. We have to hurt that bad boy before he hurts somebody else who's little. That bad boy is a fuck of a shit. We have to put him in jail. Stevie, you are the only good boy who knows what the bad boy looks like. Remember what you told me about his teeth?"

"Shiny teeth," whimpered Stevie.

Mrs. Morris loosened her grip, and Govados snatched Stevie from her and said, "This brave policeman is going to catch the bad boy and you're going to help him. We'll go inside the school and get him. You just show us the bad boy, okay? Just point your finger at him."

"Don't see him," sniffed Stevie.

"Not yet," said Govados. "We'll go inside the school and get him."

I leaned over to Govados's ear, away from the side where he held Stevie.

"He's still in two-thirteen?" I whispered.

"Yep. He's got a double period. Mo Scharff is outside the room keeping an eye on him," Govados said loudly.

"Shh," I whispered. "Take them quietly to the asshole's office and sit them on the couch."

"Gotcha," said Govados enthusiastically.

8

I took the stairs two at a time and aroused Mo Scharff, who was leaning against a hall bulletin board with his head down, looking at the floor.

"Go in and get him," I said. "We're taking him down to the principal's office. Govados has the victim and his parents downstairs."

"Maybe you ought to come in with me. You know, just in case."

"You go in. Tell him the principal wants to see him about his attendance."

"That won't work. I'll tell him Govados wants to see him."

"Good idea."

"Right."

He went into room 213 and slipped slightly on a pencil as he walked up to the teacher, who was still sitting on the desk. They talked. The teacher raised his eyebrows and waved lazily to Gandry, almost apologetically.

Without waiting for Scharff, Gandry walked out the front door. When he got fully out the door he stopped and looked at me.

"I'm looking for a chicken-lover. Where can I find one?" I said and smiled. His throat muscles started to tighten and a leer formed on his lips. He took a half step backward with his right foot as Scharff walked through the door.

"You know where the office is. Govados wants to see you down there pronto," ordered Scharff.

Gandry looked from me to Scharff and then back to me.

"Face the wall," I commanded. Both Scharff and Gandry turned to face the wall, side by side. I reached Gandry's left wrist, my thumb pressing hard enough to feel his pulse, and pulled it around behind him. "The other one," I said. I took the cuffs out of what was left of the bulge in my pocket and cuffed his wrists behind his back. The last person I had done that to was John Figaro.

"Ow," said Gandry, "they're tight. You gotta loosen them."

I patted him down and pulled a red bandanna from his back pocket; it was sticky, probably from semen.

"You jerking off in class, boy?" I said and wrapped the bandanna in my own clean handkerchief and put it in my jacket pocket, starting the bulge again.

By this time Scharff had caught on to the idea that he didn't have to face the wall. He bent at the waist and examined the handcuffs on Gandry. "I used to be in the military police," he said.

"That'll come in handy at this school. Lead the way to Darwin Hearn's office. Be our point man."

We kept the kid between us and proceeded in single file. I figured that if the kid ran he'd have to trip over Scharff.

We entered Hearn's office through the secretary's office. Scharff was the first one in, followed by Gandry. I got in the doorway just behind Gandry. The room was crowded. I can't deny that, and Scharff and I did have the kid as our prisoner. Stevie Morris was sitting on his mother's lap on the brown leather couch directly facing Gandry. Stevie looked up at Gandry's face and then turned away and grabbed the back of his mother's head.

"Is this the bad boy?" I asked.

"Uh-huh," Stevie muttered into his mother's plump neck.

I had Gandry's arm and could feel the muscles in it tighten. I dug my thumb hard into his biceps and got no reaction. John Gandry was looking at a ghost. His victim was alive. His face then tensed into a contrived look of false relaxation. His lips quickly covered his braces the way a man with a scar on his cheek might try to cover it with his hand during a lineup.

"Is there a room I can use?" I asked.

"You may use my office. We'll all leave," Hearn said solemnly.

"Thanks," I said and pushed Gandry out of the way of the door and hard into a corner. His head hit the wall, and he said "ow" again.

"Of course, I think a representative of the school should remain," said Hearn.

"Govados, stay in here with me," I said.

Hearn didn't say any more. I asked the Morrises to take Stevie home.

"Why don't you punch him in the nose?" asked Stevie

"Don't worry, Stevie, I'll do worse than that to him," I said.

As soon as they left I shoved Gandry on the couch and sat beside him. Gandry's teeth and lips were still clenched tight, and the side of his face closest to me twitched around his eye while on the other side of his face his cheek and neck shimmered like moonlight on a lake.

"I want a lawyer," he said in a high-pitched voice through his clenched braces. His breathing was rapid and shallow through his nose. Defiant terror.

"Kid, how come you're wearing a yellow shirt?"

"You didn't give me my rights," he shot out nervously. "You can't spook me. You got the cuffs too tight."

"Mr. Govados," I said, "I thought this was a high school."

"It is," Govados said.

"You hear that, kid. This is a high school. What did you think this was, a law school? Every punk kid I've talked to today sounds like Perry Mason. I hope they're not teaching you this bullshit in your Sociology and Social Problems class. Because I have news for you. I'm not the FBI, Mr. Gandry. I don't have to tell a kid like you anything about any rights. You just don't understand, Mr. Gandry. I'm about to give you the break of your life."

I reached behind him with the key. He flinched. I undid the cuffs and put them in my pocket. Gandry rubbed his wrists.

"You ain't got no evidence, right? You're letting me go."

"Far from right, Mr. Gandry I have one hundred times enough evidence. You're not using your God-given brain. You're an intelligent young man. If I didn't have you tight, why do you think I caught you so quickly? I don't even need that little boy's testimony to send you to jail forever. I'm doing you a big favor right now. I'm going to let you tell your side of this, and that might save you a big chunk of your jail time because I think that little kid is not as innocent as his mother thinks he is. All little boys like that have something to hide from their mothers. You know what I mean?" I winked. "Have you ever been tied up?" I leaned into him. "Have you ever been tortured?"

He didn't say anything.

"Come on. You know what I mean about some of that little chicken meat," I said. "Those little ones know exactly what they're doing. They might fool other cops, but they've never fooled me. Not once. He led you on, didn't he? They all do. They take their pants down 'cause they want that money or toy or ice cream you're going to give them, then the minute you do something they yell bloody murder for their mommies. You know what I mean? I know you do. You're an intelligent young man. Now here's your chance to help yourself. You're only getting one chance. If you screw up your one and only chance, the cuffs go right back on and you get no more chances. I'll have to take a more unpleasant approach with you. Listen to this question very, very carefully. Pay careful attention to what I say. Watch my lips when I speak. All you were trying to do was stick it between his legs. You had no intention of going up his ass. Am I right? All you were going to do was stick it between his legs and jerk off on him between his legs. Now I can't tell you what to answer and Mr. Govados here can't tell you what to answer, but you think before you say anything because this is your only break, your one and only chance. We're witnesses to how you answer this question. The only thing you were going to do was stick it between his smooth legs, not in his mouth, not up his little ass. Now I don't want to put words in your mouth, so you tell me."

He didn't answer.

"Maybe you did try to stick it up his ass. Is that what you're telling me? Don't be stupid. Don't tell me that." I raised my voice. "Are you that stupid? God damn it, boy, don't tell me that. Up his ass?"

His left eye began to twitch violently. "That's all," he said.

"Which? Between his legs or up his ass?" I said the last three words with precision.

"Be-between his legs," he said.

"Good. You've helped yourself here. You're a smart boy. Now this chicken led you on. You know what I mean? Am I right or what?"

"Yeah. He, he led me on. He wanted me to buy him something from the 7-Eleven."

"I knew it. I can spot one of those midget cockteasers a mile away. Here now I've helped you, right? I just let you give your side of it. But in your heart you know there's a catch. I helped you for a selfish reason. Now I need your help. Can you write?"

"Huh?"

"Can you write words on paper? Can you spell?"

"I could get by."

"Well look, boy, I need your help here, and you could help yourself, too, but you gotta be able to write."

"I could write some."

"Mr. Govados, may I have paper and pencil, or do you prefer pen, Mr. Gandry?"

"I don't care." He laughed. "Man, this is something. You're weird, man."

"Yes, I am."

Govados handed him a yellow legal pad and pencil.

"I ain't givin' no confession," he said. "I ain't signin' nothin'."

"Look, I told you you had to do something for me. If you don't write this out for me, I'm going to deny you ever told me your side of this about just going between his legs, because I'm going to have to spend all day tomorrow on my day off filling out long forms, and it's going to be all your fault. Eight hours. All day. When I could be at the beach with my family. Form after form after form on my day off. Do you want me to put it in the forms that you tried to stick it in his ass? Is that what you want? 'Cause I'll put that in if you make me fill those goddamn forms out. Now it could be all nice and simple if you would write out your side of this just like you told me. All I have to do then is fill out one form before I go off duty today, and attach your confession in your handwriting, and they give me a medal and I can go to the beach tomorrow. Then the official police version is your version. Your version. Your side of it in your own writing becomes the official police version. Not that kid's. Not his mother's. Get me? You're a smart kid, you can see nobody likes to work more than they have to. I'm not telling you anything you don't already know. Which is it? The hard way for everybody or the easy way especially for you, kid? Look how short a time it took me to get you. Less than one school period and I had the whole thing put together and the kid right there in the principal's office. You're caught, John. This is your one and only chance to explain it your way before the lawyers take over. You can give your side of it later, but then it'll look like you and your lawyer cooked it up. You give your side now and it's nice and fresh. Let's settle this between us. Here. You do for me. I do for you. Don't make me come in tomorrow on my day off. This is just another case to me. This is how I earn my living. Be smart, kid. Get it over with the right way."

I pushed the pad and pencil toward him. He took them.

"How do you spell railroad tracks?" he asked.

"Mr. Govados will help you with the spelling. I'll be in the other room. If you need me, call me."

I went into the secretary's room and called DiGiacomo in detectives. Mondale had given his speech without getting himself killed, and the police department could get back to work. DiGiacomo agreed to meet me at the clerk of the court's office to help with the paperwork and the processing in lockup. He loved it and kept saying the words "written confession" over and over again like they were some major event of the decade.

I'd traveled a full day, been up half the night with the boys, and there wasn't a tired muscle in my body. It was a thrill to be back in the race.

Govados interrupted my reverie. With a big grin on his face he handed me the collected works of John Gandry, Dangerous Pervert. I read the confession. Here it is:

> I went down the railroad tracks but this guy sold me a lude for a quarter so I done it but it dint ack like a lude it made me feel kinda funny in the stomak so I got mad and want my money back so I go looking for this guy by the shak so he aint' theire so I got <u>screwed</u> and tatood and <u>ripped off</u> ect, ect so I had me some herb. Whitch I traided it withe this other dood for some uppers 3 to be exsack which I took them and then I do'nt remember too muche cause they mess with my mind. They was bad to. So I got blackd out kinda but I do rembemer that little kid who kept pestering me but I only went to stick it in between his legs but my mind was not sharp, which was gone because the uppers was <u>bad bad bad,</u> so I ony rememeb trying to stick it between his legs lik <u>he wants and he acks me to do which he wants.</u>
>
> Yours trueley
> John Gandry
>
> P.S. I carrieyed him down to the tracks. That way he did not fall down and hurt himself.

9

So after we processed Gandry and left him in the police lockup to be "exsack" I went to the county side of the Public Building to bring my case to the attorney general's office like DiGiacomo told me, "witch" is something new after an arrest, "witch" is called *intake* and so that means that the deputy attorney general assigned for that week is supposed to review the arrest just to make sure it's a good enough case to prosecute. Yours truly, Lou Razzi in ecstasy.

In my day a cop didn't see a prosecutor until the day before the grand jury. Today the prosecutor is like any prosperous lawyer with a lot of business. He picks and chooses his cases. He "intakes" them and screens out the ones he wants and throws away the crumbs and scraps.

I walked in through the glass door marked INTAKE. The cute little blond receptionist told me that the deputy attorney general would see me shortly, took all my paperwork into an inner office, and came out and asked me if I wanted my overtime slip signed, since it was twenty minutes past four. When I told her that I didn't know cops got overtime for court work and didn't have an overtime slip, she told me that she'd seen my picture in the paper and if I just felt like going out or something before going back to Brazil, to give her a call. She'd be working until 8:00 P.M. She put a plastic pen in her mouth and played with the blue cap between her lips. Subtle, but effective.

I was feeling like a movie starlet when, after a few minutes, she told me that Ms. Gold had finished reading my reports and was ready to see me. I walked into the inner office, and then all at once I saw familiar red hair and unfriendly hazel eyes, and I stopped feeling very wanted. She looked mean, but her light-red hair was still fluffed out at the shoulders like it had been last night. She was wearing a blue suit, white blouse, and one of those female ties that look half tie and half ribbon, but all business.

"Hello, Miss Gold," I said.

"Hello," she said. "I had a feeling that I hadn't seen the last of you. It's not every day that I get sucked into a friendly conversation with a stranger so he can be insulting. Especially when he clearly doesn't know what the fuck he is talking about. You'll note I said 'the fuck he is talking about,' not 'the fuck he is indicating about.'"

She stared at me; in her hands she held my paperwork.

"This case sucks," she said.

I stared back.

"Weren't you supposed to be here for one day and then retire?"

"Let's start over. Hello, Miss Gold, I'm sorry for my attitude last night."

"You don't really have any idea what you've done, do you?"

"Not today."

"Well today," she said, getting louder, "you violated John Gandry's Fourth Amendment right to be free from unreasonable searches and seizures, his Fifth Amendment rights not to incriminate himself and to due process of law, and his Sixth Amendment right to counsel. In short, you gave John Gandry the same respect a Viking warlord would give to an Anglo-Saxon peasant. And you don't seem to realize the terrible damage you have done to any potential this investigation ever had."

I tried an old favorite all-purpose line, the one I last used on Janasek and Figaro in that hotel room full of counterfeit money. It became my philosophy of life. It got me through prison: "What are you going to do, kill me? Everybody dies."

"*Body and Soul*. Remember, I read your trial transcript. Good movie, but you're not John Garfield and this isn't 1946 anymore. Haven't you ever heard of *Miranda*?"

"Willie Miranda, the shortstop, or Carmen Miranda, the singer?" I asked. "How about 'Pigs' Miranda, the bootlegger. Is he still making bathtub gin?"

"Ernesto Miranda."

"Never heard of him."

"You know, I really believe you haven't."

"I really haven't. Thanks for your belief in me. Can I use you for a reference when I leave the department?"

"This isn't one bit funny."

"Well, I admit it could be funnier," I said soberly, pointing to my reports in her hands, "but then everything's relative. You see, this arrest, while not really funny, is not as unfunny as my last arrest."

"Yes, it is," she said hotly. "It's a tragedy. It's a tragedy that you didn't face reality this morning when you got that phone call from Mrs. Morris. The world has passed you by, Sergeant. You should not have tried to handle this alone. You're an officer for a day so you can qualify for a pension, and from the looks of this investigation they'd better get you back to Brazil in a hurry. You know," she said, changing her tone to that of a schoolteacher, quiet yet seething, "after reading your reports and talking to you, I can only conclude that you still possess the trait that every policeman sooner or later acquires. You'd think that after all these years it would have left your system. But, you are as full of self-pity as an alcoholic."

"I guess you know," I said as quietly as she, "that a man would be knocked on his ass by now."

I had her attention. I continued. "I don't know what this intake thing really is, but I'm on my own time now, and why I'm a cop or how long I'm going to remain a cop is my own business. What about this investigation? Out with it."

"Out with it? That's the point. Out with everything. It's the worst thing I've ever seen. The written confession is unusable in any court of law in any state. Ditto for the oral confession. Ditto for the identification that Stevie Morris made in the principal's office. Ditto for the red bandanna you took out of his back pocket. Sum total. No evidence. No case. Gandry walks as soon as I pick up this telephone."

"That doesn't make any sense. I don't understand." My legs felt weak. I was tired and I realized that I was still standing.

"First of all, you handcuffed Gandry in the hall and searched him without probable cause to do so under any U.S. Supreme Court definition. Next, you staged a lineup in the principal's office that was unnecessarily suggestive. There's a Delaware decision tossing out evidence of an out-of-court identification in a principal's office exactly like yours. Then, you didn't give him his *Miranda* rights. That is unbelievable. You didn't tell him he had the right to remain silent, that anything he said would be used against him in a court of law, that he had the right to an attorney, and that if he couldn't afford an attorney one would be provided free of charge. Good God, he even asked for a lawyer. Haven't you ever heard of the exclusionary rule?"

"If that's what they call it, it's an FBI rule. The FBI should have rules against them with all their power, but not us. They used to ask us to get evidence for them that they could use in court only if we got it. Are you saying all those old FBI rules now apply to us, too?"

"Oh, brother. What did you read in Brazil? Nothing but menus I bet. Those old rules and some new ones are the law of the land, and I wouldn't want to live in a land without them. This isn't Brazil. Individual liberty is what this country is all about."

"It took me awhile to learn to read Portuguese," I said. "Where I was, the people can't read. Besides, they don't publicize things like that in Brazil. I want to learn about it. Now." I sat down and looked intently at her. "This is important. If this boy walks out of jail tonight, he'll be far more dangerous than he was this morning. Explain all this law to me. Maybe I'll see some way of handling this."

"I can't do that. It's very complex. I couldn't teach you enough in one sitting to get you through a purse snatching. You'd have to take a course in it. Furthermore, the rules are hard and fast, and there's no way to finagle around them once you've broken one, if that's what you have in mind."

"Can't you think of something legal to fix this case?"

She smiled. It was a relief. I could tell by her smile she knew I was sincere.

"Maybe if we wait long enough for the taint of this identification to wear off, we can try another ID by Stevie during the trial itself."

"How long a wait?"

"Who knows? And the more I think about it, what trial? We can't get that far. My job this week is to screen out bad cases, and I wouldn't waste the office's time with a case that depended entirely on a four-year-old boy's very stale trial ID when no mention could be made to the jury that the boy originally ID'd the defendant just a few hours after the crime. I'm truly sorry, but even if the boy could ID Gandry in trial, it would probably be too close in time to the illegal ID to be allowed in as evidence. We just don't have any evidence."

"I get the feeling I'm in another time warp and you're talking a language from another time zone. I don't understand what you said. And I'm trying hard to. I've got a reason besides this case. A personal reason. If I'm lucky enough to find the needle in a haystack that I'm looking for, I hope I know what to do with that needle when I find it. Now, what about the fact that the gym teacher was there when I questioned Gandry? He saw there was no strong-arm stuff. Gandry kidnapped that boy, and he told us the truth when he said he carried him down to the tracks."

"It doesn't matter."

"All right. I can go out to the lockup, tell the little boy- killer his rights, and I personally guarantee another confession."

"Forget it. When you first started to question him, he asked for a lawyer. That's it. No more police questioning. Maybe if by some miracle he confessed to his cell mate . . ."

"All right, we'll put an undercover man in his cell."

"Let me finish, Sergeant Razzi. You are not allowed to do that. You cannot ask him a single question directly or through someone else unless he knowingly and intelligently waives his right to counsel, and in this case he's already asked for a lawyer. And on top of that you still can't do it because any new evidence you got would stem directly from the illegal evidence. It would be 'fruit of the poisonous tree.'"

"'Fruit of the poisonous tree,'" I erupted. "What about the Fruit of the Loom? Of the poisonous loom? Who the hell talks like that?"

"'Fruit of the poisonous tree' is a direct quote from a Supreme Court opinion. It's a commonsense doctrine that maintains the integrity of our constitutional rights. And this case could have been solved with today's rules if you had let someone else solve it. Now the potential evidence is so tainted only a miracle could save it."

"Like if he talks to a cell mate," I said, "and that cell mate turns him in."

"Yes, or a relative or a friend he's confessed to is willing to tell us about it."

"Hand me the phone book, please."

She did and I looked up a number and dialed.

"Mrs. Smotz, this is Sergeant Louis Razzi. I'm the one from city court when bail was set on your grandson . . . Good, you remember me . . . I'm glad that you feel that way, and we're anxious to get him psychiatric care just like you are. My job is not finished with an arrest. Believe me, prison is no place for a sixteen-year-old white boy. I'm a Christian and a human being just like you, and my regular assignment is in the Officer Friendly program in Youth Diversion. I'm here to help youth. Now the newspapers might be calling you, so I advise that after we hang up, you leave your phone off the hook . . . That's right. If you've got a heart condition, the last thing you need is reporters bothering you. You don't want any bad publicity over this, and we can't control the newspapers, so keep your phone off the hook. Getting back to John. Is he all right? Does he need anything? Did you get a chance to talk to him? . . . Good, good, that's fine, especially the part about blacking out. That proves he needs psychiatric help. Listen, I'd like to come over and get this psychiatric background down on tape for you while it's still fresh in your mind, but I've got a million things to do and I can't promise anything. Do you own a tape recorder you could speak into? . . . Oh, that's too bad. John will need all the psychiatric background you can give him. He belongs at the state hospital, not in prison. I'll try to get over with a tape recorder, but if you don't see me by six o'clock, I advise you to write down everything John said to you so you have it for later, especially the part about blacking out. Okay, now be sure and keep the phone off the hook and don't say anything to anybody about anything until we can get John squared away at the state hospital."

I hung up the phone. "What are the rights I have to advise her of?"

"None, not as long as you don't arrest her. She's a witness. Not a suspect. She has no rights. Want a Kel Kit?"

"What's that?"

"Never mind, take this." She handed me a small cassette recorder. "Hurry up back with something, because if you don't get back soon I have to release him. I probably shouldn't hold him now. And if you hadn't charmed her so quickly on the telephone, I wouldn't be letting you go back out there. And I'm not letting you go by yourself. Take someone with you."

"I can't. Speed counts. I can't close this sale with another cop there. I'm going out as a Christian and a human being. I've got to go alone."

"Mazel tov," she called after me as I left her office.

10

The Smotz house, where John Gandry grew up after his parents deposited him at the age of three and a half never to be heard from again, was a brick row home not unlike the homes in the Morris neighborhood about a dozen blocks away.

I stood on the red-brick stoop. The bricks were loose underfoot. I knocked on the door, and an elderly white male voice growled from within: "Agnes, get the door for chrissake. It's that goddamn cop from city court. Ain't we got enough trouble?"

The door cracked. The night chain was latched and it cut across Mrs. Smotz's face as she peered at me.

"My husband says not to talk to you," she said. "He thinks you're trying to trick me. He says my heart can't take it."

"The psychiatrists have determined that your grandson harbors a deep hatred for women," I said. "He wants to rid the world of women. It's not something that concerns your husband, but it should concern you, as a woman, especially when he's released."

"We ain't goin' for bail," she said through the crack.

"Good. That's smart, but in the event that he's released because he's a juvenile, certain safety precautions have to be taken in the home. All steak knives must be removed. All sharp tools and all blunt objects, too. There are certain procedures that have to be followed to protect you, not your husband. He's a man. It's the women in the house we're worried about. We've seen this pattern before and we've learned from our mistakes. Maybe you've read about some of the tragedies. Are there any other women living here?"

"No."

"I'm coming in. We've got to make the house as safe as possible for you."

"Charlie, I'm lettin' him in now. This don't concern you," she yelled.

"You're ignorant," Charlie yelled back. "Don't let him come near me."

She closed the door in my face long enough to scare me, and long enough to unlatch the chain as well. She reopened the door and let me in.

Dirty lampshades gave a yellowish tint to the lighting, and the once-white walls looked as if they had a thin layer of cooking grease on them. She waddled into the kitchen and I followed silently. It smelled like an old damp cellar and bacon. She sat at a kitchen table with a green oilcloth on it.

I poked through the kitchen closets.

"Do you have any rat poison or other pesticides?" I asked.

"No."

"Good. I want you to take all your sharp knives, your ice pick, and all your blunt hand tools like your hammer and keep them next door whenever John is home." I began piling such things on the kitchen table.

"When's he coming?"

"Maybe never. It depends on whether he's mentally ill, and that's where your information comes in. But before we get to that, let me finish what I'm doing. Count all your drinking glasses. If there are any missing, check your food for ground glass. Your safest bet is to eat food that comes from cans and packages that you yourself open. Get me? Again, it's women he hates. He's got a strange streak in him about women. Maybe you noticed it."

"He got a temper, the boy. He never went after Charlie, but he threw a whole pot of boiling water on me when he was eight. I still got burned marks on my legs. That boy is my cross."

"You be especially sure to hide your knives next door. It gives me shivers to picture him coming home here and sitting at this table for dinner and eating a piece of meat and looking at you and grinning that evil grin with his braces while he's cutting his meat with a steak knife."

"He broke my middle finger when he was thirteen. He just bent it back. He's always too strong for me. He never liked nothin'. Women or nothin'."

"That proves he needs help. Don't you agree? We've got to get him into the state hospital under lock and key getting treatment."

"He needs something. I don't know what, and I don't care what he says." She thumbed toward where Charlie's voice had been. "The boy is the best of me. I had two heart attacks. I gotta take heart pills. I'm diabetic, you know." She seemed proud of it.

"That's all the more reason to get this over with and get him into the state hospital, where he belongs. They won't release him from the state hospital until he's cured, even if he is a juvenile. It's not like prison, where you're in today and out tomorrow. They keep you at the state hospital. Let's get this over with. This is a minicassette tape recorder. I've just put it on. Mrs. Smotz, as you know, I'm Sergeant Razzi. Tell the tape recorder what your grandson, John Gandry, told you this afternoon about blacking out when he tried to kill the little boy."

"I only know he said he didn't mean to do it. Something come over him like and he kinda blacked out from some dope he took, but you never know with that boy. He ain't no dope fiend. He's sick in the mind. The male side of the family got something in their blood. They got suicides and everything in their blood. He thought the kid was dead when he ran off. He choked him with his own pants. Now, I say that ain't right, a thing like that."

11

"As Casey Stengel used to say, 'This is amazin',' " said Honey Gold as she turned off the tape recorder. "It's the kind of thing my chief deputy, Morris Dershon, thrives on. Making the illegal legal, but really legal. You're a quick study, Detective Razzi."

"What if Grandma Smotz won't repeat this at trial?" I asked.

"Nothing to it. As long as she shows up for trial, gets sworn in, and answers a few preliminary questions, we can have you introduce the tape recording."

"No rule against it?"

"None. Now that it's legal, it wasn't so bad, was it?"

"Not too bad, but there were some moments. Now what?"

"Now I think it's a case. I'll approve it for presentment to the grand jury. I may even take it to trial myself."

"That, Miss Gold, is a genuine thrill."

"Well, Sergeant, looks like you'll be staying in town a little longer than you planned."

"Not necessarily. I can always fly back from Brazil to testify. Are you married, Miss Gold?"

"Honey. And it's not a nickname. Divorced."

"The sadder, but wiser, girl."

"That's from *The Music Man*."

"Honey, I'll bet we have some things in common. I bet we could get through a meal without yawning. You hungry?"

She hesitated, then said, "Now I know how Mrs. Smotz felt. You sure work fast. Speed really does count with you, but what do I have to lose? What are you gonna do, kill me? Everybody dies. Sergeant, I'll let you buy me a meal, a good meal."

12

The plan was to meet at the Green Room in the Hotel DuPont at about 8:15, after her shift. Meanwhile, I went back to my room for an hour's sleep. My mind was full of the past two days, and sleep was slow in coming. I had just dozed when the phone rang.

"Thank you," I said.

"Excuse me?" said Marian.

"I thought it was a wake-up call."

"I don't have much time," she said. "Can I come up to your room?"

"Where are you?"

"Downstairs at the front desk. Carlton and Sarah think I went to the ladies' room. I've only a minute. I'd love to see you, even if only for a minute. Yes or no?"

"Where are they?"

"In the Green Room. You always loved the Green Room, and I thought we might see you there. Frankly, I hoped Sarah would get to meet you fortuitously without a lot of anxiety being built up on her part."

"Don't come up. It's 7:40. I'm having dinner at 8:15. The meeting can still be an accident."

"I won't leave. I'll be waiting for you."

It sounded like a sad song sung to a GI during the war. Years of trying to fit in with the fox-hunting set must have taken their toll on Marian. To be tolerable, life had to have intrigue. I couldn't get back to sleep, and I spent the next half hour cleaning, shaving, getting back into my white suit outfit, and keeping my mind empty. I reached the Green Room foyer by 8:15. Honey was sitting in a green Victorian love seat.

"See the redhead," she said.

"You're the redhead," I said.

"Not me, her. The very attractive redhead. Watch my finger 'indicate.'" She pointed toward a table with Marian facing us. Carlton Cruset to her left and Sarah Razzi Cruset to her right.

The hostess came up to us carrying menus.

"Razzi reservation for two," I said to the hostess.

"*That* redhead asked about your reservation," said Honey. "She wanted to know if you were dining alone."

"Just a minute," I said to the hostess and brought us all to a stop. "She's my ex-wife," I said to Honey. "Sitting with my ex-daughter and my ex-daughter's stepfather. I just learned a half hour ago they'd be here. Want to leave?"

"I'll stay if you want to. I don't mind. They say you can't go out to eat in Wilmington without seeing somebody you know."

"Lou," Marian called out. She was standing by her seat. In the blink of an eye she was fifteen years older. She leaned forward in her bright pink tight-fitting silk dress with three buttons opened at the top. Her bust had gotten larger, as if from surgery. Her red hair was cut short, very stylish. Too short. No gray. And bright red, not light like Honey's. Bright red lipstick, too, and pearls all over her neck. Jewelry on her wrists and fingers. Big stones and gold. No opal.

My heartbeat was rapid, and the first surge of adrenaline flowed just above my kidneys as my eyes moved from Marian to Sally. Sally with my black hair and brown eyes. She was beautiful. Except for the coloring of the hair and eyes, she looked exactly the way I remembered Marian in high school. She turned away from me back to her mother.

Honey nudged the hostess to our table as I walked over to Marian. Sally and Marian took a good long look at Honey as she walked.

Carlton stood up and I got a better look than the last time. He was thin, very erect, maybe six five. High cheekbones. Short gray hair parted neatly on the left side and combed straight across.

"Lou Razzi, I think you met my husband, Carlton Cruset," said Marian.

I shook his hand. It was bony, but strong. Under his jacket, in a handmade black leather holster attached to his belt on the right side, I could see a stainless steel .45 automatic. He made sure I saw it by leaning his body to the right when he extended his arm.

"Good to see you again." He bowed slightly. He looked to be a dozen years older than Marian. He still wore those large metal-framed aviator eyeglasses with the yellow tint.

"Same here," I said.

"And Lou, this is Sarah," said Marian.

I wondered whether I should shake her hand or hug her. It was very awkward for both of us. Daughter and father. I wasn't aware of all that she was doing or feeling as I looked at her. She started to rise and I think she said, "Hello." I instinctively stuck out my hand, but she may have been going to hug me. I vaguely recall that she had on something yellow and green because those colors seemed to be moving when she hurried out the foyer.

"High drama," said Carlton to Marian.

"For God's sake, Carlton," said Marian. "If you'll excuse me, Lou, I think Sarah needs me." She hurried out to the foyer.

Everybody in the place was looking at us. We weren't being loud, but not too much goes unnoticed in Wilmington.

"She has a refined sense of timing," said Carlton to me as we stood by their table.

"It's my fault," I said. "Will Sarah be okay?"

"I don't see why not. She's a tough competitor, but as you no doubt noticed, she is very sensitive to the slightest movement of other people. She has a keen, almost predatory understanding of people, but there is some secret part of her that no one, absolutely no one, gets close to. No doubt you would like her. You will have to come to dinner at our home to meet her in a proper way. I assure you there will be no high drama ever again."

Carlton signed for the check and left. It looked as if they were about half finished with their meal. I went over to Honey's table. She was drinking white wine with a dash of creme de cassis.

"Cheer up," she said, and toasted me.

I sat down.

"My sinuses are clogged," I said as I wiped my right forefinger across my eyes. "I must be catching something. My friends in Brazil warned me not to drink the water."

"You sound like you could use a cry. It's none of my business, but it does clean out the sinuses. Tears have an antiseptic in them."

"I need a case of Rolling Rock."

"Not if you expect to see more of me tonight."

I smiled and said, "Waiter, cancel the case of beer. Carrot juice on the rocks, please, with a twist of lemon."

"I can't believe I said that."

"It's not what you say in life that counts. It's what you 'indicate,' but don't let me change the subject. You're prettier than average for a lawyer."

"And you're prettier than average for an ex-convict."

"Bite your tongue."

A little quarter moon of her tongue peeked out between clamped teeth. Her eyes blinked rapidly in exaggeration, like a silent movie star's.

"This has been a hell of a trip," I said. "I ought to do this every thirteen years."

13

The Green Room's splendor of glass chandeliers, ornamental mahogany, and magnificently framed oil paintings was a special treat that made it easier to concentrate on dinner and not dwell on the earlier incident. A lot of mahogany comes from Brazil, and a lot of it must have gone to Wilmington. The last time I had been to the Green Room for dinner was the night the jury went out. Marian and I and my lawyer, Ed Barnes, now retired to Vero Beach, cheered ourselves that at least the jury was out a long time and that was a good sign.

Honey had never eaten there before. She had the open-face crab with melted cheese and said that from now on she wasn't driving all the way to Baltimore for crab cakes. She told me the Gandry case could drag on in the system, and I assured her again that I'd fly back to testify and at my own expense. She had a lot of questions about the poor of Brazil, the military junta, and everyday life there. She told me I was one of the most "different" people she'd ever met; and after dinner, and without discussing it, we just very naturally and casually took the elevator to my suite. I think she led me to the elevator the way she led the hostess to the table, with little nudges. All any man wants out of life is to be seduced intelligently.

It wasn't smooth for me once we got inside the presidential suite. I was exhausted and felt haywire, like chop suey. It was great to sit at dinner and anticipate and kid around, but the old central nervous system's tender emotions department had been laid low enough for one night by the way I'd botched the meeting with Sarah.

"Last night on the plane you wouldn't hold a conversation with me, and tonight you're in my hotel room," I said.

"That sounds like a complaint, Sergeant. Let's take one step at a time and see whether you're capable of holding an after-dinner conversation. You did okay during dinner, but let's see if you can keep it up."

"Where do you live?" I asked. "How old are you?"

"Humphrey Bogart, nice, but if you're going to interrogate me, at least read me my rights."

"I still don't know them."

"Well then, since I like talking about myself, I'll just fly into it. I'll be twenty-six next month, the thirteenth. I have an apartment in the city. Three-thirteen Delaware Avenue. My phone number is five-two-one, four-nine-six-three. I wish you'd take notes. I'm from Flushing, New York, of Russian-Jewish parents. I have a six-year-old son named David, who lives with his father, named David, and boring stepmother, named Naomi, in Miami. I was coming back from a visitation when you offended my profession. I've been divorced five years. Let's see, I'm an inactive Democrat in a Republican state, and despite what you think, I don't run around with every cop in town. I rarely date. My choice, not theirs. I'm usually not this outspoken, but you're about to fly away to Brazil forever, so what the hell. I haven't had sex with anyone but myself in about a year, but I am very attracted to you and I don't know why. You have confidence, even when you screw up. Certainly more than the research chemists I've been out with. One of them gave me a whistle to blow in case I get mugged. Now, buster, what do you think of me?"

"I liked you from the minute I saw you in the airport. And I've liked being with you more and more."

"I like that part about liking me. If it's true."

"It is. I'm not just trying to get in your pants. I do like you."

"Promise?"

"That was my promise."

"Then I suppose everything you say in life is under oath."

"Not everything. Once in a blue moon I lie, but I make it a point not to lie on my first date to people I'm attracted to, and it's easy to tell that I'm attracted to you."

"How?"

"The same way you can tell when a puppy likes his belly rubbed. It started during dessert and came back again when you talked about having sex with yourself."

We both looked down at the remains. She laughed and I laughed with her. We reached out and held each other's arms and then moved toward one another, with her forehead coming to rest against mine.

"You've got some kind of energy," she said. "I can feel it."

"It's the Brazilian sun," I said.

We separated, still holding each other's arms, and Honey looked at me impishly. She put my hand on the side of her left breast.

"That's not a come-on," she said. We both laughed.

"I'd like you to stay," I said.

"Don't let me twist your arm," she said, "but I was beginning to wonder."

We kissed. Softly, at first. Every part of me that was touching her felt indeed energetic. The haywire circuitry was clearing itself. I was warmer all over, and I felt she was, too, as our bodies and lips pressed harder. I wanted to make love until the cows came home.

She sucked lightly on my lower lip. The energy in my lower lip became a tingle, and the phone rang.

We separated, virtually pulling apart like a suction cup from a glass surface.

Her cheeks were red and her eyes moist. She looked at me quizzically, and that was followed by a look of grave concern on her face.

"You look enraged," she said while the phone continued to ring. "I'd hate to ever cross you. You look possessed."

I took a deep breath, exhaled, and tried to relax.

"It's got nothing to do with you," I said. I reached for the phone.

"You think it's Marian, don't you?"

I stopped my hand inches from the phone.

"Answer it," she said. "Find out what she wants and then see how you feel about it."

I picked up the receiver.

"Lou," said DiGiacomo, "I nearly hung up when you didn't answer. You in the shower?"

"Hi, Rocco" I said and winked at Honey. "No, I'm not in the shower. I could use one, a cold one. What's going on?" "Lou, I wish I could tell you this in person, but I gotta get back to dicks. Shy Whitney's just been shot dead down at the train station . . . We ain't got much. I'm leaving the scene now. I figured you'd wanna go down there and help out. Everybody's being called in off duty. Even the state and county police. You know how it is when something like this happens."

"I'll be down." I hung up.

I sat on the bed. I didn't know how it was when something like this happened. It had never happened when I was on the cops. I pictured his face in front of me. It was as big as the room, his eyes twinkling like he was up to something.

"Shy Whitney was murdered," I said. "He's a cop. He broke me in. I just saw him this morning. We talked about Mondale getting shot."

"Did Mondale get shot?"

"No. My friend, Shy Whitney."

"Oh, my God." She sat down next to me and put her arm around me. "Was that Rocco DiGiacomo?"

"Rock wants me down at the train station. It's the worst news I've ever heard in my life. I'm stunned."

"I know, but it'll do you good to get moving. Fighting back."

She got us out of the hotel and to my car.

14

The Amtrak train station is a very pale, old two-story red-brick building that was property of the now-defunct Pennsylvania Railroad when I left Wilmington. It occupies a city block in a ghost town of a neighborhood. The two main Amtrak entrances are on French Street. Over French Street is a trestle for the railroad tracks that go into the second floor of the building. The trestle is supported by a stone wall on the other end. The trestle makes the French Street entrances gray and cavelike, even on the brightest summer days.

Now, as we pulled up to a spot under the trestle near the stone wall, the area looked brighter than I'd ever seen it. Artificial lamps and the headlights and dome lights of police cars filled the area. Across the street, along with half the other buildings, Janasek's Hotel was boarded up, waiting for the merciful weight of the wrecking ball.

The far front entrance of the station was roped off, and we walked over to it.

Shy was gone. What was left was a white chalk outline drawn like an accordian on the dirty steps leading to a grim gray landing that led in turn to green doors with small glass panels at eye level. The area was surprisingly quiet, considering all the police and spectator activity. A little pool of red blood, made darker by the soot of the station, attracted a number of flies to the head of the outline. The arms were spread out, and the legs and feet cascaded down the stairs like a child's sidewalk drawing. There was a smaller chalk circle near the head. Shy's cigar.

Honey stood to my left.

"I know how you feel," Covaletzki said softly from near my right shoulder. "It's a terrible, terrible shame, a dirty rotten shame."

I turned and looked at him. He was in his chief's uniform — white shirt, white cap, and dark-blue pants. He had his lips parted and his head bowed almost religiously. His hands were clasped just below the waist. I studied his eyes. He wanted me to let him off the hook. He wanted to personally profit from Shy's death.

I looked away from him and back to the chalk outline. I still hadn't forgotten how to do time. "What needs to be done?" I asked calmly.

"You work this case with DiGiacomo," he said, his smile displaying a synthetic serenity. He put his left hand tenderly on my right shoulder. "DiGiacomo's in charge. I sent him to the Detective Division. Why don't you go over to dicks and tell him you're on the case. Shy would want you working the case. Listen, I know you didn't put your retirement papers in today, and I know you done a damn fine job on that Gandry thing. I ain't worried about when you're gonna retire. You have some fun first. Maybe I'll transfer you back to dicks for a while. I gotta replace Shy anyway."

"I'll go on up to 'dicks' now," I said, "and have some fun out of Shy's murder."

He abruptly took his hand off my shoulder. That pinched look of his took hold of his face and drew all his features toward his left eye, causing it to squint. He studied me out of the big eye. Staring like a cyclops.

"You're fucking around with me, aren't you? I can tell by lookin' at you. Your mind's gone, boy, if you think you can bullshit me," he said in his monotone. "You work this case if you wanna, but you better be on your shift at Youth Diversion at 8:00 A.M. — on fucking time — every day until you put your fuckin' papers in." He turned away smartly and took a few steps until a dark-blue Lincoln limousine pulled up alongside of us. Four men in their early thirties rushed out almost at once. Three were white, one black, but all wore gray three-piece business suits.

"Good evening, Mayor, Commissioner, Councilman," said Covaletzki.

"Are there any clues, Chief?" demanded one of the white men.

"The ass end of two black youths was seen by a civilian witness running in the direction toward the river immediately after the shot was fired," said Covaletzki. "One subject wore a green CPO jacket. The other subject was carrying a sticklike object, possibly a rifle. No clothing on the other subject could be ascertained due to the distances involved and the inadequacy of the lighting. The witness didn't see their faces. A .22 caliber long-rifle shell casing was located on the sidewalk twelve feet, seven inches from the right foot of the body. It has an S marking on it, possible Sears manufacture. Sergeant Rocco DiGiacomo's checking out Sears for recent purchases. The bullet hole in Whitney's forehead is a small entrance wound, could be a .22, but we're waiting for the ME to make it official. Meantime, we're stopping every car that moves, and we're starting a door-to-door canvass of the neighborhood as soon as all the state and county men get here. Whitney's service revolver was taken. We don't know if he had it drawn at the time he was fired upon. He was at the station picking up his wife. We had to rush her to the emergency room. Her blood pressure went off the scale. They're afraid she might get a stroke."

"Is that legal, stopping cars and going door to door?" asked the same young man. "I don't want any overreaction, especially in the black community."

"Let me check for sure with her, Mayor, sir," said Covaletzki, and he turned back to us and pointed to Honey. "She's a deputy AG."

"I'm Honey Gold, Mayor. Under the *Prouse* decision, random routine traffic checks are illegal. So are the fruits of any random checks. Make sure the men don't randomly stop cars. They've got to stop every single passing car on a given street. Like a roadblock. Remember, they're looking for witnesses. The same is true on the door-to-door canvass. Ask for people to volunteer information. Don't force anything."

"You got that?" said the young mayor to the chief. "I don't want any kicking ass and taking names, and I don't want any move without checking with her first."

"Right, sir," said Covaletzki. "I'll make sure everybody understands that, which I really think they do, Your Honor."

Honey and I walked across the cobblestoned street toward my gray Granada.

"The *Prouse* decision," I said. "What is that, more fruit?"

"I think I'll go to dicks with you," she said with a look of exasperation. "I don't know about DiGiacomo, but you could use my advice. You got that funky 'astuperious' look."

I drove the twelve blocks to the Public Building. She sat closer to me than to the passenger door. Even at the worst of times I guess you notice things like that.

"What's with you and Covaletzki?" she asked.

"He helped frame me."

"That's pretty strong. It comes out sounding a little paranoid. Can you prove it?"

"To whose satisfaction?"

She didn't answer.

I yawned. I was still tired from jet lag, much less last night and today. It was close to 11:00 P.M.

"Marian Cruset's husband is an odd duck," Honey said. "Did you notice his facial tic?"

"I wasn't paying attention to him."

She looked over at me. "She's stunning." I yawned more deeply. "He's a good friend of the colonel of the state police," she continued, "and of Covaletzki. He powwows with all the chiefs. He's a cop groupie. A real crime nut. A few years back he formed a citizen's group called the Delaware War on Crime. D-WOC. With his money behind it they put up rewards for information, and they lobby and throw parties for retiring cops and write a lot of law-and-order letters to the editor. They do some good, I guess. But his big thing is abortion. He's the head of the antiabortion forces, I think, in the whole Northeast. I expect you know about *Husband vs. Wife*?"

"No. I don't."

"The decision doesn't mention their names, but everybody around the courthouse knows it's them. He took her to court about three years ago to try to stop her from having an abortion. Of course, it was thrown out. But I guess they kissed and made up. They're still together. They say it made him suicidal, the powerlessness of it. He wanted to have the baby, but she felt she was too old to have another child. Anyway, she had a boob job right after the abortion. I'm surprised you hadn't heard about it. I never saw his wife until tonight at the Green Room. She really is stunning. For a redhead."

"I'd like to see Shy's murder solved before breakfast," I

said. "He was closer to me than you realize. I've also got to pay attention as I drive. I'm a cop, and there's a cop shooter out tonight."

"Sorry."

"When they start bringing in known cop haters and armed robbers, I'm certain Rocco would want me at least in on the interrogations. Maybe I'd better drop you off at your office."

"Sergeant, you just can't go around rounding up the usual suspects anymore. It's not that way. Even suspects are now considered to be human beings, and I told you, I'm going to stick around. I'm not your date anymore tonight. In fact, I may shortly be in charge of this investigation."

15

Two long columns of gray rubberized desks, nicked and scarred and each supporting a black telephone. A scattering of battered manual typewriters of mixed manufacture. The dicks. The big brown leather chair was gone, but not the dust. It was home sweet home. A large brown glass ashtray with cigar butts was where I knew it would be, where it had been for more than twenty years, where you could still smell Shy. There was a framed photograph of Shy and his wife, Mary, smiling on either side of Giuseppe DiStefano, Shy's favorite tenor. Giuseppe had his arms around both of them, and they were having the thrill of their lives.

Behind the main room was the captain's office, where Figaro, Hanrahan, and Covaletzki had had their little chit-chats. I opened the door a crack. Rocco DiGiacomo was sitting in the captain's chair.

"I'm glad you're here," he said. "We're gonna need your brain tonight."

That felt good. Especially in front of Honey. Little Clem Augrine was sitting at a typing table, pecking away. I thought it was early to be making out reports. Honey and I walked on in.

"I'm glad you're here, too," DiGiacomo said to Honey. "We're working on a search warrant."

"I heard they found a .22 shell with an S," she said. "What have you got?"

"Okay," said DiGiacomo, "Tony Landis is over at Sears. He got the manager out of bed, and the guy went down and opened the store after Tony told him there's ten large grand in reward money."

"Carlton Cruset?" Honey asked.

"Yeah," said Augrine without looking up, "yeah."

"Landis called from Sears," said DiGiacomo. "The shell is definitely theirs. Tony's been looking through the books, and he came across the sale of a .22-caliber bolt-action single-shot and a box of long-rifle cartridges to a burglar named Harrison Lloyd. Harrison filled out the federal firearms forms about not having no felony record, but we figure he had a felony. We're pretty sure he was a person prohibited from buying a gun under the statute."

"How do you know it wasn't somebody using his name?" asked Honey.

"The manager says it's company policy to compare the driver's license picture with the guy's face. They copy the license number right on their ledger. It's Lloyd's license. We ran it through Motor V."

"Did you type all that in the affidavit to the search warrant?" Honey asked Augrine.

"Pretty much," said Augrine, "mostly," as he handed her a sheet of paper with some typing on it. Honey picked a fountain pen from her handbag and began to make changes and additions. It took her at least a good precious three minutes while the rest of us watched. I said nothing. By now I knew better.

"What do you mean you're pretty sure Harrison Lloyd has a felony conviction?" she asked finally.

"We know he was arrested for felonies by a uniformed man, Joe Janiro," said Rocco. "Felony theft and burglary, coming out of the Shortlidge School carrying a computer, but we don't have no disposition on our rap sheet. We called Janiro at home and he said Lloyd plea-bargained, but he don't know what to. If we knew he went down for a felony, we could lock him up right now on the gun-purchase charge and go from there. Then the search warrant for his house would be easy to write up. But that's where we're stuck. We're just not sure Lloyd went down for a felony."

"Wait a minute," said Augrine. "I just thought of something. Didn't Pascal lock Lloyd's ass up last year on Clayton Street for some kind of assault that had to be a felony? It had to be a felony, that thing he had with Pascal."

"He was a juvenile last year," said DiGiacomo. "That don't count as a felony. Janiro's bust is his only adult record. Honey, do you think we got probable cause to search his house without Janiro's felony?"

"No," said Honey. "I'm glad you're steering away from the murder because you certainly have no probable cause at all on any homicide. You're on the right track sticking with the gun-purchase charge, but you don't have enough to search his house there either. Purchasing the gun isn't illegal unless he's a convicted felon, and you don't know if he's been convicted of anything, much less a felony."

"Would the AG's office records show anything? You know, how about your office records," asked Augrine, "would that be good enough?"

"Good idea," said Honey. "I'll go across the street to the main office and check."

"I'll walk you," I said. "We may be dealing with a sniper."

By sticking to Honey, maybe I could nudge this along the way she herself nudged people along. I was beginning to learn that you have to nudge before you can crawl. Things were already going too slowly for me. Whatever happened to instincts? I'd have scooped up Harrison Lloyd and questioned him the second his name came up. What'll I do with Figaro, take him to the law library? As Yogi Berra said, you can't hit and think at the same time.

16

A highly officious old white security guard rode in the elevator with us as an "extra precaution," even though he knew Honey personally. I read the signs on the wall: NO SMOKING and THIS ELEVATOR IS VOICE MONITORED FOR YOUR PROTECTION. I wondered if that was legal, and whether there was another old guard somewhere in a small closet listening to us. But I didn't say anything. We got off on the seventh floor and Honey used her key to get in. The guard turned on the lights and waited in the hall, his arthritic arms dangling like a gunfighter's. We went to a section with small file cabinets holding three-by-five cards. Honey went to the Ls and pulled out all the Lloyds until she found Harrison, DOB 11-28-57, home address being that of his parents.

"That's our boy," she said. "Look at this. He pled to burglary of the Shortlidge School on twenty-six May. La-de-da. A fel-o-ny. He was definitely a person prohibited when he bought the rifle on eleven June. But uh-oh. He was on for sentencing yesterday morning. Darn! He was probably in jail tonight when the gun was used. Let's check the sentencing lists, if I can figure out where Rosemary keeps them."

I followed her to a desk. On it were four large stacks of files, with white sheets of paper on each stack. Honey picked up the white papers and speed-read through them.

"Pay dirt," she said. "A bench warrant was issued at 11:30 this morning. He failed to show up for sentencing. Now, Sergeant, we can pick him up."

17

"Dynamite. Dynamite," said DiGiacomo when we carried the news to the captain's office. "What's the plan, go to his house and lock him up for not showing for sentencing? Then we can search around him incidental to the arrest and forget about the search warrant altogether? Hah? What?"

When you spend your remaining days before retirement trying to break serious cases in boring ways, you overexcite yourself when you smell a shortcut.

"I don't even know what Rocco's talking about," I said, "but somehow I know he's right."

"No," said Honey. "We still need a search warrant to be able to search the house for the rifle. Type in the felony conviction and leave a space for my signature as affiant on what I saw in the AG's records. It's not going to take a half hour to an hour to get the thing typed and over to a judge, right?"

"Right," said Rocco. "You're the boss. We got Judge Wyrostek out of bed. He'll wait up for us. He's a good man."

"Good," said Honey. "Let's do it."

Augrine started typing. "How do you spell 'manufacture'?" He looked up. "Give me a spelling on 'manufacture.'" Honey brushed past me, mumbling, "Excuse me," and bent down and wrote the word out for him as he two-fingered it slowly on the typewriter.

"Damn it," I said. "Nothing can be this technical. It's late. There are two cop murderers we want. And the cop they killed was closer than a brother to us. We just lost an hour we'll never see again trying to figure out whether we have the right to bring him in here, and we're now about to lose another hour. Let's get him. Maybe she doesn't know it, but everybody else in this room knows it. When you're lucky enough to get a trail, you follow it before the winds blow on it and the rains wash it away. Come on. Look alive. Get some energy back in you. When we had Lloyd's name from Sears, everybody on the street should have been looking for him. I agree, tell him about *his Miranda* rights, but get him in here and find out who his partner is. Then get his partner in here and play one against the other. Last I knew, cop killers bought the farm. Eighty-eight bullets resisting arrest. And I'm not even talking about that. I'm talking about locking them up. Am I missing something?"

"Fifteen years," said Landis, who was back from Sears. "Rest up, Lou. Grab a sandwich out of the machine."

Everybody stared at me the way Covaletzki had at the train station, out of his right eye. Like I was crazy. I leaned against the wall out of the way.

"As I said," said Honey, glaring her hazels at me, "we've got to have a warrant on the gun-purchase charge so we can search Lloyd's house for the gun. You see, Sergeant Razzi —"

"That's a mistake, Honey." I glared.

She knew what I meant. I could see it in her eyes. She continued rapidly but in a softer tone: "Look, Lou, you did tell me you want to learn this stuff. If we arrest Lloyd for skipping sentencing, we can only search within his immediate reach for weapons he might grab. But if we have a search warrant, we can search the whole house until we find the gun, and that way we might accidentally come up with other evidence on

Shy's murder." She turned from me. "But, men, if we do, don't seize it. We'll get another search warrant based on whatever you find that relates to the homicide. Unless it's Whitney's service revolver — that comes under exigent circumstances." I laughed a short grunt. She continued, unintimidated: "I hope this is clear to everybody in this room. Now, let's plug this felony conviction into the affidavit, and then I'll plug some extra probable cause for a search in the nighttime."

"Let's not forget to put in that we're looking for the bullets he bought at Sears," said Augrine, "and most definitely the sales slip. That way we'll get the right to search wallets and little places that the gun can't fit. Who knows what we'll find in those little teeny places. Probably drugs and shit. So we better put the sales slip and the bullets in. We're not just looking for the gun. Get me?"

"I get you," said Honey. "Good idea." As the rest of us watched, she sat next to Augrine at the typewriter and began to reword the first draft of the affidavit on a yellow pad. Augrine typed what she wrote. Now I understood why Augrine wore three-piece suits. He had become the dicks' law clerk. I wondered if he still wore elevator shoes. Landis went out to make sure the judge was awake.

I walked into dicks and looked again at the desk of Shy Whitney of Chattanooga, Tennessee, who had drifted down to Delaware when his navy hitch in Philadelphia was up because they were hiring on the cops. The least they could do now was retire his desk like Joe DiMaggio's number. He was one brave man, and he always got his weight on the opposite foot of his punch. You stayed hit that way. He taught me that kind of leverage when he broke me in, and with his beautiful tenor voice alone in a patrol car with the windows up, he taught me to appreciate good music. But my greatest appreciation for the way Shy broke me in came when I saw how other rookies were broken in by their veteran partners. During working hours you got your rookie partner his first oral sex. You waited for him in the patrol car. As he walked down the dirty stoop of some poor woman's place, smoothing down his jacket and wearing that pathetic boy-grin that says now-I'm-a-man, you knew you owned him. Your rookie would never report you for breaking department rules, or for anything else you did. A stunt like that never entered Shy's mind.

I wondered if Shy had kept up with all the new procedures. He must have, but if they came down all at once, nobody could have kept up with them. Poor Shy. A chalk outline on French Street. Worse than dying, he'd have hated some punk kid getting the best of him. For more than half the hours of his short time on earth, on duty and off, he carried the weight of a loaded pistol so other people could go about their business — other people giving political speeches or going to train stations to pick up their wives or just going to the Laundromat. Mrs. Smotz would say, "That ain't right, a thing like that."

Finally Honey was done. Landis called Judge Wyrostek to make sure he was still up so that we could go to his house for him to approve and sign the search warrant. It was 1:33 A.M. when we arrived. The judge, a man in his forties wearing yellow pajamas and a red robe, led us into his living room. I guessed that his wife had straightened up before we arrived.

Wyrostek had half-lens reading glasses perched on the end of his nose and looked out over them to ask Honey questions that I didn't understand. I think he asked her whether she "would agree" that some of the probable cause was "stale" for a nighttime warrant, or something like that. In the end he signed the thing.

We left Judge Wyrostek's and everybody thanked him as if he were the cavalry. In the car on the way to execute the warrant, I nodded off in the backseat, leaning against the door.

18

Car doors slammed, and I awoke with a jolt to find myself sitting in the dark in the backseat with Honey.

"It's your job to protect me," she said, "in the event there's trouble loud enough to wake you. The other guys are taking the doors on Lloyd's parents' house without backup support."

An upstairs light went on. They weren't exactly "taking the doors." Landis and DiGiacomo were standing on either side of the front door, waiting for it to be answered. I left the car and walked up the cement path of the brick home in a familiar block not far from the one in which I grew up. The fat, burly sycamore trees that once lined the street, dropping crisp bark and what we called itchy balls, were all gone. Maybe they knew something the people didn't know.

A fortyish black woman in a green terry-cloth robe opened the door. Landis flashed his shield and peeked in past her, gingerly. DiGiacomo held up the search warrant. She looked at it and stood aside. The steps they took through the doorway during this police emergency had about two hours of preparation invested in them. I followed.

Inside the front door was the living room. Beyond the living room was the dining room. The house smelled of disinfectant. Mrs. Lloyd seated herself with dignity at the Mediterranean-style dining room table, as if we were her guests. Beside the dining room was a small kitchen. DiGiacomo walked into the kitchen and let Augrine in through the back door. Augrine acknowledged my presence with a nod, opened a door off the kitchen, and hurried down to the basement with his gun drawn.

"Harrison's not been home for two days," she said wearily. "I knew that boy was heading for more trouble. He just don't listen. You-all have a look for him, but he ain't here."

"Who else is home?" asked Landis.

"My husband and my two other boys is upstairs sleeping. They're both good boys. What's Harrison done?"

"He didn't show up for sentencing," said Landis.

The stairs to the second floor were in the living room. DiGiacomo headed for them but stopped short when a very tall and dark-skinned muscular Negro male in his forties, wearing eyeglasses, white boxer-type shorts, and a tight black T-shirt with a white Playboy rabbit on it, started down the stairs. He was followed by two skinny boys in their early teens. Both boys wore eyeglasses and were over six feet tall. They had on tan chino pants and no shirts and were wiping sleep away from their faces.

"He didn't show up for sentencing, huh?" said the man in a very deep voice. "He ain't showed up for a lot of damn things, but I ain't never seen no houseful of po-lease at two in the morning." He sat down on a gold crushed-velvet sofa. "Shit." He lit a mentholated Benson & Hedges.

The boy who appeared the older and taller of the two opened the screen door and rushed outside. The door had no spring and he slammed it shut hard. Nobody tried to stop him.

"He's got hypertension," said Mrs. Lloyd from the dining room. "These two are good boys."

I stood by the door and watched him get into a green Plymouth with wide wheels and the rear jacked. He sat in the car with the door open and played soul music on the car radio. It was loud. Honey rolled up her window.

"Are you Mr. Lloyd?" asked Rocco.

"Yea-yah," said the man.

The younger boy sat on a blue crushed-velvet chair directly across from his father. He looked more like his mother than the older boy.

"I know you," said Tony Landis to Mr. Lloyd. "You got a numbers bank on Jessup Street. They call you Tramp."

"Bust me. Search me. But please don't bore me," said Mr. Lloyd. "Not in my own home."

I took a step toward Tramp Lloyd, but DiGiacomo stepped into my path with his back to me.

"Somebody's gotta come upstairs with me," said DiGiacomo quickly. "You mind coming, Mr. Lloyd? We've got a search warrant for your son Harrison's rifle. It seems he bought a rifle after he was a convicted felon. You gotta witness what we do."

"It ain't here. I got a rifle, but it ain't his. I'll show you mine."

Tramp Lloyd got up and led the way upstairs. Landis sat at the kitchen table and began to question Mrs. Lloyd in a conversational way. Augrine came up from downstairs.

"Nothing down there," said Augrine, and he headed upstairs. "Not a thing."

I sat next to the young boy who looked like his mother.

"How old are you?" I asked. "About sixteen?"

"Thirteen," he said without looking at me.

"Harrison a good brother to you? He treat you right?" I asked.

He didn't answer, but the tension in his cheeks and forehead showed that he had something more against his oldest brother than sibling rivalry.

"You know what first-degree murder is?"

"Yea-yah. What you sayin'? Harrison kilt somebody? I ain't got nothin' to do with him."

"His rifle upstairs?"

"No."

"How do you know?"

"I seen him take it out the attic round about yesterday. He had it in a suitcase in two and he carried it right out of here and he ain't been back. I don't know nothing about no first-degree murder."

"Who was he with, that shorter dude, what's-his-name?" I figured most dudes would be shorter to the Lloyd family.

"Yea-yah, Jack Stiggs."

"The one with the green CPO jacket?" I figured Stiggs to be the one running without the rifle, the one in the jacket.

"If you be knowin', why do you be axin'?"

"What time they leave?" I asked quickly and firmly.

"In the mornin'."

"Where were they goin'?"

"I don't be knowin' his business and he don't be knowin' mine."

"You've seen him use that rifle. I know that, and you know I know that."

"One'st. That time he shot the black dog in the throat. With some white fur on his throat. With it over by the lots. One time, maybe 'bout last week."

"Where does he keep the bullets?"

"With his shavin' cream and stuff. What you axin' me all this for?" He got up and walked out to join his brother.

I went upstairs. DiGiacomo, standing next to Tramp Lloyd, was holding a .30-.30 army surplus carbine rifle. They both watched Augrine pick through drawers in a small bedroom.

"Harrison's room?" I asked.

DiGiacomo nodded.

On a bureau was a black vinyl shaving bag. I walked past DiGiacomo, picked up the bag, and emptied the contents on the bureau. Along with deodorant, shaving cream, and loose change, there was one .22 long-rifle round with an S stamped on it. I picked it up and held it near Mr. Lloyd's eyes for emphasis.

"Where's the attic?" I asked.

Mr. Lloyd pointed with his thumb to a spot above the bureau. Augrine climbed onto the bureau and pushed aside the wooden hatch.

"Is there a light switch up there?" Augrine asked. "Any light?"

"Over your head there's a string," said Tramp Lloyd.

Augrine hoisted himself into the darkness and in a few seconds had the light on. Papers rustled.

"I got the Sears bag and the sales slip," he said, "but I don't see a weapon up here."

"I ain't never seen no gun in this house e'cept mine. The one he's holdin'," said Tramp Lloyd.

Augrine jumped to the bureau and then the floor, and we all went downstairs. Landis had searched the entire downstairs and had finished questioning Mrs. Lloyd, and they were standing, shaking hands.

Landis said, "I got possible places he could be. He doesn't own a green CPO jacket."

"Mr. and Mrs. Lloyd," said DiGiacomo, "the best thing Harrison can do is turn himself in. He's a convicted felon and he's got no business buying a gun at Sears. Understand? Besides, he's in enough trouble missing sentencing. Understand that?"

Tramp scowled.

"I do," said Mrs. Lloyd.

DiGiacomo gave Mrs. Lloyd a business card. "Call me," he said, "if he contacts you." DiGiacomo turned and left, with Landis and Augrine following.

I stayed in the doorway. "Hear about that cop getting shot and killed at the train station tonight?" I asked.

Mrs. Lloyd didn't answer. There was a sudden hardness to her look now. She raised her eyebrows as if I had shortchanged her at the grocery store.

"A Wilmington police officer was shot in his brain tonight," I said. "There's a very large army of armed and dangerous policemen on the street. They're what you'd call enraged. Harrison's a prime suspect and their tempers are boiling over. A lot of the cops on the street were good friends of the one who was killed. See that woman in the police car with the red hair? She's a deputy attorney general, a lawyer with the state. We've been assigned to work for her tonight to find Harrison before anybody else does. The safest place your son could be tonight is at the police station in responsible care. We don't want anything ugly to happen. If he shows up, for God's sake get him to us. For his own good."

I walked out to the car before she could ask questions or respond. All eyes in the car were on me.

19

I got in the backseat. The cacophonous blare of the rock music from the green Plymouth was distracting. Instead of ordering the boys into the house or threatening to arrest them for breach of peace, DiGiacomo drove two blocks away from the noise and parked. I told him what I'd learned from little brother.

"Lloyd's probably thrown the rifle away by now," said Honey.

"Kids never throw guns away," said Landis. "They maybe threw their clothes away. It's been a few hours. But not the rifle. Let's go see if Jack Stiggs is at his mother's house. I know where they live. If we catch him off guard he might talk to us."

"What do you think?" DiGiacomo asked me just the way he always used to. "What's our next move?"

"I think you drop Honey and me off at the division, and the three of you go see Jack Stiggs's mother and lay it on thick about cops full of vengeance roaming the streets. Maybe mama will bring her little lamb in so that we can talk to him about his friend Harrison Lloyd. Is that legal, Honey?"

"It sounds okay to me, but if Stiggs does come in on his own, don't detain him or restrict his freedom, and the safest bet is to give him his warnings."

"We understand," said Landis.

DiGiacomo switched the ignition and it wouldn't start. He

tried and tried again. He cursed the mayor for buying economy cars and radioed for two black-and-white patrol cars. The first one came in less than five minutes, and the three detectives went off in it. Fifteen minutes later our ride showed up, and Honey and I were driven to the Public Building by a uniformed man, a boy. He couldn't have been seven in 1961.

The Public Building was practically empty. All the men called in were out chasing other leads or had been sent home to save on overtime pay.

Once we got upstairs to the hallway with my old locker in it leading to dicks, I saw Mr. and Mrs. Tramp Lloyd sitting on the oak bench that Figaro, Janasek, and the Darvi girl had been cuffed to. Between them sat a young black male bent forward at the waist, with his face in his hands. He was skinny, but he wasn't tall like his father and brothers, and he didn't wear eyeglasses. The black sheep. He was wearing a white nylon T-shirt, army fatigue pants, and high-top black sneakers. Converse All-Stars. He smelled like a sewer.

"Harrison," I said.

He looked up lazily.

"Stand up," I said.

He did so.

"You're a lot shorter than your little brothers," I said.

I walked up to him and patted him down. He came prepared for jail. Empty pockets. I thought about checking his underwear for hundred-dollar counterfeits.

"You've done the right thing, Mr. and Mrs. Lloyd. I'm going to take your son in the other room. Kindly wait here. Let's go, Harrison."

When we got into the main room I led him straight into the interrogation room, my favorite room in the whole world since I've been alive, if I ever start to rate rooms. It looked the same.

Even the old manual typewriter looked as if it hadn't been replaced. The only thing new I spotted was a Sony cassette recorder near the typewriter on the gray table. Metal folding chairs surrounded the table. The see-through mirror on the wall next to the polygraph room was in place just as I remembered it, fooling no one.

The sight of it all gave me a feeling I couldn't suppress. It had a life of its own and it made my heart race. I was excited the second I walked toward that room with my prisoner in front of me. Just my prisoner and me and Honey makes three in a little room the way it was supposed to be.

"Harrison, I just hate you," I said affably. He had that look of bewilderment when you first throw them off balance. "I hate your friends, too. And I think that tonight you are going to find out that you have one less friend in life than you think you have. Tonight you are about to find out that it's every man for himself in this dog-eat-dog world. Which reminds me, Harrison, please don't let me forget to ask you about a little incident involving a dog. It's such a minor thing I could forget to ask you about it. Would you remind me about it, Miss Gold?"

"Excuse me," said Honey as she followed us into the room. She positioned herself between Lloyd and me.

"Sure, go ahead," I said. "She's going to tell you your rights, boy. Listen up. And then I'm gonna tell you some things."

"Harrison Lloyd," said Honey, "you are under arrest for possession of a deadly weapon by a person prohibited and for failure to appear at sentencing. Do you understand that? Well, do you?"

"Yea-yah."

"You are also a suspect in another crime, murder in the first degree of a police officer. Do you understand that?"

"Yea-yah," but a little tighter in the larynx.

"Mr. Lloyd, you have the right to remain silent. Do you understand that?"

"Yea-yah."

"Anything you do say to us can and will later be used against you in a court of law. Do you understand that?"

"Yea-yah."

"You have the right to the presence of an attorney during questioning. Do you understand that?"

"Yea-yah."

"If you cannot afford an attorney, one will be provided for you by the state free of charge to you. Do you understand that?"

"Yea-yah."

"Understanding all of the above, will you freely and voluntarily answer our questions?"

No answer. He peeked up at me out of the side of his face. His lower lip hung down.

I waited. She waited. He said nothing.

"Harrison, my friend," I said slowly and smiled and tried to look halfway amused. "What kind of bullet do you think we found in the dead dog in the lot? You know, the black dog with the white fur on its neck in the lot? Well, what do you think, buckaroo? Do you think we're matching it with another bullet we found inside somebody's head? Maybe you think another dog came along and ate that dead dog all up and that bullet, too?"

"Excuse me," interrupted Honey with her patented edge to the voice. "We need a waiver. Understanding all of the above, will you freely and voluntarily answer our questions?"

He looked at me trying to size up the situation. I pressed to regain possession of my prisoner. "Harrison," I said firmly, "if you've got nothing to hide from me, you better understand all of the above and begin answering my questions right quick."

"Wrong!" Honey bellowed. "Lou, just be quiet. You can't do that. There's case law on it. He's got to freely and voluntarily waive his rights. Mr. Lloyd, do you want a lawyer or not?"

He looked at me as if he had just found out that while I had four hearts showing, all I had in the hole was a diamond, and a low one at that.

"I ain't saying nothin'. I want a lawyer."

"What for?" I demanded. "Your lawyer going to hold your hand? What are you, a little Mary? Harrison, asking for a lawyer is the first, absolute first, sign of guilt. You've told me all I need to know, young man. Now, I'm giving you five seconds to change your mind and give your side of this. After that, I'm taking Jack Stiggs's side. You know Stiggs, the one who wears a green CPO jacket. Don't ever trust a man who wears a green CPO jacket. You know we hang murderers in this state. You get five seconds or I'm going with Stiggs, and that puts your neck in a world of trouble."

"What that chump be knowing about me?" Lloyd jumped at the bait. "He think he be knowin' my business, but he don't be knowin' my business, not my business."

"Excuse me," Honey said calmly, yet deliberately. "We absolutely must step outside, Lou. Please."

I followed her out of the room and she shut the door behind us.

"You can't ask him another thing. He's asked for a lawyer. That's the law, Lou. Period. The only thing left to do is book him on the weapons charge and for missing sentencing. Try talking to his parents. He might have confessed to them, like Gandry."

"I'll try, Honey Gold," I said, "but look at 'Tramp' Lloyd. He wouldn't tell us this place was on fire."

She sighed. I patted her shoulder and then dropped my hand.

I took Harrison Lloyd to the basement lockup and, with help from a uniformed man, put him in the first cell. I went upstairs to the Lloyds, but my heart wasn't in it; and while Mrs. Lloyd was subdued, Mr. Lloyd treated me like a hired hand. "It was her bright idea to bring him in here," Tramp Lloyd said coldly. "What's the difference you burn him on the street, or you give him a trial and then you burn him? He ain't gonna get justice."

I got DiGiacomo on the radio and told him what was what. He had nothing on his end. They had found Stiggs, but he refused to come in for questioning. He wanted a lawyer. DiGiacomo said he was coming in to handle the reports on Lloyd and to douse Lloyd's body with benzidine to see if he had any of Shy's blood on his body from when they stole Shy's weapon. If he had any blood it would turn blue. I said I'd never heard of the stuff. He said it was a giant long shot, but maybe Lloyd would get cancer from the chemical. He told me to turn in and get some sleep. He'd see me in the morning.

When I finished talking to DiGiacomo, I went upstairs and looked for Honey. She was in the captain's office sleeping in his big chair. I awakened her by walking in.

"Go on back to the hotel," I said and put my room key in her hand, "please."

"What are you going to do here? You can't go back in on Lloyd."

"I get the message. Ernesto Miranda. I'm catching on. I just want to talk to Rocco about something I thought of when I looked at you all curled up in the captain's chair. We should try to find the dead dog with the white patch on his throat."

"Very funny. Is this another one of your stand-up insult routines?"

“No. I didn’t mean it the way it sounded. I’m very tired. I just thought of it when I saw you. Besides, you don’t have a white spot on your throat.”

“Oh boy, you mention my throat and I want you to hold me again. This is confusing. I guess I’m uneasy about coming between you and Lloyd. I want you to solve Shy’s murder, and I don’t want to have to be the one to stand in your way, but what can I do? Anyway, there are other ways to solve this crime, and that happens to be a great idea about finding the dead dog. If the bullet in the dog matches up with the bullet in Whitney, that could do it.”

“Right. If the bullet didn’t pass through the dog into forever, or if neither bullet fragmented on a bone, or if the dog’s carcass hasn’t already been picked up by the SPCA and burned, or if Harrison’s brother wants to identify the empty lot.”

“That’s all true, but it’s worth a shot and you know it, or you wouldn’t be waiting to tell Rocco. I think Lloyd’s brother would show you where Lloyd shot the dog if you got him alone. You’re very good at that sort of thing. I’ll see you later, Lou. I’m tired, too. Dinner at the Green Room feels like two weeks ago. Wake me if you break the case, or whatever.”

She left, and I decided I could just as easily leave a note for Rocco and follow close behind Honey, or whatever. I sat at the typewriter and started rambling in a note about how we could call the SPCA in the morning to see if they’d picked up a murdered dog’s carcass, and I fell asleep in the captain’s chair.

20

Digiacomo woke me. It was 4:00 A.M.

"I seen your note," he said. "Good idea. Landis and Augrine took a coupl'a uniform men out looking for the dead dog. I let you sleep a little bit while I figured something out. Come on down with me to the lockup."

"Benzidine," I said.

"Nah, I got a better idea."

"Honey says we can't go near Lloyd."

"She don't mean we can't process him, *paisan*. Besides, she don't know everything about the law. Hey, remember how the three of us used to go up to the Phillies games with passes from the Philly cops?"

"Shy, you, and me. I'll never forget those days. How about Shy coming up with tickets for that final series game in Pittsburgh? Hal Smith and Mazeroski. That was my last World Series, Rock. I don't even know who won last year."

"The Reds. They beat the Red Sox. What a series. Bernie Carbo and Carlton Fisk. Like Smith and Mazeroski, only the Red Sox lost. Did I ever tell you I pitched against Carl Furillo? It was a charity game in Reading for the milk fund."

"No, Rocco, I don't believe you ever did." I grinned and got out of the captain's chair.

We headed out for the walk down to the lockup. In the

hallway near my old locker, he put a big arm around my shoulder. "You know," he said, "the thing I missed most about you being in Brazil is talkin' baseball. No one wants to hear my baseball stories."

"Maybe I did hear about the time you pitched to Furillo. Did he ground to short? Wasn't there a movie on that with Tab Hunter playing you? Or am I thinking of the time you walked Billy Cox in Montreal and then you struck out Preacher Roe, Bobby Morgan, and Wayne Belardi? I know they made a movie out of that one."

"Hey. What?" he said and squeezed me, and we both laughed on the way to the basement.

When we got to the small, brightly lit processing area next to the dimly lit disinfected cells where I had put Lloyd, DiGiacomo suddenly banged his fist hard on the wooden countertop, and all talking in the cells stopped abruptly. A pale-skinned, thin young uniformed patrolman with buck teeth responded on the short flight of stairs behind the counter linking lockup to the radio room.

"Who are you?" asked DiGiacomo belligerently.

"Patterson," said the cop.

"Where's Scagle?" DiGiacomo boomed.

"He knocked off sick a half hour ago."

"Look, kid, I want one of your prisoners, Harrison Lloyd."

"What for?"

"Never mind what for. Because I'm a sergeant." DiGiacomo sounded like ten sergeants.

"Oh yeah, well, you know the rules. I can't give him to you."

"Kid, you're screwing up the Shy Whitney homicide investigation. I hope that means somethin' to you. This Lloyd here knows where the .22-caliber rifle is that killed a cop. There are no rules for cop killers. Harrison Lloyd's coming with me."

DiGiacomo punched the countertop again and sweat flew from his hair. Patterson didn't look impressed.

Then a door buzzer sounded, and Patterson scurried down the rest of the steps, reached under the counter, and pressed a button that released the lock on the entrance to lockup from the outside courtyard.

Two uniformed black patrolmen escorted a thickset white male in his forties wearing cuff's on his wrists, a brown plaid suit, and a green-and-brown-striped tie hanging loosely from around his white button-down collar. He had thick, greasy black hair and bushy eyebrows and wore black horn-rimmed glasses with heavy lenses. His skin was very oily from perspiration.

"A flasher," said the tallest of the uniformed officers. "He's the stud we've been getting reports on in the hotel parking lot. We nailed him with his pecker in his hand in plain view, sitting in a blue Seville, and this mask was on his face."

The officer put a blue bandanna and a small jar of Vicks on the countertop.

"What's the Vicks for?" asked Patterson.

"Ask him. He had it all over his pecker. It must be good for his sinuses."

"Right on," said Patterson, looking at the prisoner. "You can catch a bad cold with your dick hanging out. Is 'at why you need the Vicks? One of the tools of your trade? Hah, hah, hah, hah. One of the tools of your trade to put Vicks on your tool. Hah, hah, hah, hah."

"I know my rights," the prisoner said.

"That he does," said the tall officer. "This man's a counselor-at-law. We've got us the flashing lawyer. I'm serious, man. This guy's in the DuPont Company legal department. He's really a lawyer."

"I'm terribly sorry," said Patterson, coming around from behind the counter. "I'd like to give a man of your status your own room, but we're booked solid tonight. You should have called for a reservation. That's always how it works in the summer season. One night you can't fill a cell, the next night you're booked solid."

"Fuck the lockup humor, Patterson. You can let him have Lloyd's cell," said DiGiacomo gruffly. "He's coming out with me right now. He's gonna show me where he hid the rifle that killed a police officer. It's as simple as that."

"Look, Sergeant, I don't want no problems. You ask my captain's permission and I'll let you have him," said Patterson. "Meanwhile, I'll just stick this lawyer in here with Lloyd in the first cell. You don't mind spending the night with a cop killer that smells like he's been hiding in a sewer, do you?" The tall uniformed officer unlocked the lawyer's cuffs, and Patterson grabbed him by the arm and unlocked Lloyd's cell. The lawyer was given a little shove by Patterson and disappeared through the cell doorway into the cell where we couldn't see him but could hear him mutter, "Motherfucking pig." Patterson locked the cell, went back behind the counter and up the steps to the radio room. The two uniformed officers left the way they came in.

DiGiacomo and I were alone. Rocco put his finger to his lips and tiptoed over to the side wall of Lloyd's cell. I followed his lead, and we stood where we could hear the lawyer muttering about the cuffs having hurt his wrists.

"You really a lawyer?" asked Lloyd in a soft tone of voice.

"What are you?" asked the lawyer loudly. "The FBI?" He sounded big-city.

"Shh, man," said Lloyd. "Listen, lawyer, you gotta be my witness if they take me outta here."

"What do you mean take you out of here? The only way anybody can take you out of here is if you make bail or they have a writ of habeas corpus. They can move you to another cell, but nobody, I repeat, nobody can take you out of this building. Not as long as I'm here. The only thing is, I'm not going to be here very long."

"Oh, yea-yah."

"Oh, yeah. I've been arrested before on this charge. It's a sickness not a crime. I'm a sick man, and when my father learns I'm here he'll make two phone calls, at the most, and they'll destroy every record of this arrest and I will go home. It's a piece of cake. Daddy dear doesn't approve of my sickness, but then again he doesn't want any publicity, and he's a big enough man that everybody in this town does what he wants."

I wrinkled my face as if something smelled and looked at Rocco. He put his finger to his lips again and motioned with a tilt of his head for us to keep listening.

"Yea-yah," said Lloyd, "and me I'm sitting here facin' murder and you're walkin'. Ain't that the motherfuckin' way it is? What are you, a DuPont?"

"Never mind my name," said the lawyer.

"You gotta help me they try and take me outta here."

"Sure, kid. I'll help you. I hate these fucking bourgeois pigs. They treat a man like a jungle animal."

"Dig it. I help you and don't never say nothin' to nobody 'bout your thing, you know, and you help me. Like you find me a real lawyer, right. Listen, dig, I help you keep the publicity down, and you pay for my lawyer so I don't have to use no public defender."

"Listen, kid." There was a rapid tapping noise coming from the cell.

"What you tappin' for?" asked Lloyd.

"If they have this room bugged, it keeps anybody from making out our words," said the lawyer as he continued the hard rapid tapping. "Listen, kid, it sounds to me as if your biggest dilemma is that rifle the obese fucking pig was talking about. I hope you destroyed it." *Tap, tap, tap . . .*

Silence from Lloyd, but the tapping went on.

"Oh, kid, you're not too smart, are you? Did you finish high school?" *Tap, tap, tap . . .*

"Quit the jive, man. And I ain't your kid. If I was gonna be somebody's kid, I'd be your poppa's kid."

"That's not all it's cracked up to be, young fellow. But I like you. I'll help you. Is this rifle located anyplace where the pigs can find it?" *Tap, tap, tap . . .*

Silence.

"Whisper in my ear" — *tap, tap* — "where the thing is, and I will arrange to have it destroyed. Don't worry. I'm an attorney, and right now you are my client. I am trying to protect you, and nobody had better try to stop me."

There was a brief unbearable silence, then talking resumed for two to three minutes, but no distinct words could be made out of the whispers and the tapping, no matter how hard I tried to listen.

Abruptly the tapping stopped.

"Don't worry, kid, I will take care of you."

Rocco tiptoed back to the counter and I followed. Patterson reappeared from the radio room.

"Okay, lawyer," said Patterson, "you must be a real big shot. My captain said to send you home."

Patterson ambled to the cell, unlocked it, and the lawyer came out and went up the steps with Patterson.

DiGiacomo and I followed them up the same steps. When we got to the top and into the radio room, DiGiacomo shut the glass door behind us.

The lawyer took off his thick glasses, squinted his eyes a few times, and said, "These fucking lenses are killing me, you obese bourgeois enemy of the people." He turned from DiGiacomo and pointed at me and asked, "Who's he?"

"Don't worry about his fancy spic clothes. He's my partner," said DiGiacomo. "He's a stand-up guy."

"All right, he says the rifle is at his 'ahnt's' house at twenty-three-oh-one Connell, third house from the hairdresser. Name's 'Ahnt' Esther Vesper. Esther doesn't know it's there. It's broken down in two parts. The barrel's tied to a bed slat with a nylon stocking, and the butt's behind the refrigerator. When are you releasing my men from the other cells?"

"It's gotta be gradual over the next half hour," said DiGiacomo. "We'll have the four of youse back home in bed in two hours tops. If we can do anything for you guys in Philly, ever, call me. Day or night. This one means a lot to us down here. Shy Whitney was somethin' to us."

"Anytime, Rock. Nice meeting you," he said to me and sat down in a wooden chair and tilted his head back and closed his eyes.

"I don't want you to think we do these tricks and traps all the time," said DiGiacomo to me on our way back up to dicks. "Only when it counts."

21

Daybreak. It was a-coming as I walked down the steps of the gray Public Building, the color of daybreak itself. The air brightened when I stepped onto the morning-wet green grass of Rodney Square on the way to the Hotel DuPont. The faint early rays of an unseen sun bothered my eyes.

Before I'd left, Landis and Augrine had reported back. The murdered dog's remains and whatever other evidence they'd held had been cremated and melted two weeks ago by the SPCA.

I had told DiGiacomo that I wasn't going with them to the Lloyds' to question the parents and brothers on the whereabouts of the .22-caliber rifle. He was disappointed. He wanted me in on the hunt, but as far as I was concerned the hunt was over. Of course, I didn't say that.

Honey was right. Time had passed me by. To me, there could be no thrill, no pride, in cruising all over Wilmington to "look" for a murder weapon in a dozen different places when I knew all along where it was, just so I could "prove" my lie if I ever had to deny with a straight face that I knew it was at Aunt Esther's. And just so I could gaily laugh and say that Lloyd was having hallucinations if he ever told his public defender about a phony perverted lawyer with a jar of Vicks who tricked him into telling where the rifle was. In case the story ever surfaced, and it never would. It would be Lloyd's parents themselves who would unintentionally "give" DiGiacomo the "clue" where the rifle might be. The Lloyds would be coddled and questioned and manipulated into giving possible locations of the rifle, and all the vacant leads would be followed until, lo and behold, the rifle would be found. Surely Aunt Esther's name would come up and surely she'd give consent to search her house. A lie with an ending in the beginning, and truth that could never be told. Puke. It's the kind of thing that gives an investigator a nervous twitch. They didn't need me. I'd have handled it in a *maneira mais simple e rapida* to a bossa nova beat. I'd have gone straight to Aunt Esther's.

I had a little more than two hours to kill before I was due back in Youth Diversion and so went straight to my hotel room and Honey. Who could blame me?

22

Half of a fresh Puerto Rican pineapple scooped out in the center and stuffed with fresh strawberries, honeydew, cantaloupe balls, apple chunks, blueberries, walnuts and honey, and fresh pineapple pieces shouted at me when I opened my hotel room door. A large glass of freshly squeezed orange juice with the pulp risen to the top stood at attention next to the pineapple on the room-service tray resting on one of the beds. Honey slept under the covers of the other, with the air-conditioning on full blast. Her red hair looked perfect against the white pillow.

She had eaten her own tray of fruit, which was on the floor, and drunk her juice and now looked as cozy and contented as a sleeping three-year-old.

I quietly lifted my tray from my bed and went into the bathroom, shut the door, put the tray on the makeup vanity, and began to eat standing up, starting with the blueberries and working my way through each fruit. It was the first free and unblemished pleasure I had experienced by myself since being back. In Korea there was nothing I liked better than opening a can of peaches. I doubted that "fruit of the poisonous tree" tasted this good. When I finished the last drop of orange juice, I went out and got the phone, brought it into the bathroom, and asked the desk clerk to wake me at 7:30. I stripped to my boxer shorts and opened the door.

Honey had switched to my bed. She turned her head and smiled a closed-lips smile.

"Let's just cuddle," she said. "I'm beat. Don't wake me in the morning."

I smiled and climbed in beside her.

"Is it solved?" she asked sleepily.

"I think they're about to recover the murder weapon," I said and fell asleep as the warmth of her body made me feel cozy, too.

23

The first phone ring sounded like an air raid drill at Wilmington High. I leaped to silence it, and my momentum carried me stumbling into the bathroom, where I'd left the phone. I found myself on my bare feet, standing on the cold white tile. The phone receiver and its long extension cord were dangling from my hand. I literally forced my eyes open by moving the muscles in my forehead up and down. I looked at Honey through the bathroom doorway. She was still asleep, the bird. The clock on the nightstand said 7:15.

I lifted the receiver to my face and I heard Marian's voice: "Lou, Lou. Don't hang up."

"Yeah, Marian." I kicked the door partially shut with my toe and sat on the toilet.

"Am I calling too early? You were always an early riser. I'm dreadfully sorry about last night. I really am. You're a sensitive paradox to Sarah. She wants to know you, but she's afraid to know you. Perhaps I built you up too much for her."

"Marian." I was trying to get awake. "What are you talking about?"

"Sarah. I'm talking about Sarah and you. I created an image of you for her. I told her how wonderful a detective you were, that sort of thing. Frankly, I sculpted a masculine image for her out of the clay of our existence."

"Maybe it's me, Marian, but I've been getting the feeling that you're on the verge of telling me something. Are you trying to tell me something about Carlton?"

"No. I'm not trying to tell you anything about Carlton, per se. It's not that. Certainly Carlton is an eccentric person, and I suppose that adds to the overall picture, the gestalt, if you will. Carlton can be loving and masculine to Sarah one minute, a total father, and then without warning or reason he can become a withdrawn, suspicious stranger the next, and he has such strange beliefs. She reacts to his moods by trying to please him, the way I used to. It's not the best situation for her."

"I guess it is hard on . . . " I didn't know whether to say Sally or Sarah, and I didn't know what I was doing sitting in the bathroom talking about her husband to Marian. I decided not to totally waste my time. I slipped my shorts down to my ankles and sat down on the john.

"I made such a thing out of providing her with a good name, a father, and a secure life. It's strange. What was once important to me is not so important now. Wilmington was the only world I knew in 1961, Lou. I hope we get a chance to talk . . . before you leave."

"In a small town like this it's important to have a good name. Razzi was not much more than blue-collar so-so even in the best of times."

"Lou, I'm trying my best to make all this work, but I keep bumping into your bitterness. I didn't call to quarrel with you. We've all read the article, and we want you very much to come to dinner tonight. We want you to bring your lady friend if you would like. Sarah was positively exhilarated by the article. She read it before catching the school bus. And Carlton thinks you'd make a terrific character in a novel he's been writing for a number of years."

"What article?"

"Don't tell me you haven't seen it. Lou, you are a hero. The front page says: FRAMED COP SOLVES ASSAULT ON CHILD. Can't you see now what I've been saying about Sarah? One day back and you're already the hero I told her you were."

"What about Shy? Isn't there anything in the paper about Shy?"

"You mean Shy Whitney, the one who used to smoke those big Winston Churchill cigars at the Policeman's Ball. The one with the lovely voice. His wife's name is Joanie or Susie or something like that. The article says you solved the case by yourself, without a partner."

"I did. Shy's been killed. I thought it would be in the paper.

"Oh, my God."

"Shot in the head at the train station waiting to pick up Mary."

"Oh, my God." She was crying softly into the telephone. I could hear a male voice that must have been Carlton's. They began to have a heated conversation. "I'll have to get back to you," she said into the receiver and hung up before I could answer.

I called the front desk and canceled the wake-up call so as not to disturb Honey. I finished on the toilet, shaved, and quietly dressed in the same clothing I'd worn almost continuously for twenty-four hours. It was 7:45 and I was due in at 8:00. From my overnight bag I removed the retirement and request-for-pension papers the union lawyer had sent me. I put them in my breast pocket.

24

After reading the article about the Gandry investigation, I tossed the paper back on Gronk's desk. It built me up too much. I had started my second cup of machine coffee when an unshaven Rocco DiGiacomo filled the doorway.

"Where's your bodyguard?" he asked, pointing a thick finger at Tim Gronk's empty desk. "Seen the paper yet?"

Before I could answer either question, he walked over to my desk and picked up the retirement and pension papers that I had set out.

"Filled them out. Why?" he demanded.

"On the flight from Belém to Miami."

"You ain't signed them yet. Give yourself some time. Stick around and testify in Gandry. What are they gonna do without you? Besides, Mendez from the FBI just called me. The article on the Gandry case got to him. He's willing to meet you at noon in the steam room at the Y. Strictly confidential. Here's a day pass for the health club. I don't know if he'll tell you anything about Figaro, or what, but at least he'll talk to you."

My face was expressionless, but my heart was circulating enough blood for a mountain climb.

"I've got the Gandry preliminary hearing at two," I said.

"You'll be back from the Y in plenty of time. Lou, if you need me on this thing with Covaletzki, I'm on your side. You know that. But I think it's a dead end. If Mendez had anything, he'd have used it. He's a good boy. Anyway, you'll get a steam out of it. You seen the article? Hah?"

"Yeah, it was nice, Rock." I picked up the retirement papers and put them in my pocket.

He smiled at me. "You sure are something, Luigi. I'd like to see you back in action. You know where I'd like to see you? In a hostage situation."

I looked at Rock over the edge of my coffee cup as I drank. A habit I'd picked up in jail. I wondered when he was going to tell me about the rifle.

He continued, "I wish you hadda stayed with us this morning. That old fox Tramp Lloyd wouldn't let us back in without another search warrant, and he put the word out for nobody to talk to us. He's tougher than I thought. We went over to Aunt Esther's house, but she wouldn't answer the door. We could use some ideas."

Before I could answer him the phone rang. It was Marian again. I cupped the phone and told Rock I was sorry, but I didn't have any ideas, I needed some privacy just now, and I could see him in court at the preliminary hearing at two if he still needed me. He looked worn out and disappointed, but he left. I couldn't help him. He needed Honey or somebody.

Marian apologized for hanging up so suddenly. She explained that she was overcome with grief over the news about Shy and that Carlton had walked in on her. He had to know all the details of her sorrow. She thought the scene would probably appear somewhere in his novel.

"It's super how we're talking. It's just as if you'd never left. I know Sarah, or Sally, or whatever, is going to simply love you."

"Wouldn't it be better if we all called her Sarah? That's what she calls herself, I'll bet. Settle down. You're unhappy with some of the choices you've made in life, but who isn't? We all are. Don't let all this excitement get to you. Everything's going to be all right."

"You're right. You've always understood me. Please say you'll come tonight after work. We'll eat at eight, but you get here as soon as you can."

"Okay. I'll be there. I know where you live." We said good-bye, and I hung up and walked over to the Y.

It felt like a child's game, waiting to meet Mendez in the steam room in the nude. He sat down next to me and draped his white towel over one thin leg. We were alone. He had short, straight, yellow hair parted like Calvin Coolidge's and a hard-to-see mustache. No other hair on his body except a little fuzz around his large penis.

I looked at it and wondered if he was showing off. I asked, "Why the steam room?"

"I just don't want any wires. Understand? I'm doing you a favor."

"I understand."

He began, his voice sounding like Walter Cronkite whispering the evening news. "Figaro has always believed that your present chief was in some way implicated, but at no time was Figaro directly or indirectly told that by Hanrahan or anyone else. I am simply relating Figaro's personal belief." He stopped and took hold of his towel as if to leave.

"Is that it?" I whispered.

"Yes."

"What occurred between them?"

"Your lawyer can subpoena the reports."

"I'm not suing anybody. Everything's settled. For God's sake, don't play with me. Give it to me straight. If it's in the reports anyway, why not tell me now?" The room was getting hotter and the sweat was dripping from my lip as I whispered.

"All right." He dropped his towel back on his lap. "Figaro handed Hanrahan the bogus bills and said, 'Here's a thou the hotshot missed. He thinks he's so great.' Hanrahan grasped them in his hand like they gave him inspiration. He said something to Figaro about college boy Razzi being too much of an altar boy for his own good and making trouble for people. He told Figaro that he'd heard that Figaro knew how to play ball and that he might be rewarded. He put his arm around Figaro's shoulder and whispered in his ear: 'We'll just forget about these little bills, now won't we?' It was then that Figaro smelled a little whiskey breath masked by Sen-Sen. Figaro said, 'What bills? I don't see no bills,' and winked at Hanrahan, who said, 'You'll go far in this world, my boy. You're nobody's fool,' and walked out of the room. That is it." He got up quickly and cracked the door that opened out to the lockers.

"Why did Hanrahan come in that night, Agent Mendez?" I said it loud enough for everyone in the locker room to hear, and loud enough to make him close the door and sit back down.

"This better be your last question," he whispered through gritted teeth.

"It isn't," I whispered back. "I also want to know where Figaro is."

"Then that better be it."

"Deal."

"Figaro actually did ask Covaletzki to get brass in that night. Covaletzki chose Hanrahan. It was just stupid talk out of a little twerp. You know, 'I want to talk to your supervisor,' that sort of thing, but Covaletzki took it seriously. That's that part. As to Figaro, he skipped out of the Witness Protection Program and left some townspeople somewhere holding a lot of unpaid bills. He had used his new identity to set up a landscaping business. He ran up beaucoup debts. He went around taking deposits and never did the work, and the locals think he did a few burglaries the day he left. I will deny everything I told you if you ever quote me, and I won't forget your cheap trick at the door. If you yell my name this time, I'll get back at you. You can count on it, mister."

"Just don't try to attack me with that thing of yours," I whispered.

He couldn't help himself. He started to smile, suppressed it, shook his head, and then left. Altogether we had spent two minutes in the steam, and I sweated it out two more to give him a head start. When I got to the lockers he was gone.

I got back to Youth Diversion by 1:30 and called Honey at the hotel.

"Sorry to wake you," I said.

"That's okay. I should be getting up. Where are you, can you come over?"

"I wish I could. I've got the Gandry prelim at two with your boss, Morris Dershon, and then I've got dinner tonight at the Crusets'."

"Oh, crapola, I was going to invite you to my place for some Jewish lasagna. How about tomorrow night?"

"Deal. Call me tomorrow at work."

"At work, at work. I love it. Bring all your arrests to me in intake."

"I divert youth," I said.

"Then come empty-handed," she said. "But if I know you, you'll figure out some way to get in the action. What about Shy Whitney? Did they find the dog?"

"Dead end," I said. "See you tomorrow, buttercup. Fettucine and gefilte fish."

"Deal," she said.

25

IN THE MUNICIPAL COURT
FOR THE CITY OF WILMINGTON
STATE OF DELAWARE vs. JOHN GANDRY,
PRELIMINARY HEARING TRANSCRIPT . . .
JUNE 30, 1976, 2:00 P.M., BEFORE THE
HONORABLE VINCENT TALLY PRESIDING:

By Morris Dershon, esq., Chief deputy attorney general, for the state: The State calls Sgt. Louis Razzi.

Q. By whom are you employed?

A. (Being duly sworn) Wilmington P.D.

Q. I direct your attention to the twenty-ninth day of June, 1976. Did you have an occasion to investigate an alleged assault on a three-and-a-half-year-old boy whom you determined to be one Steven Morris?

A. Yes.

Q. Please indicate to His Honor what you observed about little Stevie.

A. You mean you want me to tell the judge, right?

Q. Yes, please go on.

A. I saw petechial hemorrhages on his face and strangulation marks on his neck.

By Bernard Jones, esq., Assistant public defender, for the defendant:
Objection. This witness is not qualified to give a scientific opinion on strangulation marks.

By Mr. Dershon:
I'll rephrase the question, Your Honor.

Q. Please share with us any marks you observed on Stevie without going to the extent of characterizing those marks. Is my question clear? You look puzzled.

A. No. I get what you mean. You want me to tell the judge. Okay. Stevie had multiple red dots on his face and red splotches all around his neck.

Q. Did you interview the boy?

By Mr. Jones:
Objection. I recognize that hearsay is admissible at a preliminary hearing, but it has to be reliable hearsay, and there has been no showing that this three-and-a-half-year-old boy, a child of tender years, would be allowed to take the stand and testify in a court of law.

By Mr. Dershon:
That's a matter for the trial judge to determine, Your Honor. We're merely here to determine whether there's sufficient probable cause to believe a crime occurred and this defendant committed it so as to bind him over to the Superior Court for presentment to the Grand Jury.

By Judge Tally:
Objection overruled. I'll hear the evidence. Whether the child could qualify as a witness to testify at trial, in view of his tender years, is a matter for the trial judge in the event I bind your client over.

By Mr. Dershon:

Q. What did little Stevie indicate happened?

A. He actually told me. He said a bad boy took him to a shack behind Shelton High School in the City of Wilmington, State of Delaware, and choked him. He referred to the boy as the "bad boy," and by making comparisons to my own body I learned that the "bad boy" was my height, thin build, white, with short light-colored hair and something shiny on his teeth, apparently braces.

Q. What did you do with that information?

A. I went to the area of the shack and questioned a few truant boys who were hanging around. I got the name of a friend of theirs who attends Shelton and who wears braces and fit the description. I went to Shelton and observed the defendant sitting in class.

Q. Let me stop you there. At some point later in the day did you have occasion to interview a Mrs. Smotz, the maternal grandmother of the defendant?

A. Yes. I met with Honey Gold of the A.G.'s office, and after talking with her it was decided that I ought to interview Mrs. Smotz because the defendant lives with her and she might have some evidence to offer. The A.G.'s office gave me a cassette tape recorder to use.

Q. Do you have the recorder with you in court, or did you give it back to my office?

A. I'm sorry, but I still have it in my car. I'll bring it in tomorrow.

Q. No problem, but you ought to get it out of your car before it gets stolen.

A. The tape's in records.

Q. Fine. What did you learn from Mrs. Smotz, and I take it your interview of her was tape-recorded.

A. Yes it was, and I told her I was doing it.

Q. That's all right. It's legal even if you didn't tell her. What did she tell you?

A. She said that her grandson, John Gandry, told her that he choked the boy with the boy's own pants but didn't mean to do it as he was under the influence of drugs and had blacked out. He said he thought the boy was dead when he left him.

Q. Your witness.

By Mr. Jones:

Q. Detective Razzi, you are a detective, aren't you?

A. No, I'm not. At least I don't think I am.

Q. Yes. I believe I read in this morning's paper that you are temporarily assigned to Youth Diversion pending the processing of your retirement papers. You have been away from police work for quite some time now, haven't you?

By Mr. Dershon:

Objection. Irrelevant.

The Court:

Mr. Jones, how is any of this relevant? Besides, I don't think there's a person connected with the criminal justice system in Delaware who isn't familiar with Sgt. Razzi's unfortunate case.

By Mr. Jones:

Very well, Your Honor. I'll move along.

Q. You have been advised by the prosecution, have you not, that an alleged confession you obtained from my client is inadmissible at trial because you arrested my client and did not give him his *Miranda* warnings before questioning and, more importantly, because you proceeded to question him despite the fact that he affirmatively asked for a lawyer?

By Mr. Dershon:

All of this is irrelevant at this proceeding, but if Mr. Jones is trying to make a record for a future suppression hearing, he's wasting his time. The State concedes that the confessions given by John Gandry directly to Sgt. Razzi, orally and in writing, are inadmissible under *Miranda* and *Escobedo*. Furthermore, under the current state of the law the out-of-court identification procedure in the principal's office is inadmissible under *Wade-Gilhert*, as interpreted in *State v. Clark* by the Delaware Supreme Court. Additionally, the fruits of any search are inadmissible. Our case at trial will consist of what we presented at this preliminary hearing, relying solely on the confession the defendant gave to his grandmother, Mrs. Smotz. We will introduce her tape-recorded statement to Sgt. Razzi under 3509 by producing her at trial and making her subject to cross-examination.

By Mr. Jones:

May it please the Court. This is an interesting concession by the State and, I might add, a correct statement of the law. It is especially interesting in light of what happened to Agnes Smotz last night.

The Court:

You look as if you expect us to say something, counselor. Do you have anything more to say or are you waiting for the Court to fish it out of you?

By Mr. Jones:

I am sorry, Your Honor, but I assumed that the State would have heard by now that Mrs. Smotz suffered a heart attack at 9:45 last evening and tragically passed away en route to the Delaware Division.

By Mr. Dershon:
Are you serious?

By Mr. Jones:
I wouldn't kid about something like that. It's easily checked, Your Honor.

The Court:
I suggest we do that right now. The Court stands in recess until the call of the Court.

26

Chief Deputy Morris Dershon, the man Honey said thrived on making the illegal legally legal, said he'd think of something. When we shook hands and said good-bye, the young lawyer looked me in the eye and told me not to worry, that it wasn't my fault, that he'd think of something. He'd call me. I gave him my hotel number and Cruset's number. But instead, he just let Gandry go.

I turned off the car radio. I breathed deeply and relaxed my stomach. The news account hadn't mentioned my name. I told myself that it really wasn't Dershon's fault that he had to drop the charges and release Gandry to the public. My face felt hot.

It was an hour after the prelim, and I was on my way to Woodstone, the Cruset estate, in Centerville, millionaire chateau country, west of Wilmington, and a half mile from the Pennsylvania border.

I had just passed Olde Blayne's Tavern and a strip of a dozen boutiques and specialty shops that had sprung up in century-old stone houses. It was 5:15. Rush hour. But there was never anything as ugly as traffic to worry about in this part of town. I stopped on the road, made a U-turn, and headed back to the strip, knowing there'd be no chance of another public phone along the road to Woodstone, just fenced-in rolling fields and horse pastures, with an occasional brown and white stone mansion high on a hill in the distance.

As I got out of the rented Granada, I felt the first drops of a summer rain. It smelled green and alive. I walked to the pay phone in Blayne's parking lot. It was an outdoor, open-air phone booth that provided little shelter as the rain developed into a fine misty drizzle.

I took out my pocket notebook, found the number, and dialed Mrs. Morris's. The line was busy. I tried four more times, but no luck. I called the emergency operator, and she told me that nobody was speaking on the line. The phone was either out of service or off the hook. The rain stopped.

I called dicks and DiGiacomo answered.

I told him what I was trying to do and he told me it wasn't necessary. He had already sent Augrine over to the Morrises'. The boy's mother was out of control with fear.

"He's bound to make another mistake soon," said Rocco. "We'll be on him. He'll be back for another bite out of the apple." Rock was sure that Gandry's lawyer had told him what everyone else already knew: The charges would never be reinstated regardless of what hope Dershon might hold out in the newspapers. No new evidence would ever be found because there was no more evidence anywhere in the world unless it came from Gandry's mouth, and that was extremely unlikely, and nobody in authority could question him. "I love it when they announce that so-and-so is wanted for questioning like it was still 1955 or somethin'," said Rocco.

The Morrises were packing to spend two weeks with relatives in Baltimore. Augrine was staying with them until they got to their relatives'. "They might never come back, and we want to know where to pick up their trail if they try to disappear," is the way Rocco explained it.

"Partner," said Rock. "Are you all right? You been through a dose of stress. How about we meet at the Y and hit the heavy bag and then go to a ballgame?"

"Whatever happened to real outdoor phone booths?" I asked.

"I don't know. Too much upkeep. Vandalism. Broken glass. Piss and vomit on the floor. Who cares? Come on, let's go to the Y. This thing ain't your fault."

"That's what Dershon said, but I don't believe it. Mrs. Smotz, with her weak heart, never had to be a witness against her own grandson, except for my presence in the U.S.A. I should have called you from the emergency room. No. I take that back. I should have called you that first time I was in the principal's office. I should have had you pick up the Morrises, and I should have stayed at the school and kept an eye on Gandry. You'd have done it right, or you'd have figured out a way around these Supreme Court rules."

"I wasn't around. I was out watching Mondale."

"I should have called for somebody. Any rookie would have known better than to do the things I did."

"God damn it, Lou. You're second-guessing yourself like we all done, and I don't wanna hear it. You just did your fucking job the way it's supposed to be done. You went with the fucking flow. Come on, asshole, I'll meet you at the Y, then we'll go see them beat up on the Cubs. Hah? What? After that we'll go to the club and get loaded. Shoot some eight ball. Make a night of it. C'mon."

"What about the rifle? Did you get it yet?"

He sighed. "We had a meet, but every idea we come up with was too risky. While we was plannin' our next move, we put a couple of undercover guys to watch Esther Vesper's house, and then around two o'clock Tramp Lloyd shows up. Stays in the house about a half hour and then comes out with a saxophone case. We gotta figure the piece is in the case and by now it's el gono."

"How can anybody just watch that man walk down the street with a saxophone case in his hand?"

"Come off it. What are you gonna do? If one of us was there we'd a thought of something, but we wasn't there. They were young cops. Ya gotta take these things in your stride. C'mon. We both need a break. We both lost one today. Let's forget about it. When was the last time you went to a baseball game? We'll get these guys. Lloyd. Gandry. They'll be back. What goes around comes around. Let's go to the Y. Hah?"

"Thanks, Rock. I've been invited to Marian's. It's starting to rain again. The game'll be rained out. I'll see you tomorrow."

"Snap out of it. This trip ain't been good for you. Too much at once. You gotta readjust. Get a good night's sleep. Get your sense of humor back. You hear? Hah?"

"I hear."

27

"As my father says, confession is one of the necessities of life, like food and shelter. It helps . . . it helps . . . eliminate psychological waste from the brain and is necessary for proper functioning of the mind and body. Catholics and psychiatrists agree, and still those in our system who should confess are discouraged by the police."

I could hardly believe this was my fifteen-year-old daughter talking. It sounded like catechism. At first I thought that if you grew up with a professor for a father, you learned to express yourself. But it wasn't just the words. There was something unnerving about her. She seemed high-strung, and striving to keep it under control. We hugged naturally enough when I arrived. She acted as glad as everyone else to see me, and she sounded so grown-up I half expected her to take a drink when Carlton started pouring the twenty-five-year-old scotch.

It was only chitchat and a raw vegetable dip before dinner, and everyone tried to pitch in and lift my spirits about the Gandry thing.

But once dinner started, Sarah went into electric overdrive and attacked the conversation as though points were to be tallied after dessert and she had no intention of coming in second. Her demeanor resembled the large painting of

Carlton's father that dominated the dining room wall. Hard and uncompromising.

Marian looked at me a couple of times as if to say, See what I mean?

I put down my fork and said that I always thought that confessions were a good economic way to solve crimes, but that sometimes weirdos liked to confess to things they didn't do and you had to be careful with confessions, and that I liked the rack of lamb very much.

It was then that Carlton offered me a job. Nobody said thank you for my comment about the rack of lamb because nobody in the room had cooked it. I thought I'd pop into the kitchen before I left to thank the cook. I didn't want a goddamn job from Carlton Cruset. I wanted to call Honey and meet her at the hotel.

"What kind of job?" I asked and drained my red wine. Carlton refilled the glass.

"Confession-taker," he said.

"Whose?"

"Silent men with deadly secrets. Sirhan Sirhan. James Earl Ray. Arthur Bremer. John Gandry. Harrison Lloyd. No one in particular."

"I thought you were serious for a second."

"He is," Sarah said suddenly and gravely. There it was. Dancing darkness in and around the eyes. High-strung out in the open. All her nerve endings plowing right through her muscles to the skin surface, her teeth and lips clenched, she defied me with her eyes.

"I am," Carlton said calmly.

"What do you have, a private police force?" I asked, looking away from Sarah's glare to Carlton.

"Not a whole force," he said. She was still staring at me.

"That's the way Hitler started out in Munich," I said.

"And Hitler was very kind to his German shepherds," he said icily, "but because he was doesn't mean we shouldn't be kind to dogs."

"Hitler did not have a private police force," Sarah said. "He had a private army, not a private police force." She was moving way ahead of the field. I doubted I would finish a respectable second, and she had just passed Carlton.

"Right you are, darling," said Carlton. "Tell me, Lou, is Honey Gold Jewish?"

I put some dessert in my mouth to keep what I was thinking from coming out. Their dinner conversation was far from what I'd expected for the evening, and they were turning me into the table liberal. The horror of the release of John Gandry was becoming the furthest thing from my mind.

"Really, Carlton," said Marian, "what's the difference what she is?"

"Mother's right, Daddy. You have a way of losing track of what you are doing. Lou, is it appropriate for me to call you Lou?"

"That makes sense," I mumbled through my chocolate soufflé. I took a slug of wine.

"Lou, what do you think of Father's proposal that you work for him?"

"Delaware War on Crime?" I said.

"Yes," she said.

"I have a job," I said. "I do all that now." I drank some more wine.

Sarah looked at Carlton as if to say, What's the use, but you may try if you like — and turned back to her dessert. We all ate silently for a few seconds.

"Sarah, honey," said Marian, "wouldn't you like to get to know Lou better?"

"Perhaps."

"How about the two of you meeting for lunch sometime soon. How would that be?"

Sarah looked at Carlton and he nodded approval.

"Perhaps," she said.

Marian swallowed hard and fortified herself to go on with this. "Let's set it up now, shall we?"

More out of some unnamed pity for Marian than because I wanted to, I jumped back into the thick of it. "Let's do it, Sarah," I said. "It's hard for me to plan lunch because I don't really know what assignments I'll be getting, but how about breakfast, say this Thursday, day after tomorrow?"

"Great, that's settled," Marian gushed. "I'll have Arthur drive Sarah to the Green Room. Will seven o'clock be fine with you? That will give the two of you almost an hour alone together, and Arthur can wait and drive Sarah home."

"What do you say?" I asked.

"It would be interesting to hear your thoughts about changes in police procedure," said Sarah. "Daddy says we are witnessing the Vietnamization of the war on crime. He says we left it up to the South Vietnamese to fight the war while America gradually withdrew. It is now left up to the citizens to fight the war on crime as the police gradually withdraw."

"Fine," I said, "then it's a deal. We'll finish this talk at breakfast. You are some mature and knowledgeable young lady. I'm very impressed."

"Yes," she said and looked back to Carlton, who smiled at her.

"Lou," he said. "I'd like to see you for a while in the study, if you don't mind. I'd like your reaction to a project I've done some work on."

"Marian tells me you're writing a novel."

"Not currently," he said. "It's in abeyance right now, but it is the project I'd like your reaction to. It's a crime novel. I've suspended writing on it temporarily while I research a history I am planning on atrocities. The burning of Joan of Arc, the Spanish Inquisition, contemporary African tribal warfare, ad infinitum. The excesses of the Nazis are, after all, nothing novel in world history. Worse genocide goes on in so-called abortion clinics right now as we sit here, don't you agree?"

"Please don't start," said Marian.

"I haven't kept up with things," I said. "Let me see what you've got on your crime novel."

I got up too quickly and felt a little woozy from the scotch and wine, steadied myself, and waited for him to get up. I thanked Marian for the dinner and smiled at an unsmiling Sarah.

28

Carlton led the way out of the dining room. He wore a dark-blue blazer, white button-down shirt, red-and-blue striped tie, gray slacks, and stiff black loafers. New shoes. *Sapatos novos*. And that same .45 automatic. At home.

"Is it true," he asked, "that airline search dogs are trained to sniff out certain drugs by being addicted to them?"

"I don't know," I said, "but that ain't right. A thing like that." Gandry was creeping back.

I followed him into a foyer as big as the late Mrs. Smotz's ground floor, which now, no doubt, Charlie would own outright. On each wall there were worn antique tapestries and on the floor two antique Oriental carpets that served to keep people from tracking mud onto whatever lay beyond the foyer.

I followed him beyond the foyer to a wide gray marble staircase in the middle of a hall. To the left I could see what looked like a south parlor or a museum. He guided me to the right and we were in the study. More antique Orientals, but thicker and more ornate. Brown leather sofas and chairs. They brought back memories of the brown leather chair in detectives. It's the only real leather chair with which I'd ever had any close contact. There were eight mahogany tables with a lighter-wood inlaid mosaic design. There were crystal glass lamps on the tables. But most of all there was an impression of books. Walls of books reaching sixteen feet into the mahogany-paneled ceiling. Collections of Dickens, Hardy, Thackeray, Sir Walter Scott in old leather-bound sets with gold-leaf lettering. Other, more contemporary books in their best-seller book-of-the-month-selection jackets, books about spies and war and crime. Rows and rows of books about crime. Novels with the words *executioner* and *murder* in their titles, with knives and guns on their spines. Beyond the crime books were what appeared to be complete collections of esoteric magazines like *Soldier of Fortune*, *Guns & Ammo*, *Street Survival*, *Martial Arts*.

He handed me a scotch on the rocks he had poured from a wet bar along the wall.

"I have every issue of *Soldier of Fortune*," he said.

"My partner once pitched to Carl Furillo," I said. The scotch was that same twenty-five-year-old very smoky-tasting stuff.

I picked up a *Soldier of Fortune*. I did not know they made such magazines in this country. When I left, *Look* was still big, with pictures of Adlai Stevenson on the cover. This cover had a color photo portrait of a middle-aged man with a jaundiced complexion, an eye patch, and a red beret. It read: "Col. Trader on Dirty Tricks." The good eye looked like it had a one-track mind tucked behind it. I put the magazine back.

"Do you hunt animals?" he asked.

"No," I said.

"I don't anymore either. There's no longer any challenge to it."

On a mahogany table in the far corner was a white cardboard architect's model of what looked like an ancient Greek or Roman palace.

"Are you planning an addition?" I asked.

"Don't you recognize it?" he said, punctuating the question

with a sharp and surprisingly loud suction click from the left corner of his mouth, as if he were reaching up with his lower lip to snap up and suck in his mustache.

"Well, it looks familiar, but I can't place it."

"It's the capitol seat of the domestic government of the United States of America." He was smiling, and sort of squinting into my eyes, as if my eyes gave off a light that hurt his. And he has a seven-inch height advantage, I thought. "What is it? A building in Washington?"

"Only partially correct," he said. I was merely a student with an incomplete answer. He clicked a suction snap again. It had a military precision that must have taken a great deal of practice. "Can't you be more specific?" he asked.

"Capitol of domestic government? Is there some kind of cabinet post for domestic affairs like the Secretary of State for foreign affairs?" I was trying to be polite, and it really was a pleasure to be in such a room with brown leather chairs. But I was realizing more and more that this professor was not the Mr. Chips I had imagined over the years was taking care of my little daughter. He tapped his foot.

"You mean you honestly don't recognize the United States Supreme Court Building?" he said as he lifted the roof clean off in two parts. He put the pieces on a stack of typing paper on another table.

"Come, look. These are the chief justice's chambers and here's the famous robing room, where the justices shake hands before going out to the bench to rule the land. Here's the winged bench itself, with all eight associate justices and the chief in the middle, and here's the main conference room across from the courtroom."

"Incredible. So detailed. What are these things? Metal detectors?"

"Yes. Metal detectors. Very good. Their security is really quite primitive, you know. It is positively amazing to see Supreme Court justices milling around the courthouse with the general public. Yet no one gets into the courtroom itself unless one passes through a metal detector."

"What's your interest in the court?"

"It is the subject matter of my novel." He pointed to the table with a word processor and a very small number of typewritten pages next to it. On an adjacent table were research volumes on the Supreme Court.

"Do you have a name for it?"

"*Sounds of the Rude World*," he said. "It's a line from the song 'Beautiful Dreamer' by Stephen Foster. What do you think of the title?"

"Boffo. What's it about?"

"Very succinctly," he said, clicking, "it is about a patriotic retired professor, of all things, named Andrew Bliss, who while headquartered at the Union Hotel in Harpers Ferry, West Virginia, stages a series of raids on the members of the United States Supreme Court and ultimately attacks the court itself." He said it very quickly, as if he had said it very succinctly many times before.

"Harpers Ferry. Like John Brown, the abolitionist," I said. "Didn't he raid the government arsenal at Harpers Ferry to arm the slaves, and didn't the government hang him?"

"Precisely." He glanced briefly at my eyes, looked back at my lips, and said again: "Precisely."

"Why is the professor in your novel doing this?" I asked.

"Ah, motive! The detective in you beginning at the beginning."

"Actually, that's not a good beginning question for a detective. I was taught to never look for a motive in the beginning.

It can sidetrack you. In real life it's mostly a waste of time to try to figure out why people do some of the things they do even if they tell you why."

He looked offended. Easily hurt, but quick to recover, he said, "I never looked at it in quite that way before. What a splendid observation." He clicked.

"Who would know in the beginning, for instance, why Gandry did what he did," I explained. "Time should pass before you look for a motive. Then beyond motive there's motivation. For example, I know that Gandry's thinking he's invincible now because of his triumph over me. But that's now. If he kills now, I'll know that he knows to squeeze harder and longer on his victim's throat rather than risk being identified by a half-dead victim. He's got the same motive, but more motivation."

He looked inside the court replica and poked a few pieces of furniture with his long finger before looking up.

"You just answered your own question about Professor Bliss's motive."

"You mean he's assassinating the whole court because of some case that got tossed out."

"Not some case that got tossed out, man." He was very disappointed in me. "The exclusionary rule," he half shouted.

"Your hero would make nine men a target over a legal rule?"

"A target of nine," he clicked. "*Target Nine*, a good title. Yes, all nine."

"Aren't any of them against the exclusionary rule?"

"Indeed, four of the nine are, but not militantly enough, that is, to suit Professor Bliss, a man who never once compromises with evil. As Black Panther leader Eldridge Cleaver was fond of saying, 'If you are not part of the solution, you are part of the problem.'" His eyes were burning a hole in the Oriental carpet.

"Sinners in the hands of an angry God," I said.

"Precisely," he said and clicked his lower lip and clapped his hands once for double emphasis. "Do you see these little metal caps?" He pointed at the caps in a rapid darting fashion. They were the size of a pencil eraser and resembled the bottom of a silver bullet. They were attached to the foot of nearly every wall in the model. "They are standpipes for the connection of fire hoses." He lifted one of the caps. It was on a miniature hinge, and it stayed up, creating a tiny hole in the wall. "In my research, I have personally lifted open each and every one of these standpipes at the court any number of times."

"Dynamite?" I asked.

"With timing devices. The horizontal pipe continues under the marble flooring behind the walls. Minimum damage to only those bystanders standing near the standpipes themselves — acceptable losses, if you will — but incredible damage to the building. You see, in my final scene, while the explosions burst at the justices' feet during oral argument, Professor Bliss stands tall in the visitors' gallery and fires from a nine-shot revolver made of white metal, the kind used on car door handles, the kind that can pass through a metal detector undetected. His bullets are laced with live rabies virus."

"I can't wait to read it." I grinned.

He looked as if he were about to drop a few sticks of miniature dynamite into the teeny-tiny standpipes.

He obviously wanted to tell me more, so I said, "However, I am curious, how does Professor Bliss get away after the shootings?"

"He doesn't." He brightened. "It's what I believe would be properly termed a kamikaze mission. He makes the supreme patriotic sacrifice. He is motivated to atone for an act of cowardice, draft dodging during World War II and hiding out in South America."

"Not Brazil, I hope."

"I haven't decided yet," he said softly. He blinked his eyes tightly and instantly transformed his body into a relaxed state, as if he did it with the flick of a lighter switch. He looked as if he had just had sex. He even took a deep breath. "Perhaps some day you will be kind enough to tell me about Brazil. Perhaps I may use Brazil in my novel."

As I drained the last drops of my scotch, he went to the booze table and poured me a cognac. It tasted fifty years old. Smooth as water and not smoky like the scotch. The taste disappeared in your mouth like a bubble. The glass snifter had a fox-hunt scene on it that you wouldn't find on a glass in Mrs. Lloyd's house or in Mrs. Smotz's, rest her soul, or in Mary Whitney's.

He poured himself one from the same bottle but didn't put the bottle down. With bottle and glass in hand he led me to the south parlor, which was opposite the library.

Even after being in the library and the dining room, I was dazzled by this room. There were old oil paintings in gold-leaf frames, with little lights shining on the pictures. On top of the Knabe grand piano was a bust of Beethoven carved from a solid piece of wood. Other statuary in the room included a bust of Shakespeare on a black marble pedestal. If I'd known anything about the value of Oriental rugs, I'd have been afraid to step on the carpet.

Carlton sat in a high-backed wing chair near one of the three fireplaces in the room. He motioned me to sit in a matching chair, about eight feet from his, on the other side of the black marble flooring in front of the fireplace.

Carlton reached into the breast pocket of his blazer and pulled out several sheets of typing paper folded in half the long way.

"I would like to read to you the first chapter of my novel."

I raised my glass in approval and took a sip. Carlton waited until I stopped sipping and then he began reading. I looked outside and noticed that it had stopped raining.

Since he later gave me the manuscript of this first chapter, I am able to reproduce it here as I heard it, word for word. It took about eight minutes, and Carlton appeared to have the thing memorized. Part of the time he spoke the words from memory while looking at the Oriental rug. Here's what he read to me:

Sounds of the Rude World

by Carlton Cruset

White. Hospitals seem to be whiter than most places, thought Chief Justice Lindsey Dankworth as he pushed the lever to lower his reclining bed.

He was not going to sleep, he told himself. He was simply going to think. Occasionally, a new law clerk not knowing the legend of Dankworth would be startled to encounter His Honor flat on the deep gray carpet of his chambers. Later in the course of his year's service with the Supreme Court the young clerk would learn what court scholars and the eight justices already knew: Dankworth worked best either reclining on the floor or standing at an antique podium desk. On the desk was a green wooden sign, a handmade gift from the first female clerk ever to labor for the Supreme Court. It said many things about both Dankworth the unpretentious man and Dankworth the lord of many domestic issues facing the American people. The sign stated: "'. . . there is nothing so conducive to brevity as a caving in at the knees.' O. W. Holmes."

The C. J. craved thought. He used his mind continuously. It never rested. It burned with the fuel of his surroundings. Whatever he saw, touched, or heard made him think.

Yes, white is medicine, he thought. Blue is police. Gray is prisons. Black is crime.

Yes, that was straightened out in the orderly processes of his mind and under the influence of medication, and almost against his will he began to sleep. He snored.

If sleep had not come, the process of free association might have led to the solving of some intellectual or legal problem or the genesis of a thought new to him, as in 1972 when he had found the power to make abortion a constitutional right during one of the silent and lonely voyages of his creative and dynamic intellect. The vote at the court had been four to four, with Dankworth uncommitted, until he closed his eyes and allowed his mind to float as if it were Galileo's feather falling from the Leaning Tower of Pisa.

As the chief justice slept on this night, a very tall and skeletal silver-haired man with a scholarly manner quietly entered Dankworth's room at the Walter Reed Army Hospital. The man was two years younger than Dankworth, who was fifty-seven, and in keeping with the white hospital motif he wore a white surgical mask, white jacket, white slacks, and white buck shoes with red rubber soles. He noiselessly reached the bed in two strides of his six-five frame.

The tall man in white who stood by the bed and stared down at Chief Justice Dankworth was Professor Andrew Bliss. His blue eyes slowly adjusted to the semidarkness as Dankworth snored softly. Although the hepatitis appeared to be on the mend, rest was important for Dankworth.

Professor Andrew Bliss reached into his white coat pocket and pulled out a pint of domestic vodka and a small can of odorless cleaning fluid, the kind sold in any drugstore. He slowly poured all of the fluid on the bedding and pillow surrounding his victim's head. Using a hypodermic needle and large syringe he injected several ounces of vodka into the clear plastic bag of intravenous solution. He increased the rate of fluid passing through the IV by turning the black dial from 24 to 65cc's per minute.

Dankworth inhaled the fumes of the cleaning fluid into his lungs as the vodka entered his blood stream. By morning the combination would empty his already deteriorating liver of all its blood.

On the nightstand the good and graceful professor placed a 5 × 8 index card with the following typed message:

> "The germ of dissolution of our federal government is in the . . . federal judiciary; an irresponsible body."
> — Thomas Jefferson, 1821

Carlton Cruset closed his mouth, closed his eyes, and lifted his fox-hunt snifter full of cognac to his lips. He drank a good healthy swallow.

"That's pretty interesting," I said politely. "Can you really kill somebody that way?"

"Certainly," he clicked. He hadn't snapped one off since we left the study. "Nitrobenzene is a common household ingredient. It's found in liquid shoe polish, metal polish, dyes, and cleaning fluid. Alcohol hastens its deadly effects. People die from it accidentally all the time and it is diagnosed as hepatitis."

"That's pretty interesting writing," I said and remembered too late that I had already said that.

"You don't know what to make of me," he said, "do you?"

I tried to stifle a yawn, covered my mouth with my hand, removed my hand, and drank some more cognac. I knew what to make of him. He shifted in his seat, waiting for me to speak, and took another swallow. I drank again.

"I'd like to see chapter two," I said. "Don't take offense if I appear listless. I'm still in a lousy mood and I didn't get much sleep last night."

He said, "That's all I've done. There is no chapter two." He clenched his fists and held them up away from his body. "Writing and talking will not accomplish much in this world." He stared at his fists. "But I presume you know that."

"No. I don't know that," I said.

"Come now. You are a man of action, not words."

"I don't know what I'm a man of anymore. For a long while I just wanted to be a man with no cares in a new tropical land with a lot of new things to eat and learn."

He grunted and said, "Here, you may have this," and handed me the manuscript.

We both stood up as Marian and Sarah entered the room. I hadn't noticed before, but Sarah's black hair was very long. She wore it straight, with bangs neatly trimmed. She had a lovely, graceful walk.

"I think it would be best for all concerned," Carlton said and started walking, "if I went up to my room for the evening."

"Oh for Christ's sake, what's the matter?" demanded Marian.

"I haven't been real good company," I offered. "I've got a lot on my mind."

"I can imagine," said Marian.

Carlton kept walking, ignoring our conversation, as if we couldn't say anything to change his mind.

"I'll go up to my room too, Daddy," said Sarah without looking at me.

Marian said, "Sarah, won't you even say good night?"

Sarah turned and faced me. She said, "Good night," turned again, and followed her father up the stairs.

This was harder on me than I'd expected. I'd had the right idea before I got on the plane in Belém. I should be across the street merely watching my daughter. Or I should be in an insurance agent's office taking out a ten-million-dollar policy, with her as the beneficiary. I should be looking out for her from a distance, and I shouldn't be this close to her new life, for my sake.

"She looks a lot like you," said Marian as she sat in Carlton's chair. I sat, too, and poured another cognac from the bottle. "She has a mannerism of yours. You know the way you touch the corners of your mouth with the tips of your thumb and middle finger. Sometimes she gets lipstick on her fingers from doing it." Marian took Carlton's glass and drank from it.

"It's funny," I said. "I forgot I did that. I don't think I do it anymore. I work in dirt. Where do you suppose she got it? The time she saw me she was too young to pick up something like that."

"Genes. She's your daughter," said Marian as she rubbed the edge of Carlton's glass with her middle finger, the way people used to get music from a glass on Ted Mack's "Amateur Hour."

I finished off my drink and poured another inch while she fondled her glass.

"You know, Lou, you were right today on the phone. There is something I have been trying to tell you. But it's not about Carlton, it's about Sarah, and it's something I've never told anybody. Can I walk you to your car?"

"Sure," I said, and we went out into the foyer and through the massive mahogany front door to the outside nighttime.

When she closed the door behind us, she said, "You are interested in her well-being, aren't you?"

"I suppose I deserve that."

"Sorry. I shouldn't have asked that. Did Carlton talk to you at all about Sarah?"

"No."

"Did he say anything about me?"

"No. He just murdered Chief Justice Dankworth for me." She laughed and said, "He thinks you're somebody special. He's very impressed with you and I think a little intimidated by you. He wanted me desperately to invite you tonight. He looks up to policemen, you know. He likes to be around them. That may be why he married me in the first place, a detective's ex-wife."

We stood by my Granada in the cobblestoned courtyard. "Reach down the back of my dress," she said and turned her back to me. I pulled her dress from her skin, peeked in, and saw paper. I reached in and pulled out a folded manuscript similar to the one Carlton had handed me. "Dankworth," I said and waved my own copy.

"No. Unfortunately this one's not fiction."

"Is what you want to talk to me about in here?"

"I don't even want to talk to you about it. I just want you to know it. You must never let on that I gave you a copy. Please destroy it once you've read it. He chronicles everything. After Sarah confided in me what actually happened, I searched Carlton's room until I found this, then I copied it and put it back in place. He's never told me the truth of what happened, and she would never forgive me if I brought it up with him, and she'd probably never speak to me again if she knew I'd told you or anyone about it. She's quite capable of that kind of retribution. She doesn't know about Carlton's written account, and she would probably accuse me of having written it myself to smear Carlton. Carlton long ago quite effectively won her over from me. Brainwashed her with his charm, generosity, and false sincerity. I can see by the way you're looking at me that you mistrust my motives in giving you this. I am not looking for a knight in shining armor. At least I don't think I am. I simply want you to have a better understanding of Sarah and Carlton and me in the future. I think you'll understand when you read it."

"Sure," I said, shook her hand, got in my car, and wearily drove onto the highway.

29

As I drove I pictured Sarah's intense face saying good night to me, and I thought how different everything could have been. I made a mental list of how things were. Shy's chalk outline. Stevie Morris's polka-dot face. Mendez sitting nude in the steam room. Covaletzki and the mayor at the train station. DiGiacomo shaking hands with the "lawyer" from Philadelphia. Tony Landis and Clem Augrine staring at Judge Wyrostek's floor. Honey curling up in my hotel bed. Tramp Lloyd sitting on his crushed-velvet chair. Marian standing up at the Green Room and calling my name. Gandry sitting at the defense table during his preliminary hearing and smirking. Carlton poking his finger in the cardbord Supreme Court Building. What a mess. The mess I'd left behind in 1963 was a trickle from a rainspout by comparison. I looked at my watch. It was early.

If I got to my bed by 10:30, I could get nine hours' sleep. How can you divert youth on less than nine hours?

I pulled onto the shoulder of the road, put on the dome light, and began to read the papers Marian had handed me. Again I reproduce what was written:

The Target Manifesto

Prologue:

On September 28, 1953, six-year-old Bobby Greenlease was abducted from his Catholic school class by a woman posing as his aunt. She and her boyfriend, a morphine addict, collected $600,000 in ransom, killed and buried the boy, and raised suspicion about themselves in St. Louis by flashing big money to a cab driver and a prostitute who reported their suspicions to the St. Louis police who kicked their door in. On December 18, 1953, eighty-two days after the kidnapping, they were executed in Missouri's gas chamber. Tempus fugit.

Episode:
You might say I was naive. It would be cruel to say I was anything more than that. One never imagines that the proper thing to do when one picks up one's thirteen-year-old daughter after Girl Scouts at Christ's Church, of all places, is to check the backseat floor for strangers when one returns to the locked car after being inside the church getting the girl for no more than five minutes. And so I prefer to say that as I drove away from the church, I was naive and nothing more.

The first I knew there was a problem of any sort was when he put the gun to my head and ordered me to make a right off the Kennett Pike and to head for Chester. I never did see his face clearly, but I did see and hear handcuffs on his wrists.

I told Doris not to worry and that when we got to Chester I was sure he would let us off somewhere safe and sound.

I told him that I had over $500 in my pants pocket and he could have that. In fact, I said he could have the car for all of that. It was a '73 Eldorado and easily disposed of for cash, I thought. He never replied to any of this and spoke only to give directions. When we got to a deserted spot in the middle of nowhere he hit me on the back of the head with the gun, behind my right ear. I made a suitable noise and collapsed on the car seat.

Doris didn't scream. She said, "What are you going to do to me?"

And he said, "Climb in the backseat, white bitch."

And she said, "No. What are you going to do to me?"

"If you don't climb in the backseat I'm 'onna shoot your fucking brains out and then I'm 'onna shoot your papa in the balls."

I felt her climb over. Actually she stepped on my hand in her haste but I cleverly suppressed any reaction.

"Now, little pussy," he said, "suck on 'is and swallow the come."

I heard the noise in the backseat and felt the car rock after he ordered her to turn over and began to thrust into her dry virginal anus. She sobbed, almost quietly, the whole time. She never once screamed. What a brave girl.

You see, she recognized the importance of quiet, of not agitating the demon holding the lethal weapon trained at all times on our vital organs. In many ways over the years I had prepared her for this moment.

She did as I did. No one could or should fault me for my inaction in this time of crisis. I won't use grogginess as an excuse. Indeed, I need none. Strategy was my game. And Doris instinctively played the same game with her soft silent sobbing, as he rocked the car with each painful thrust of his penis.

My erection was a normal healthy reaction to an incident of sexual explicitness. Neither do I make apologies for that. My father's credo "Never Explain, Never Complain" is part of my formula for living.

No, not cowardice, not painful inaction, not grogginess, not preoccupation with sexual acts foreign to me. No, none of these called into play my silent passing of the tragedy played out behind me in the backseat.

It seemed like hours.

My motive was twofold. First, to come out alive. Second, to get justice.

Alive we were when he pulled away, leaving us in the night of a Pennsylvania hillside. He had pushed me clear of the car and I wasn't certain he had released Doris until after the car pulled away and I heard her faint silent sobbing near my right ear.

"Daddy, Daddy, are you alive?" she pleaded. I waited a respectable time, groaned and rolled over, holding my right ear.

"What happened?" I asked.

I made a promise to her in no uncertain terms that very night, as we stood there in a soybean field holding each other while she described to me the things he did to her mouth and anus, that I would never rest until he suffered greater harm.

Next, we agreed to keep our secret sacred. We would report the theft of my car, our kidnapping, the

> blow to my head, and nothing more than that would we say. The penalty for victimization vis-à-vis rape would be a matter not left trusted to those in the modern rehabilitation industry.
>
> Epilogue:
> And so was born out of intense personal tragedy, forged in the fires of hell itself, a bond between man and girl that would last the ages and would found a movement so large and so strong and so powerful that the very foundations of American society would quake. Upon the back of this young girl, this thirteen-year-old sacrificial virgin, would rest the future course of the social history of the next quarter century.

I put the pages on the passenger seat and stared at my own reflection from the interior light hitting the windshield.

30

The high-beam lights in the rearview mirror broke my reverie, and the car pulled up dangerously close behind mine.

I rolled down my window and watched the state boy approach. He was awfully, awfully young and very cautious. Probably these days they had to be cautious. He was tall and trim, with a prominent Adam's apple, and brown hair frizzing out from the blue forest ranger–type hat that went along with the dark-blue coat and the gray trousers with gold side stripes form-fitted into big black boots. There were gold buttons on the jacket, black leather straps across the shoulder and around the waist, and what looked like a stainless steel .357 cannon in the holster.

He held a foot-and-a-half-long chrome flashlight in his left hand and shined it directly in my eyes as if it were an immobilizing ray gun.

"What's the matter?" I asked. "Jumpy?"

"License and registration," he snapped, still shining the big beam in my eyes.

"Don't I have any rights?" I squinted. I handed him my Brazilian license and the rent-a-car registration.

He didn't reply but focused the beam for a quick look on the passenger seat and the floor, then back to my eyes, then a flash on my Brazilian license.

"I'm on the job," I said. "Wilmington dicks. I don't have my shield with me. I gave it to a little kid yesterday to play with."

"To play with? Are you kidding? Have you been drinking?"

"I was just about to ask you if you've been drinking?"

"Kill your ignition and get out of your car."

"All right," I said as I got out, "but don't push it."

"Is that a gun in your belt?" he barked at me.

"You're one sharp cookie," I replied.

"Turn around and put your goddamn hands on the roof of your car and spread your goddamn legs, hotshot, and be quick about it. Pronto quick. *Comprende*, amigo from Brazil?"

I stared into his eyes as best I could, considering the beam of the flashlight. "Make me," I said. He stepped back and lifted his cannon from his holster with his right hand. He pointed the muzzle at K-5, the highest score on the paper targets of the human body at the firing range.

"Hands on the roof of your car, José. Turn around and spread them." But something in me wouldn't let me.

"Make me," I said again. Adrenaline shot through the alcohol in me.

He stood and stared at my clothes for a few seconds, trying to figure me. It was cricket quiet. He walked backward to his car and put the flashlight on the hood while he kept the gun at K-5 and used his radio with his free hand. He was calling for backup. This was getting to be something. I didn't care how light-headed I felt. I didn't much care about anything right then. All I knew was that I wasn't getting arrested again in my life.

"Are you related to Covaletzki or what?" I called over to him.

He said, "Hands on roof. Spread 'em."

"Don't give me any of that 'spread 'em' shit. Elmo Covaletzki. You know who I'm talking about."

"You're drunk, and you're no Wilmington detective. Not out here in that pimp getup."

He walked back to me and stopped when he was four and a half feet away. He sniffed at the alcohol in the air coming from my breath. I leaned my backside into the Granada door.

We stood that way for a little while, a goddamn Mexican standoff. He kept a hard grip on his piece of gun and aimed it, more or less, at my heart.

Two cars arrived at the same time, one behind the other and both behind my trooper's car. A heavyset sergeant got out of the first, and a younger trooper with a big thick neck got out of the second. I smiled, very relaxed. My trooper turned his head for a quick glimpse of them getting out of their cars, I guess to make sure it was his backup and not mine.

"You better take my gun before your sergeant gets here or you'll wind up on charges." I leaned my right hip toward him. He reached for the gun with his left hand and I swept his front foot with my left foot, continuing my body into his. At the same time I banged up on the elbow joint of his gun hand, and the instant his grip on the gun loosened I peeled it from his palm with a backhanded sweeping motion of the fingers of my left hand.

A radiant Taiwanese doctor I lived with for eighteen months in the jungle until the WHO transferred her would have been very proud of me. I was the sole possessor of his .357, and his body shielded mine from the other two. I flipped his gun through my open window and laughed, probably insanely.

I wrapped my arms around the trooper, and the force of his body trying to get into my car window pinned me against the Granada.

"Sergeant, he took my weapon," he yelled. "He threw it in his car."

"I got him, Sergeant," I said. "He was impersonating a state trooper. No trooper would let me take department property." I laughed some more.

The sergeant reached in the window and picked up the .357. I let go of the trooper, caught my breath, and held the roof of my car to steady myself.

"Look, mister," the sergeant said, pointing his finger at my nose and ignoring the embarrassed trooper, "you're under arrest for driving under the influence of intoxicating beverage. You can come easy or you can come hard, but you're coming. Now put your nice little fuckin' hands on the roof of your fuckin' car. We're gonna pat you down, then we're gonna put you in the police car."

"Don't I know you? Didn't you transport me to the workhouse fifteen years ago?"

"Yes, sure," said the sergeant. "Sure I did, but you were a good boy to me then. Now just turn around nice and peaceful and be a good boy now. There we go. You know how it's done. That's it, now face the car."

"He's crazy, Sarge," my trooper said. "Be careful."

"No, wait a minute, Sarge. I'm serious. It was fifteen years ago." I turned back around to face the sergeant.

At that point the other trooper with the big neck engulfed me from behind in a tight bear hug. Sarge snapped a cuff on one wrist. Hard and tight. Neck released me and pulled my free wrist behind my back, and Sarge cuffed that one to the first. Ouch.

"Ground him," said the sergeant. Neck tripped me, and Sarge kicked me in my left thigh on my way down. I landed mostly on my chest and chin.

Th sergeant frisked me and pulled my .38 from my pants.

"Oh yeah," said my trooper, "I forgot. He's got a gun." The sergeant held it in his hands and looked pointedly at the first trooper for not having told him about the gun. The sergeant kicked me again. This time in my triceps. But I knew on that kick he was really mad at the trooper, so it didn't count.

"Carrying a concealed deadly weapon, resisting arrest, and driving under the influence," the sergeant barked at my trooper. "You had the legal right to search him, trooper." The sergeant then stepped on my right ankle and said to me: "You could've got yourself killed, asshole."

I was put in the rear of Big Neck's car to be taken to Troop One.

"I am drunk," I said from the backseat. "I haven't been locked up in years."

The trooper said, "Tough shit."

When they got to the troop they put me in a cell within earshot of the front desk. They took my belt and shoelaces to keep me from hanging myself. I could tell from their conversation they knew by now who I was.

"Can he drive in Delaware on this Brazilian license?" I heard the original trooper ask. No one answered him. "What's 'The Target Manifesto'?" asked another. "I don't know, I'm reading it now" was the reply. "It looks like a short story he wrote, but it jumps around a lot." The thought of them reading it hit me hard in the stomach, and I grabbed a cell bar and squeezed. I heard bits and pieces of other things they were saying, and the word *Gandry* came up more than once, and the original trooper said a couple of times that he didn't recognize me.

He came back and asked me if I wanted to take the omicron intoxilyzer test, and I refused. I guessed I'd stay there until they could figure out what to do.

I was feeling the effects of the alcohol metabolizing and mixing with my lack of sleep, and I put my body down on the cot very gently to keep from throwing up on myself. I pictured Sarah for an instant just as my head hit bottom. She didn't look very happy with me, but at least she was looking at me. I fell asleep before she could speak.

31

DiGiacomo looked like a giant from Greek mythology when I opened my bleary eyes and saw him glaring down at me in my cell. When I did my bit a prisoner referred to his cell as his house. My first thought was to wonder excitedly what DiGiacomo was doing in my house. Why was he in my house? Had Figaro and Janasek confessed? Was I cleared? It was an old recurring fantasy I'd had in prison before Janasek died, that the boys would get me out. When I finally adjusted my senses I asked Rocco what time it was, and I got up and sat on the edge of the cot and yawned.

"Ten-fifteen," he said.

"A.M. or P.M.?"

"A.M."

"I must've slept twelve hours. Am I free?"

"Yeah, they're not pressing the resisting charge. They all want to forget what you did to their rookie trooper. It just embarrasses all concerned, and you got a right to carry a gun, so they're dropping the CCDW. But they are pressing the DUI."

"Why?"

"Probably 'cause you were DUI."

"No accident. No witnesses. No cop arrests another cop for drunk driving. What's going on? Did the sergeant call Covaletzki?"

"Nobody said. I'm sure they probably called their troop commander at home and he probably called Covaletzki, especially since you were throwing Covaletzki's name around. We know the sergeant pretty good. We could've handled this, but it's too late now."

"What happens next, do they book me?"

"No, I talked them into giving you a summons. Here's your ticket with your trial date, and here's your jacket, your weapon, your shoes, your belt, your wallet, and your stuff." He handed me a green plastic bag with my stuff, and among my things were Carlton's writings.

"What now?" I said as I looked over my bruises from the sergeant's kicks. "What do they have on me? Drunk sitting? I wasn't driving when he rolled up on me."

"Your interior light was on, and that drew the trooper's attention to check up if you needed help. Then he smelled the booze. You had the key on and you were behind the wheel. They got you for actual physical control. It's the same as drunk driving. They have half a dozen troopers who will say you were loaded. Plus you told one of the troopers in the car ride back here that you were drunk. Plus you refused the test."

"Can they use that stuff against me? He didn't read me my rights."

"You don't get rights with drunk driving."

I suction-clicked like Carlton, but not as well.

"Anything turn up on Harrison Lloyd?" I asked.

"None of the witnesses at the train station saw the perpetrators' faces. Only their backs running away. At least we got him for a few years on that other shit. Something'll turn up. Maybe Shy's service revolver'll turn up in some Saturday night shooting, and we deal for information and trace it back to Lloyd. Meantime, we got money out on the street. We might not have to wait for a shooting for Shy's weapon to turn up."

We walked out of the cell. Leaving jail is one of life's truly underrated highs.

We passed the front desk. There were state troopers in the area, but nobody looked directly at me. It reminded me of a scene from the movie *Lady Godiva* where no one in the village looks at Maureen O'Hara in the nude on her horse, but every little boy in the movie house is straining for a peek.

When we got outside I said, "I bet that rookie is Tim Gronk's brother."

DiGiacomo said, "Lou, I feel like hitting you where you stand. You're lucky. They figure you tied one on over Gandry's release. The whole Gandry thing is in the paper this morning. They can relate to that. And they don't like it that Covaletzki took some cheap shots at you in the paper. He said that Gandry was bungled by an old-style cop who took it on himself to go outside his assigned duties and investigate a case he had no authority to investigate. He made it sound like you were washed up. And now you played right into his hands with this drunk driving. Lou, I'm pissed off. I gotta tell ya, I'm pissed. You promised me you'd get a good night's sleep."

We picked up my Granada, paid the towing fee, and I locked Carlton's writings in the trunk. By the time Rocco got me to work it was half past noon. I was four and a half hours late, and a mess, but I was strangely looking forward to work. I needed something. I thought about what Honey had said that time in intake about cops, self-pity, and alcoholics. Rocco gave me shaving gear. I fixed myself up in the mezzanine bathroom and hurried over to Youth Diversion at one o'clock, still wearing my soiled and wrinkled white linen "amigo" suit.

Covaletzki, Gronk, and the two lieutenants who tagged along behind Covaletzki, Flopsy and Mopsy, were crowded into the room, and all four stood up when I arrived. I opened the glass door and looked directly at Covaletzki, waiting for him to speak.

"Sergeant Razzi, you are on administrative leave with pay for two weeks from today," he said. "At that time, at oh-nine hundred hours, I am convening a departmental Trial Board in my office. The charge is conduct unbecoming in that you were arrested for the offense of driving under the influence, together with surrounding circumstances. As of right now this minute you are suspended from police duties. Please turn in your service revolver and your ID to records by thirteen-thirty sharp. If you are cleared, you will be reinstated. If you are found guilty by the board, your maximum penalty can be dismissal, and you will lose your pension if so convicted and dismissed. You have the right to be represented and the right to call witnesses on your behalf. These are your charge papers." He put his hand out to me with sheets of paper in it. There was unconcealed joy at the corners of his mouth, as if he were turning over four aces and telling me to read 'em and weep.

I ignored his hand and he put the papers on my ex-desk.

"Laugh at the misfortune of your fellow man," I said, "and at least thirty percent of the world laughs with you."

"If you want more charges, try being insubordinate," he said. "You're a fancy talker."

"Actually, Chief, I'm a fancier listener. When I find Figaro I'll be doing some fancy listening. I bet you know where he is. Old Fig's dumb enough to be calling you for money."

Covaletzki abruptly led the Gang of Four out before I had a chance to say any more. I'm not sure I would have anyway. My head was splitting and my sinuses were killing me. When you don't drink much normally, you can't drink much once in a while.

I climbed up to records with heavy feet and dropped my gun and ID on the counter. The uniformed cop in records already had a receipt made out for me. He crossed off the word *shield* on the receipt and initialed where he had crossed it off. He gave me the receipt without asking where my badge was, which was decent of him.

I said, "I gave it to a little kid who took it to Baltimore." He shrugged.

DiGiacomo peered out from behind the wire fence in back of records. He motioned me to come back and the records cop pressed the door buzzer.

DiGiacomo whispered, "Don't worry. I can get the whole thing handled. The Trial Board's gonna be rigged with Covaletzki's own people, but his fuckin' charges depend on the state police convicting you of drunk driving at the justice of the peace, and they can't convict you if they don't show up. Don't worry, I been making some calls and I can get that straightened out. I'll get you an appointment with a good lawyer next week. But don't worry," he repeated. "If you beat the DUI in court they won't fire you in a Trial Board. They could, but they never fired a guy who beat his criminal charges and they ain't got the balls to make you the first. Believe me. Just don't do anything stupid, you guinea bastard. *Capisce?* Shithead." He messed my hair with his meaty hand. His eyes were wet. "*A più tardi,*" he said.

"*Arrivederci,*" I said, and I went back out to the mezzanine elevators, straightening out my hair. I walked over to the hotel; bought some brown loafers, new gray slacks, a yellow sport shirt with an alligator, undershorts and socks, and a blue blazer like Carlton's; went up to my room and showered; pushed aside a tray with a room-service tuna fish sandwich on rye, a

Heineken, and fresh fruit salad; tried to reach Agent Mendez, who wasn't in or wouldn't take my call; put my meal outside to be picked up so I wouldn't have to smell it; and went right to sleep.

I slept from 2:00 P.M. until 5:30 A.M. the next morning. I called and learned that the Green Room didn't open until 6:30.

I showered, watched a talk show about school busing as I shaved, and dressed slowly in my new clean clothing. And at 6:30 I went down to the Green Room for breakfast. Rain began to hit the windows. I was the only one eating. I opened the newspaper and discovered that I'd made the paper again, this time on the DUI charge and the suspension. Star quality. That's what I've got. Charisma.

Still, breakfast at the Green Room in the rain wasn't exactly life as a prisoner of the Cheyenne, and DiGiacomo seemed to have everything figured out. It's just that my bowels were rotting and what I ate of breakfast tasted like fungus on tree bark. I thought, as I made designs with my scrambled eggs, that what I had done to that trooper was the worst kind of cop's bravado. And it was the kind of extraneous sideshow that deflected my focus from the increasingly irresistible pursuit of Covaletzki.

Sarah walked in. I had forgotten about our breakfast date. It was seven o'clock and I'd eaten without her.

32

"My father drove me here, not Arthur," she said after ordering a poached egg on a heavily buttered English muffin, and black coffee. "He's picking me up out front at eight."

"I can drive you home. I don't have to be anywhere."

"I know, Lou, I read the paper. My arrangements have been made and my father doesn't mind."

"I didn't mean that he did. I just thought we'd be together longer if I drove you home."

"Ten minutes longer at the most. My father will pick me up."

"I'm sorry that I put my hand out to you when we met here Tuesday night. I wanted to hug you. I've wanted to all your life."

"That isn't why I left the table." She spoke very deliberately. "A handshake would have been okay. Just so you know and you don't have to wonder about it, before Mother stood up and shouted your name out loud so everybody in the whole place could hear it, she said to me: 'Sarah, honey, it's your father. You'll finally get to meet him.' I saw the look on my father's face when she called you my father, and that's why I went away."

"I'm not pushing to be your father. I only want to be what you want me to be."

"I don't care what you are."

"You are a very precocious and outspoken girl. Why are you here?"

"I'm curious. I'm descended from you. Aren't you curious about me?"

"Yes, but I feel something else. I hoped maybe I could be available to you, like an uncle. Help you pick out your college, have you visit me in Brazil, and maybe more than that." Against her will she softened very slightly around the eyes. "I even fantasized that you might be willing to have two fathers, or one and a half."

"I think that's against the law even for Mormons. You ought to know, you're a cop," she said without humor.

"You're a tough cookie. I don't like it, but if that's all you're offering me, I'll take it. If all I can ever be to you is an ancestor, then I'll try to be a good one. If you have any questions, fire away."

"What were your parents like?"

"I never met my father. He came over from the province of Marche in the summer of 1929, just in time for the Depression. He married my mother in Scranton, Pennsylvania, in 1931 and went back to Italy to get his old job back with the railroad while she was pregnant with me. He was supposed to send for us, but he was never heard from. At least that's what she told me. For all I know, she made him up. During the war I would save newspaper photos of captured Italians and ask my mother if he was in them. She never remarried. She supported us by giving piano lessons and making and serving Italian food for other people. Her parents were from Marche and died of influenza when she was seventeen. She died of breast cancer when I was seventeen. I don't think anyone who knew her would say anything bad about her. Her death crushed me. I still miss her."

"Why did you leave Delaware in 1963?"

"Why do you think?"

"An act of cowardice."

"Maybe. The judge who sentenced me —"

"I know all that."

"Your mother wouldn't let me see you. I was denied visitation."

"Did you try, not that it matters to me, Lou, but I would like to know my background."

"I sent for a lawyer. He came to the prison and told me I had no chance to get visitation because of my record. That was the way it worked back then. This is very hard on me, Sarah."

"If you'd rather not . . ."

"No, I'll tell you what you want to know. Before they released you in those days, they let you out on job interviews. I couldn't get in the door anywhere. Everybody knew about me. I was big news in this little state. 'Rogue' Razzi, the crooked cop. Before my arrest the newspapers used to call me 'Rapid' Razzi. Two of my homicide cases made *True Detective*."

"Yes, I know. I've read the articles. Why won't you work for my father?"

"Do you want me to?"

"Of course. Why do you think I'm really and truly here? I could find out all I want to know about your mother from my mother."

"I hoped that you wanted to get to know me a little bit."

"Maybe. But my father's work is more important to me than anything."

I put my hand gently on hers. Her hand was ice cold, not just cold.

"I never should have left," I said. "I wish with all my heart and soul that I had stayed. I'll never run away again from anything. You're a brave person to be sitting here telling me the truth about myself."

"Look, Lou, don't make a big deal out of this conversation. You can hold my hand all you want, but I have no intention of holding yours back. Do you know what my father is trying to do for this country?"

"Fight crime."

"No. Wrong."

"Bring criminals to justice."

"Not hardly. He is trying to eliminate crime."

"Come on, Sarah. That's like eliminating hunger."

"Yes, I know. And we're the first country to do that. No one has to starve in America. *Sixty Minutes* would show it on TV. There isn't any reason why we can't be the first country to eliminate crime."

"That's a tall order."

"Low aim, not failure, is the crime. That's what my father says."

"Where would you start?"

"Drugs. Did you know that the word *assassin* derives from the word *hashish*. Assasins were *hashishin*. They were a band of Muslims in twelfth-century Persia who smoked hashish and killed people when they were on the drug. My father says we should make drugs illegal again before they permanently brain-damage our nation's youth. We should allow the cop on the beat to frisk the junkies and pushers, and that would be the end of drugs. We had no drug problem when you were fifteen, except for doctors and jazz musicians."

"Okay I'll think about it."

"Drugs have destroyed black neighborhoods. Our automobiles are made by speed freaks on the assembly line."

"I will think about it. Really I will. Cross my heart and hope to die. Dela-WOC."

"D-WOC."

"D-WOC." And then I sang to myself, D-WOC, a-woc a-bomp, a-bomp, bomp, bomp, and then I looked into her eyes and tried to figure out how I could reach her. I squeezed her hand, winked at her, and sang, "D-WOC, a-woc, a-bomp, a-bomp, bomp," and watched her frown.

If I could ever help her get over the rape and get out from under Carlton's influence, it would take time. I once found an old runaway dog who had obviously been beaten regularly. I named him Luke. It took months of petting to get him to stop flinching at the sight of my hand. After a year I could touch his closed eyes without sending nervous ripples and twitches across his eyelids. I guess you could say I cured his paranoia, but there was a difference. Luke wanted to be cured. Besides, when Luke and I found each other we had no history.

33

After shaking hands good-bye with Sarah, her choice, and promising her again that I'd think about it, I strolled through the lobby to the front desk. On the way I looked in the jewelry store window at the ceramic Boehm birds. There was one big, infinitely detailed owl. The outgrowth of each feather was precise. Its face reminded me of DiGiacomo's. I was in his massive capable hands and soon the DUI charge would be "handled." What were they gonna do, kill me? Everybody dies.

The girl in the pink sweater at the lobby desk picked up my spirits even more. There was a message from Honey. She was calling from intake, and I decided I might as well return the call in person.

The rain was just a slight drizzle, and it felt good as I left for the Public Building on foot in my new shoes and clothing.

The large metal statue on the concrete pedestal twenty feet off the ground glistened in its wetness, especially the horse's rump. It was Caesar Rodney, a Delaware delegate, on his gelding and galloping to Philadelphia to vote for freedom and the birth of a nation. Caesar was suffering from cancer of the mouth when he made his historic ride. He was Italian.

My mother had been very proud of him, and when I was a small kid I thought the statue was religious.

At intake the bunny-rabbit receptionist cooed to me that Honey had given orders to send me right in. "Bye." She waved as I walked past her. She was going to remain loyal to me no matter what.

Honey sat up straight behind her desk. She was alone.

I said, "Hi."

She said, "Hi, Lou."

She handed me a typewritten police report from a WPD detective whose name I didn't recognize. The report was dated yesterday, and the incident had occurred at 1750 hours, while I slept. It was a witness interview of Billy Jerome, nine-year-old white male:

Q. Can you tell me what happened by the shack in the woods by the railroad tracks, Billy, in your own words?

A. Me and Johnny Mastropolito was coming over from the school where I showed you and it happened just like I told you. I don't wanna tell it again.

Q. Yes, but now you got to tell me about it again into this tape recorder, Okay.? Then the nice lady's going to type it up for us to read, Okay.? Go on now. You and Johnny were coming through the woods.

A. And we seen this dirty picture like on the path like I told you a million times.

Q. Excuse me. Now when you say "we" you mean you and Johnny Mastropolito, your friend, is that right? There were no other subjects with you, is that right?

A. No. Just my friend, and we picked up this dirty picture and this picture was this girl putting a cigarette out on this guy's private penis, you know, and

I think Johnny was the one that picked it up 'cause he was first, but we was both looking at it and all. Then we seen another one and it was grosser and a little bit down aways and it had a picture of a German shepherd dog and a colored lady without no clothes on and then we seen another one, all these gross pictures. I think Johnny picked them up 'cause he was ahead of me. He always was talkin' about gettin' a German shepherd when he got big. He was gonna' name it "Prince." It was like a trail of dirty pictures, you know. So Johnny picked them up and then he was near the open clearing where the hangout shack is and Johnny was way in front of me going down the hill and all of a sudden I heard this real loud voice coming from the clearing. It was screaming out real weird and loud like he didn't care who heard him. He yelled, "Halt, kid, in the name of the law, you're under arrest for possession of dirty pictures," and I ducked behind a tree, but Johnny had the pictures and that must've made him froze there and so then I was scared and I heard the same guy yelling out real loud, "I got you. You're under arrest." Then I figured he wasn't no cop. Then I started hearing Johnny saying "ouch," you know, squealing like. But I had to keep still. Then I didn't hear no more squealing. Then I started worrying about Johnny, and if it was the cops and all, so I snuck back around through the bushes and weeds which is behind the shack kind of. So I didn't want to get too close or nothing and I seen Johnny was tied up to this tree and he looked real scared, like terrified, and this dirty picture with the cigarette burning on the man's thing, you know, was stuck under the rope like a target around near his belly but up more, and I seen there was a rag or something stuck in Johnny's mouth so he couldn't squeal. All of a sudden I seen Johnny's eyes get real scareder and this arrow come whizzing out of the shack and sticks in the tree right near Johnny's head. Like two inches. It was really, really close, and this weird laugh is coming out of this guy in the shack after he shoots the arrow. So I figure I'll go for help and I start moving out backward real slow, an inch at a time like an Indian, and I'm looking behind me so I don't step on a twig or nothin', in case this guy's got a friend or somethin', and then I hear this other arrow go whizzing and then it goes plunk into the tree and I look up at Johnny's eyes but he keeps looking in the shack and Johnny's eyes are all sticking out like and bugging wide open and then I hear this guy yell out, "What're you looking at? Didn't you ever watch anybody j'ing off? What's the matter with you, boy, can't you answer me when I ask you a question? I'm gonna make you my slave. You're gonna live in a dungeon and be my slave."

Q. Jerking off, Billy. You can say it.

A. Jerking off. So I thought he was talking to me when he said that slave stuff. So I froze and crouched down. Then it was real quiet and I could hear this guy making these weird kind of sounds like groaning and moaning and laughing kind of funny at the same time, and saying "ooh, la, la" real spooky like. So I started moving back out and you know, backward, 'til I got near Shelton and then I took off and run home and called my mom at J. C. Penney's and she called you guys and then you guys went lookin' for Johnny which was too late, but there was nothing I could do. I had to go out slow or he'd a gotten me too.

Q. You did good. I just wish you had seen the subject's face.

A. I never seen him. Johnny seen him. If you find Johnny and he's dead, ain't there some way you could take a picture of Johnny's eyes showin' what he last seen when his heart stopped before he died. Wouldn't that stay on Johnny's eyes when he died like the food in his stomach stays still when he dies, you know, like on *Quincy*? That would be good if they could invent something like that. But Johnny ain't dead, right? Maybe he won't keep him as a slave. Maybe he'll let him go after he's through with him. That's what I think.

I said, "It's Gandry. It figures. I knew his release would go to his head."

"That's what they think," said Honey. "But there was nothing left at the scene. The arrows were gone. So was the pornography. The rope was left behind, but it won't be of any help. It was rope that was there for years. All the kids used it to swing on."

"Any semen?"

"None found. Maybe he didn't come. Or he used a handkerchief and took it with him."

"Like the one I pulled out of his back pocket. Any hair or fibers?"

"The scene's been vacuumed, and the mattress in the shack is on its way down to the FBI lab, but even if we find fibers, so what? Gandry's one of a hundred kids that goes in and out of that shack. We need some excuse to arrest him or search his house for Johnny or, God forbid, Johnny's body, and we don't have any legal excuse."

"What's being done?"

"A neighborhood canvass. They're hoping a neighbor saw a teenager with a bow and arrow and can ID Gandry from a photo display, or saw a teenager with a young boy near the woods. The cops at the scene figure either Johnny's dead and he's buried somewhere in the woods, or the two of them walked out together. The terrain is not conducive to Gandry's carrying a boy that age, dead or alive. They're also checking on Gandry's whereabouts yesterday afternoon. They're checking bow and arrow sales. They're digging up anything that might look like a grave in the woods. I don't know all the things they're doing. Dershon is handling it. Something'll turn up. Cripes, DiGiacomo called Dershon to tell him that his no-good son, Rocco, Jr., is so worked up he's volunteered to follow Gandry around the neighborhood. They'll get him. I just thought you ought to know about it before it hits the paper. What are you doing this afternoon?"

"I'm going to Shy's funeral."

"After that?"

I tried to smile, to look relaxed. I thought it would be a good idea to show her I hadn't lost my sense of humor the way I had with Marian during visiting days at the workhouse.

"Stay away from Gandry," she said, seeing through my smile. "It's not worth fucking up your life over."

"Don't worry. No more sideshows for me. Every time I touch something in this town it wilts."

"Like Rappaccini's daughter."

"Who?"

"Boo. Hiss. I recognized John Garfield's line in *Body and Soul*, and you don't know this story by Nathaniel Hawthorne. She's the beautiful daughter of a scientist, and she spends her days in a lush garden caring for strange and beautiful flowers and plants, but one kiss from her lips spells death for the kissee. Come on over tonight. I'll read it to you."

"You're a brave one."

"I'll just be careful not to kiss you. Seventeen hundred Pennsylvania Avenue. Seven o'clock. Bring red wine. Dry Italian red wine, but not Chianti, unless it's a real good Chianti, and I mean real good as in expensive."

"Yes, sir, Captain."

"Lou, this isn't your fault."

"Yes, it is, my sweet. It certainly is."

34

"Sounds of the rude world heard in the day, / Lull'd by the moonlight, have all passed away." Shy's burial was held in Silverbrook Cemetery across Lancaster Avenue from Wilmington High School.

The rookie state trooper who'd arrested me came up as I walked to the gravesite and told me he wanted to talk to me "straight out" and "from the hip." He wanted me to know "up front" that he was showing up in court and testifying against me. He said that he was getting pressure from DiGiacomo not to show, but he was getting more pressure from his own supervisors, and, as we all know, "shit flows downhill." I said okay, and he moved on uneasily ahead of me.

Mary Whitney in a black dress and her four teenage sons in blue blazers stood near the grave under the green portable canopy. Rocco and Rocco, Jr., and the rest of Rocco's family stood behind the Whitney boys. Rocco, Jr., looked away as soon as he saw me. Clem Augrine, Tony Landis, and John Judson stood near Rocco. The sun was out now and the drizzle had left the grass a little wet. The boys and Mary were trying not to cry too much and were staring down a lot at the grass. Her hair was gray and thin and tied in a bun. A young priest stood next to her.

The mayor and his whiz-kid staff, Covaletzki and his moron staff, and the chiefs, colonels, and other high-ranking officers from Philadelphia, Trenton, Chester, and neighboring jurisdictions were in the crowd close to the grave with the close friends and relatives. That's where I was. I knew that every time anyone looked at me they were thinking of Gandry and Johnny Mastropolito and they were wondering whether I was now drunk — the way people used to wonder about poor Mamie Eisenhower.

The uniformed contingent, the ordinary patrolmen and troopers from all over the country, wore black mourning ribbons on the badges of their uniforms for a man they'd never met.

The young Catholic priest talked about our sense of loss and society's loss. He recited the Twenty-third Psalm and told us that in His Father's house are many mansions. He told us that we live in times in which we accept as fact that our public parks and public places are not safe at night, as if that is the way God intended it.

"Speak, and my spirit healed shall be." I looked at Covaletzki.

"Yea! Shall He lift up my head above mine enemies around me." Mine, too.

"In the name of the Father and the Son and the Holy Spirit, amen."

There was relative quiet for about sixty long seconds. You could hear birds chirping and traffic noises in the distance, and then the serenity of the scene was exploded by a rifle-volley salute in the background. It was coming from behind me and sounded like a half-dozen rifles. It was very touching. Three volleys. Well synchronized and well meant. Mary's body shook with each volley and she began to lose her composure.

At the tail of the echo of the last volley, a bugler played a mournful taps in the distance. He was a state trooper standing on a little knoll against the overcast sky. He played with feeling, and then I heard Mary sob out: "Oh, dear God, dear Jesus, Mary, and Joseph. Why? Why did this happen? Oh dear, I'm sorry. I'm okay, I'll be fine."

A line formed to pay respects to Mary. I joined it. She was sitting in a lawn chair, with the priest grasping her shoulders from behind and two boys on each side of the chair.

When my turn came I bent down and kissed her cheek. I said, "I'm sorry, Mary." I meant not just Shy's death. Facing Mary with neither one of Shy's two killers headed for the gallows, and facing her without ever being able to tell her why or how it happened, made me sorry. Maybe if I'd gone with Rocco back to Lloyd's house instead of meeting Mendez in the steam bath, I wouldn't have felt that way.

She said, "It's good to have ya back, Lou. Shy was so happy you were home. I'm glad he lived to see it. Everything's gonna work out for you, Lou. You're overdue." She touched my shoulder. "You're overdue for luck, Lou."

"Thanks, Mary."

She turned to her sons and said, "Lou Razzi's working on your dad's case." They nodded and smiled. She turned back to me. "Shy always spoke well of you. Always. He looked up to you when you were partners in the old Robbery Unit, even though he was older than you, Lou. He missed you something terrible when you left. Oh, he missed you so, Lou."

I kissed Mary's cheek again and moved away to my right. When I straightened up I was three feet from Carlton Cruset, and tears had formed in my eyes.

35

"I was hoping to see you," he said dryly. He had shaved his mustache, and his upper lip looked bleached.

"Let's take a walk," I said and wiped my eyes with a fingertip as we blended into the subdued procession of policemen leaving the cemetery. We walked on the auto path, through the black iron gates, and onto Lancaster Avenue. A patrolman had the street blocked to traffic.

Teenagers, boys and girls, black and white, stood on the grass in front of Wilmington High School and watched. Some of the girls giggled as a few of the boys covered their mouths and said barely audible nasty things about dead pigs. When I went to Wilmington High we'd have taken a collection and sent flowers.

"Sounds of the rude world," I said to Carlton.

He nodded and said: "'Gone are the cares of life's busy throng, / Beautiful dreamer, awake unto me.' . . . Let's go for a drive and talk. I'll show you where Sarah goes to school. Perhaps there are other mutually beneficial things we can talk about." He was very calm. His eyes were placid. His skin, especially on his forehead, looked tight.

"Did you ever hear Shy sing 'Beautiful Dreamer'?" I asked. "He had a magnificent voice."

"No," he said gently and led me down a side street to a big dark-blue Plymouth Fury II, similar in effect to an unmarked state trooper's car, with two big antennae whipped back and fastened to the rear.

"Pretty snazzy," I said.

He unlocked the passenger side for me, and I had to laugh under my breath at the expensive police radio and microphone under the dash. The rear doors in the four-door sedan had no interior handles so a prisoner couldn't jump out and escape, just like the real thing.

He got in and started the car. It sounded like an oversized engine designed for hot pursuit. It was an irritating stop-and-go for foot traffic until we cleared the area. He drove like a cop, glancing in all directions, not just straight ahead like most people.

"Did you know Shy Whitney?" I asked.

"I'm quite certain I met him once after a 7-Eleven robbery. The medical examiner who did the autopsy told me this morning that Shy Whitney suffered from undiagnosed terminal lung cancer. I don't suppose many people are aware of that. I try to keep close to law enforcement personnel in Delaware. D-WOC helps in many ways. My organization helped with the funeral expenses and the reception for the out-of-town policemen at the Delaware Police Club. Would you like to stop by for a sandwich and a beer?"

"No."

"Neither would I. Frankly, I drank too much the other night."

"So did I."

"No, you didn't, and I'd be willing to testify to that." He clicked with his mouth. "My testimony at your Trial Board would not go unnoticed."

"I wasn't drunk when you went up to bed, Carlton, but I was over the limit when I left."

"Well, let them try to prove it. You have no doubt heard about the boy who was reported missing from the scene of the Stevie Morris assault?"

"Yes."

"My sources tell me there is no evidence against him."

"I take it you mean Gandry."

"Clearly he did it," he said with a little suction click for emphasis. "Clearly he knows where that little boy is."

"Probably."

With the police radio keeping up a fairly constant chatter, Carlton drove us to the Friends School in Alapocas Woods. It's not the kind of school that a cop's daughter would ordinarily go to. Old stone construction. Plenty of everything. Carlton seemed to know a great deal about it. He made a point of telling me how much the school meant to Sarah. "I've tried to make her life a happy and successful one," he said. "She has a few very close friendships at school. Her friends and what they think of her mean a great deal to her. Her friends only know her as a Cruset, you know. She has only known herself as a Cruset. You understand, don't you?" Looking down at me, he gave me a professor's glance as he drove slowly, as if on routine patrol.

"Friends at Friends School," I said. "It fits. Look, Carlton, I'm sure her friends have no idea that she has any father other than you, and I'm sure that's the way she wants it. Don't worry. I'm not going to do anything to unhinge her life. I'm on her side. And she's on your side."

On the way out of Alapocas Woods he said, "The exclusionary rule has no application to civilians, you know. Private investigators, corporate security, concerned citizens — we may all gather evidence without regard to the exclusionary rule."

"I wouldn't think cops would like being shown up by private eyes," I said. "That kind of thing might tend to make cops competitive and overzealous."

"What do you mean by overzealous?"

"You're overzealous," I said.

"You always say what's on your mind, don't you? You think I'm overzealous and you say so. I like that in a man." He started the clicking again. Two in a row after that comment. He didn't seem as intentionally relaxed anymore.

I didn't reply, because he gave me too much credit. I really hadn't fully said what was on my mind.

He said, "It's probably not merely a kidnapping. Johnny Mastropolito is very likely going to be killed, if he's not dead already. You know, we can make Gandry for this, you and I. You are suspended and I am not a policeman. We are civilians. We need not concern ourselves about the exclusionary rule, about search and seizure or *Miranda*. We can barge our way into the Smotz house and search it. We may, with impunity, pick him up and question him without worrying that he will ask for a lawyer. If he sued us I would handle the expenses, and no jury in the world would award him damages. My sources tell me that you were an artist when it came to interrogation. A great user of words to motivate your subjects. I would be curious to see you break him twice in the same week. That, I suppose, is the zealot in me. Of course, I would not want any of the reward money. You would have it all."

"What reward money?"

"The ten thousand dollars that was put up for the solving of the young boy's disappearance. Ten thousand dollars merely for an arrest. No conviction necessary."

"You mean the ten thousand dollars that was put up by you just this second?"

"The very same." He moved his lips and cheek into a position to click, but held them in suspended animation. He looked over at me and saw me waiting for the click. He looked back at the road ahead of him and laughed.

Carlton stopped his Fury in front of the Smotz house.

"Why not have a try?" he said, fishing into his glove compartment for a minicassette recorder and handing it to me. "Surely, he still thinks you are a policeman. He and his grandfather will just as surely let you in and search their house, thinking you're still a policeman, and it will all be to a good end. What have you to lose? Johnny Mastropolito may well be in there right now as we sit here. Perhaps being tortured. Frankly, this one has been your responsibility all along, Lou Razzi. It has been your baby from the start. Try to fix it. Sarah would be pleased to hear you tried. Yes, the Mastropolito boy may still be alive. Inside that door as the police sit idly by, their hands tied. Do it, Lou. Do it for that little boy. Just go through that door as you would have fifteen years ago. Ring the bell, they'll let you in. And whatever you find will be legal."

I got out without saying a word. Carlton stayed in the car. I walked up the crumbly brick steps and tried the locked handle and then rang the bell furiously and continuously and rapped on the door at the same time. I had the feeling I was being watched from the inside and from the outside. I stopped ringing and banging. I pressed my ear to the door, listening for any sounds from inside, scratching on a closet door, anything. As I waited, straining to listen, I wondered whether plainclothes cops were watching the house, because somehow my instincts told me that we wouldn't have a free "civilian" rein to investigate if anyone could construe for a second that we were aware of the presence of police in the area or that we were somehow under their direction or control.

The thinking soured me. Here I was starting to play out the ritual of worrying over rules. I squatted down and picked up a loose brick from the stoop and tossed it through the living room window. After the sound of breaking glass subsided, I called out: "Johnny, if you're alive inside this house, make a noise. Make a noise, Johnny. It's the police." And then I listened for any reaction from inside the house. Nothing. I walked back to Carlton's phony police car and got in, but not before spotting a head staring straight ahead in an old Buick on a side street with a view of the Smotz house.

"What's the matter?" he asked. "Shouldn't we take the door? I've a sledgehammer in the trunk."

"Don't be a fool," I snapped.

"Fool," he gasped. "Now a fool. I can imagine what you must think of me. I can imagine what personal things Marian has told you about me."

"Carlton, you're not the kind of person anybody has to tell anything about. Let's go on back to my car. Now. Gandry's under real police surveillance. There's a real cop in a Buick right down the street. The poor fuck doesn't know what to do. He can't blow his cover, so he's got to sit tight and watch me break a window. Thanks for the ride and the talk about Sarah. Let's keep things on that level and stop putting screwball ideas into my head and wasting my time. I'm no more a cop than you are. Let's both face it. We're playing cops."

"You are right about one thing. It is my fault for not realizing it. To that extent I am a fool. You are simply not ready for the things that need doing. You observe surveillance down the street and you feel sorry for yourself and you become infantile. You give up too easily. You go into exile."

"And you're a fucking whacko, Carlton," I said. I came close to telling him that I knew what a coward he was, when the chips were down, but I couldn't do that. Merely considering it for an instant made me wonder what this trip was turning me into.

When we got to my car he said, "Look, Razzi, we've gotten off on the wrong foot. That is a shame because we are very much alike, you and I. We even married the same woman. Maybe there is something I can do for you? What might you need? You name it. I would like to help you. Perhaps I can help you in your quest of Covaletzki."

"You want to grant me a wish, Carlton?"

"That is correct. Make a wish. If I can do it, I shall do it. I have the right contacts and I am a powerful man in this state, your opinion notwithstanding."

"Leave police work to the professionals. Stay out of the street. You might hurt someone who doesn't deserve it, or you might get hurt yourself and Sarah would be fatherless. Finish your novel."

"You fail to take me seriously. You think I am a physical coward. A man of the pen, not of the sword. Mazzini, not Garibaldi."

"Yea-yah," I said in my best Harrison Lloyd accent.

"I am deadly serious, and I am in a position to do things for you."

"Good. Bring Figaro to me. Alive."

I got in my car and drove to Honey's, exhaling heat all the way.

36

When I walked in the door we shook hands, and there was no doubt about what we were going to do next. Here was something that didn't hold the promise of a dead-end brick wall like everything else I'd butted into since my return from exile. There was that same warm bodily energy that passed between us that first night we kissed, which seemed like years ago, the kind of energy measured on a polygraph from wires attached to fingertips. We both felt it at the same time and looked into each other's eyes when we did.

"That's some handshake you got there," she said.

I asked, "Is this a come-on?" and we walked together to her bedroom. We first sat on the edge of her bed, fully clothed, and kissed, still holding hands. The tingling feeling of excitement in our hands had not gone away. Our kiss was riveting and sent the first waves of warmth through us.

Our hands reached around for each other. I could feel the heat of her hands on my back. It was more intense than our embrace at the hotel the night Shy was killed. Our lips became hot and our cheeks flushed. I wanted to drink her in. She put her head against my shoulder.

"I never felt anything this strong," she said. "My heart is racing."

"Mine too." I found her lips and kissed her firmly.

We made love repeatedly and with a sense of adventure. It was so clearly perfect that we didn't have to say anything about it, ask any questions, or wonder what the other liked. I can't remember ever kissing as much or feeling so good from head to toe.

It was also clear when it was time to lie still. We held each other the way runners in a close race wind down together after passing the finish line.

"I had a thought that maybe you led some kind of monastic life in Brazil," she said, "but it appears you've been keeping in touch with things."

She lay on her back with her orange hair spread out on the pillow. I was propped up on one arm beside her, lightly stroking the bare skin below her breasts with my fingers.

"Well," she said when I didn't say anything about my life in Brazil. "So you won't talk, eh? Ve haf vays to make you talk."

She turned toward me and tickled my belly. I grabbed her wrists.

"I never remarried if that's what you're wondering. I could never figure out how to say 'I do' in Portuguese."

"It entered my mind that you might be a married man, but I decided to wait to ask until after we'd made love. We are finished for a while, aren't we?"

"I came here for food and conversation. The sex was your idea." I let go her wrists.

She laughed and got up and put on a bright snow-white terry-cloth robe. It fluffed out on her body. I put all my clothing back on. We left the bedroom and I could see that she had a nice little apartment. Very colorful. On one wall in her living room she had one of those posters that you see in movie theaters. It was framed. I'd never seen one outside a movie house before. Pretty good idea, I thought. It was *Casablanca*, with Humphrey Bogart and Ingrid Bergman. I remembered seeing it as a boy with my mother, and I remembered being disappointed because I thought it was going to be a war movie and it turned out to be a love story. My mother had loved it.

Honey had a stereo, with a couple hundred record albums on a shelf, arranged alphabetically. Cannonball Adderley. Mildred Bailey. Count Basie. Art Blakey, with the legendary Clifford Brown from Wilmington on trumpet. Jazz like that. My stuff.

And she had books. It reminded me of Carlton's library. Only her books were mostly paperback and looked like they'd been read. They were everywhere.

"I feel like I'm on vacation," I said. "I'm so happy to be here."

She came up and kissed me.

"Read any good books lately?" I asked.

She went to a shelf and handed me *In Cold Blood* by Truman Capote.

"Any good?"

"Very," she said. "There's an interrogation scene in it I'd love to hear your comments on. I doubt the murders could have been solved today with *Miranda* and *Bruton*. It reminds me of the Stevie Morris case without Mrs. Smotz's role, and I hope you don't think I'm just trying to make you feel good."

"The Morris case would probably have been solved with today's rules if I hadn't done the solving, and you may be just trying to cheer me, but it's well meant and I appreciate it."

"Anyway, I'd be curious to watch you go about solving murders like those in Capote's book."

"Where? In America or Brazil?"

"Are you really going back?"

"Eventually."

She turned and went to the kitchen, and as I browsed through *In Cold Blood*, she got dinner ready.

In a little while she came out and said, "I thought we'd eat in the kitchen."

There was a candle on the wooden butcher-block kitchen table, and my bottle of expensive Chianti. She served up a sizable portion of some eggplant Parmesan and followed that with an excellent baked lasagna.

"I haven't had Italian food in years," I said. "This is really good."

After dinner she put out some Bosc pear slices on a plate with Brie cheese. She switched to white wine and asked me if I wanted some, too. I switched with her.

We scraped plates at the sink and nibbled on the pear and the cheese.

"Everything's been so good tonight," I said. "My dear, you have been responsible for the two best times this tourist has had in the old country. Tonight and eating the stuffed pineapple."

She turned from the sink and said, "Lou, come away with me this weekend."

"Where to?"

"New York, for the Tall Ships on Sunday."

"Fourth of July Bicentennial?"

"Yep. I'm driving up tomorrow and staying overnight at the Plaza Hotel and getting an early start on the Fourth for a good view of the ships. Let's do it. My treat."

I sang the words to "Just a Gigolo," nodding yes.

"Bravo," she shouted, and clapped and whistled.

"Louis Prima. Before your time."

"Up yours," she said and pushed me toward the bedroom. When we got there she undressed me and held my hand, and we lay down together and she began kissing my abdomen very softly, causing tension I didn't know was there to come out in great quakes and tremors and nervous ripples. It scared me, embarrassed me really, but she acted as if it were normal. She made love to me once I settled down, and we went to sleep with all the lights on in the apartment. Talk about heaven.

37

"Shh," said Honey, "I want to hear this." She tilted her head closer. Wisps of orange hair gently touched the glossy brown plastic of the clock radio on the kitchen table.

"This is history," she said, turning up the volume and sipping on her black coffee.

I stopped talking and helped myself to a mouthful of the peppers and eggs she had fried for breakfast.

I began listening:

> " . . . by a five-to-four vote overturned the mandatory death penalty statute of the State of North Carolina while at the same time upholding the discretionary death penalty statute of the State of Georgia. The United States Supreme Court decision makes it clear that some form of the death penalty is permissible under the Constitution. It appears that those states wishing to have the death penalty must now model their death penalty statutes after Georgia. More on that story at eight. The time now is a rise-and-shine six-thirty. We'll have the sports and weather in half a minute as we count down to one day before the Bicentennial, but first —"

She turned off the radio.

"What does this mean?" I asked, holding on to Honey's hand.

"I'm not sure, but it's a landmark case. I can't wait to get a Sunday *Times* tomorrow to read the decision. Lucky we'll be in New York." She put a forkful of her eggs into her mouth.

"What does it mean for Harrison Lloyd," I asked, "if by some remote chance they make him for murdering Shy Whitney?"

She looked into my eyes. "You're pressing my hand into the table," she said.

"Sorry." I removed my hand.

"It means he wouldn't hang. That's all. He'd get life. There're nine men on death row in Delaware right now that are celebrating. I put one of them there. Delaware's death penalty is gone until the legislature passes a new one."

"Why?"

"Because Delaware guessed wrong after the *Furman* decision in '72. Georgia guessed right. Delaware and North Carolina and I guess some other states guessed wrong. We all made death mandatory because that's what we thought the court wanted."

"What do you mean 'guessed wrong'? You have to guess?"

"Sometimes, Lou, to use your favorite lawyer word, they rule by 'indicating.' Relax, Lou. The *Furman* decision in '72 was worse. That decision kept Charles Manson and Sirhan Sirhan alive. You should have been around a few years ago when a new decision came down every week."

"I was just thinking of Mary Whitney."

She bent over to kiss my cheek. I felt my stomach start to flinch. It hadn't done that since last night. She pulled away before her lips touched my face.

"Finish your eggs," she said. "Let's go to New York. Look, Lou, why don't I take a few vacation days next week? I'll call Morris Dershon and get some time off. He'll give it to me. I think he's got a little crush on me anyway."

I got up from the table and then realized there was no place to go in the small apartment but back to the bedroom.

"I need some time alone," I said.

"Sure. I planned on going to New York by myself anyway. I'll miss you, but I'll see you when I get back. See, that was easy. And they say Jews are pushy."

"I want to go with you. I just need a little time now. I'll drive us to New York. And I want to see you next week, too, if you can get the time off. How about if we meet at the Howard Johnson's near the bridge at, say, eleven? I need to get my things anyway for the trip."

"That's fine. I understand." She took my hand.

"I'm not so sure I do. Crazy cloud formations are rolling around my brain, and I'm just not sure of myself for the first time in a long time. I just need a couple or three hours to myself. I know we haven't talked about it, but I keep thinking about Johnny Mastropolito. Cruset thinks it's my responsibility."

"That bastard," she said and kissed me on the cheek, and I left.

38

Honey sat locked inside a yellow Subaru in the Howard Johnson's parking lot near the entrance to the Delaware Memorial Bridge. She saw me pulling up and she got out of her car and relocked it. She probably wouldn't believe, I thought, that when I went to jail no one in D-WOC locked his house, much less his car. But no one in 1961 would have believed that in fifteen years the whole U.S.A. would be unsafe. So it was even on both ends.

"Sorry I'm late," I said. "I hope you'll add ten minutes on at the end of the weekend. I don't want to miss any of my time with you."

She tossed her overnight bag on the backseat and got in beside me. It was clear now, but gray clouds were in the north and rain was expected in New York.

"Spiffy," she said. "New threads?"

"Just bought 'em, but I'll need more when we get to the Plaza. Traditionally, I charge small items of jewelry and clothing to my escort's room. I assume you have no objection, but if you do I want it ironed out right now before we cross the bridge and I become a white slave."

"Clothing is okay, but jewelry depends on how good you are in the sack." She kissed me on the cheek. "What's that smell? Have you been smoking cigarettes?" She pulled a partially used pack of Luckies from my shirt pocket, crunched them into a ball and tossed them overhead into the backseat, and said, "You have got to be watched every second or you become one royal pain in the ass."

"I had a couple. For old time's sake. You can't get Luckies down my way."

"Lou" — she looked troubled — "I guess you heard by now they found Johnny Mastropolito under a fallen tree in the woods next to Shelton High. Strangled."

"I heard it on the radio just after I left, but we knew it anyway, didn't we?"

"Is that why you bought the cigarettes?"

"I bought them first, but maybe that's more or less why I smoked them. I hadn't thought of it like that."

I started the car, drove out of the parking lot, and headed for the highway and over the twin suspension bridges that cross the Delaware River. Chemical plants are close to the bridge on both the New Jersey and Delaware shores. White smoke. Gray smoke. Take your pick. This is the same river that Washington crossed at Christmas a hundred and ninety years ago. I kept thinking that, despite my efforts, my thoughts were tinged with darkness like the chemical smoke. Negative. Gloomy. I didn't dare open my mouth too often.

While we were crossing the Delaware, Honey said, "Do you want to play a game?"

"Not really."

"I admire your courage in standing up to me, but we're playing anyway. If you had seen a face last night when I kissed you, when your stomach convulsed from the tension, who would it have been?"

"Covaletzki," I sighed, trying to be sociable. "With a smirk on his thin lips. And behind him would be everybody else in single file except you."

"Everybody?"

"Harrison Lloyd, Marian, Sarah, Carlton, DiGiacomo, Tim Gronk, Agent Mendez, the whole board of directors, and especially John Figaro."

"Crap," she said. I guessed she didn't think I was taking her Psych 101 very seriously. "I can understand the rest," she went on, "but why DiGiacomo and Sarah on your list and not Gandry?"

"Honey, I'm grateful for what you're trying to do for me. Open me up and all that. You're a very nice person and very sincere. Very honest."

I pulled her closer to me and put my arm around her. We sat as teenagers going to a prom.

"Yucch. You smell of cigarettes," she said and moved away to face me. "Are you really going back to Brazil eventually?"

"I've got a business there," I said. "And a pet monkey."

"Do you really have a pet monkey?"

"Roberta."

"Oh, God, that's neat, but it sounds like stiff competition. I'd better start pampering you. You look a little tired. I know just what you need before you start getting cranky. It's nap time. Why don't I drive for a while?"

"Now that's something Roberta can't do." I pulled over to the shoulder south of Camden. We switched places, and she drove with the newsradio station on while I slept.

I woke up near Newark and with one eye open said, "What the hell is a drug abuser?"

"Huh?" she said with surprise.

"Is it somebody who treats drugs mean? Beats up on his cocaine? Talks nasty to his heroin?"

"Did you dream that up while you were sleeping?"

"All by myself."

"I shouldn't have had the radio on." She turned the station to music — "Feelings" by Morris Alpert, a hit in South America before it came to the States. "I have to be careful what your little ears pick up."

"I prefer the term drug addict," I said.

"How about dope fiend?"

"That's my girl. Promise me you'll dedicate your life to stamping out 'drug abuser.' "

"I'm having enough trouble with 'indicate.' Now shut your eyes and go back to sleep. No more newsradio for you today. I should have learned my lesson earlier this morning. Schmaltz is all you get on the radio."

39

Dinner at the Algonquin Hotel that night was New York, New York, and the rest of the world was just the rest of the world. The sole with white grapes and cream sauce was excellent, but it was something they just tossed your way. You were paying for the privilege of being there, and gladly. They had a skinny guy in a tux playing the piano and singing sophisticated songs in a high-pitched voice. The guys in the audience clapped the loudest after each song and shouted, "Bravo." It was the Big Apple to the core.

When we left, it was a little after two. Honey wanted to walk up Fifth Avenue in the warm night air rather than take a taxi. It was all right with me. It was her city.

"When we get to the Plaza let's take a hansom cab through Central Park," she said as we turned left onto Fifth Avenue and started walking north.

"Bravo," I said. "I had my afternoon nap thanks to Mother, and I'll have no problem getting up at six for the Tall Ships."

"Neither will I, my relic."

"Relic? Hell, by the time I was born, women already had the right to vote for twelve long years."

We walked on the other side of the street from Saint Patrick's Cathedral and window-shopped along the way. We turned into Rockefeller Center to look at the golden statue that overlooks the ice rink. We came back out and ambled north again. We stopped in front of 666 Fifth Avenue, wondering if we could get a drink at the Top of the Sixes, and walked into the outdoor hall of windows leading to the building entrance. No soap. The entrance was closed. Before we got back out to Fifth Avenue we stopped to look at a travel agency's pictures of Italy. We were somewhere on the Amalfi Coast when a white male in his thirties with a few days' growth and an old-fashioned light brown crew cut stepped up to us. He was a couple of inches taller than me and wore a black Ban-Lon shirt, dirty dark-blue pants rolled up at the cuffs, gray tennis shoes, and a red handkerchief tied around his neck.

"Spare some change, man?" he asked in a hushed voice, flat and low. His eyes were watery blue. His pupils dilated and he smiled wickedly. "Just got out the joint, man. Off the motherfuckin' Riker's ferry. Need some money, man, to get started. You know what I mean?" He stuck his right hand into his pants pocket and moved it about menacingly. "That's a nice ring the lady got."

"Are you begging for money or are you threatening for money?" I said and got in front of Honey.

"Good question," he said and flashed clenched teeth. He lifted his right hand, casually snapped out a black stiletto switchblade, and pointed it with his right arm at my heart. I saw the right arm as a gift, the way my little doctor from Taiwan had taught me. With my right foot I took a quick sinking step toward that gift. Lowering my weight into my right leg, I jutted my left foot forward, kicking his shin. My hands moved at his right arm as if I were clapping two cymbals, but about a foot off from making a direct crashing contact. I jammed the palm of my left hand into his right elbow joint and the palm of my right hand into his wrist, avoiding the knife. The movement of my hands working in opposite directions, combined with the sinking of my weight, snapped his elbow at the joint, making a loud crack in the otherwise noiseless corridor. He groaned sharply, dropping the knife, and his right arm hung lifelessly at his side. I had the knife the instant it smacked the cement and came up with it on a vertical line into the softness of his left underarm, cutting through the left shoulder joint ligaments and hitting bone. His left arm dangled like the right, and I pulled the knife out. He groaned as pain overcame narcotics. I held the dagger near his mouth and held him by his belt.

"Open up," I said, "say 'ah.' "

His eyelids closed. I put a foot on one of his, yanked his belt toward me, and threw him past me to the ground on his belly, his chin striking pavement. I frisked him and found nothing worth taking. He was still groaning, but he wasn't going anywhere.

"Let's go," I said, taking Honey's arm. She hesitated and I pulled her out onto Fifth Avenue. We walked north toward the Plaza, with me holding her arm and moving at a good pace.

"What happened?" she asked. "It happened so fast, Lou. What did you do?"

"It'll come back to you. We'll talk about it later."

"We've got to report it."

"I will."

I dropped the knife through a sewer grate as we crossed over it.

Before we got to the Plaza, I called the NYPD from a corner pay phone and gave them an anonymous tip that a robbery victim had stabbed his mugger and told them where to find him. Honey stayed by me until I finished.

We walked into the hotel and rode in silence to our air-conditioned room. She double-locked the door.

We talked as we undressed. "Lou, what are you doing? I don't understand."

"I'm not getting tied up in any more courts. Anyway, he's had his punishment. He doesn't need jail."

"What did you do to him?"

"I broke his elbow, and I tried to cut the strings on his other arm with his knife. I think I got that arm too."

She sighed. "You're right. It's coming back to me. Why did you slam him down so hard after you had his knife?"

"Don't ever assume that the weapon he shows you is the only weapon he's got. It could cost you your life. What'd they teach you?"

"What'd they teach me?"

After we undressed she got into one of the beds without looking at me. With cold water I washed the drops of blood off my shirt and pants. When I finished I asked, "Should I turn out the light?"

"Yes," she said and then shifted to the center of the bed, making it clear that I had no side in her bed. I turned off the lamp and plopped into the other one.

Everything had now gone wrong. I felt like I was in an avalanche, going down with the rocks. Love and sex couldn't stop the fall for long. It was something inside me, some turmoil that kept me from standing safely on the mountain, kept me from staying put. It was like a little worm inside a Mexican jumping bean. When Honey had kissed my stomach and I was convulsing, I really had seen Covaletzki's face. With his lips pressed shut. Committing a continuing crime of silence against me. But I knew, as I lay in bed listening to Honey try to sleep, that Covaletzki wasn't the worm. The worm was inside of him, too. It was the unanswered question of why they had framed me. I wanted that worm out of him so much I could cut it out of him. But there was nothing I knew to do about it.

40

The Tall Ships moved slowly under sail in the dark-green water of New York Harbor as they entered the Hudson River.

We had arrived at Battery Park before the huge throng came, early enough to get a spot on the black iron railing, but by 9:00 A.M. we were part of one of the biggest crowds ever to stand and face a body of water.

We had to speak loudly to hear each other above the noise of the crowd — the rock music from big-box portable radios tuned to competing stations, the children crying and being scolded, the congas and bongos, and the inevitable firecrackers.

There had been a cold war between us all morning. I thought I ought to explain the nightstick justice of last night, to at least talk about it, but during breakfast at the hotel Honey was hard to talk to. She said she had ambivalent feelings that she had to work through herself. All she would say was that she experienced it on different levels — fear of his knife and relief at his downfall, the sheer excitement of it, the speed of it — and she could understand why I would want to leave him, yet something wasn't right about it. I offered that it was like seeing cattle slaughtered. You know it goes on, otherwise you wouldn't have meat, but you don't like to see it. She said that wasn't it entirely, although it undoubtedly had something to do with it, and repeated that she had to work it through herself.

Sailors on the Italian ship stood in the rigging and waved. A huge roar came up from those of us on shore and we all waved back. I marveled at the Verrazano Bridge, but to Honey it was no big deal. Neither was the smell of joints, nor the grafitti painted on the trees.

We left the park and spent the rest of the day in downtown Manhattan at the Little Festivals of Celebration, small units of people dressed in foreign peasant costumes performing dances of their own lands and selling their own national foods. We ate snacks from Greece, Pakistan, Italy, Mexico, and India, all served with Coca-Cola. Just like in the old country.

Honey and I held hands without feeling, dodged episodes of rain, and finally decided to go home to Wilmington.

On the drive home on the turnpike, after about an hour of silence, Honey said to me: "I think I'll call Dershon back and cancel my vacation days. I don't think it's a good idea for me to be taking any time off next week."

"That's disappointing. I guess you've worked through your ambivalent feelings."

"You put me in a hell of a spot last night. A deputy attorney general running from the scene. Actually covering it up, when you think about it. I could be disbarred."

She looked over at me, but I didn't say anything.

"You were brutal last night and I think you overdid it. You could have killed him."

"He deserved death. Kill anybody who pulls a knife on you, Honey. Pass it on."

All of a sudden I didn't feel like having to explain that I wasn't a sadist, that I never went out looking to hurt anybody, that I was going back to Brazil for chrissake, and that I couldn't be bothered arresting him and getting involved in New York

City justice. The man drew a knife on me. He made the rules of the game deadly, not me.

After a while she wanted to know if I was angry about John Gandry, and did I think that since the law wasn't working for me I had to take it into my own hands. It appeared that she wanted me to have some psychological excuse about the way I'd handled the robber. Like I was taking my hatred of John Gandry out on him.

I said, "I just wanted to force the man into a safer line of work. You could say he had an on-the-job accident. God help you people when all the old cops retire."

"If there are any left that have your police-state mentality, the sooner they retire, the better," she said. "I'll bet you fit in just peachy in Brazil."

"We didn't live in a police state in my heyday," I said, "but let me tell you what these new rules of yours are leading to, all this unfair fairness." I told her how Carlton had recruited me to work on the Gandry case now that I was suspended and not subject to the new rules.

"A suspended cop is still a cop," she said indignantly. "Your friend the vigilante professor is dead wrong on the law. Until fired or retired you are a cop, and any evidence you might manage to get on Gandry by playing by your own rules would be absolutely useless at trial." When she told me that tidbit she had the superior look I'd seen when I brought her the first Gandry case.

All we said the rest of the way down the turnpike were things like "How's the gas?" and "Do you mind if I turn up the radio?" Mostly we listened to news of the Israeli raid at Entebbe. We pulled into the Howard Johnson's, she took her overnight bag and her *New York Times*, and we said good-bye and politely kissed on the cheek.

41

The two young girls in pink sweaters standing at attention behind the mahogany reception desk in the lobby had nervous smiles. I checked with them to see if there were any messages, and I got a feeling similar to the one I'd had about the surprise party. Something was up. The girls tried to look as if they weren't even with each other behind the desk, much less know whatever it was they knew.

I did have messages. They were on slips of pink paper. Three of them. The messages said: "Call Marian." I crumpled and stuffed them in the refuse hole in the aluminum ashtray near the elevator door.

When I got to my room it was 10:05 P.M., and even though I had already decided not to, I dialed Marian's number from memory. Her phone rang and rang with no answer. With each ring I felt my heart get stronger from the blood pumping through it, the way flowing water generates power at a hydroelectric plant. I hung up, pleased that no one had answered. I undressed and went to bed and slept quickly and deeply. At 11:06 there was a hard knock on my door. I pictured Marian. I considered ignoring the knock.

"Can we come in, Lou?" It was DiGiacomo.

I got up and opened the door to see DiGiacomo standing next to Chief Deputy Attorney General Morris Dershon, a wiry little man in his early thirties with an effeminate voice, smooth, nearly hairless pink skin, a narrow pointy nose and tapered chin, large round blue eyes, and naturally curly brown hair parted in the middle. His long, thin manicured fingers fiddled with a large red bow tie. There were two big-lug weightlifter-type plainclothes cops I didn't recognize and Covaletzki standing behind them. The delegation looked very official.

"Speak up," I said, "out with it."

"Lou," said DiGiacomo, "you know why we're here. They want to come in."

"That's an order," said Covaletzki. "You're still under my command."

"Wait a minute," said Dershon. "Let's not create legal issues here. Mr. Razzi, do we have your expressed consent to come in?"

I stood in my undershorts and looked at this quintet of fools in the hallway, and my curiosity got the best of me. I let them in. I gave my "expressed" consent.

I sat down on the bed, with my back leaning against the headboard and my legs crossed comfortably on the bed. Covaletzki had shut the door behind him. DiGiacomo was the only one to sit down. The rest stood around.

The slightly larger of the two plainclothesmen — and it took a sharp eye to see the difference — took out his identification and showed it to me. He was a real Wilmington cop, another to come on since my frame. Maybe he'd been hired to fill my vacancy. He took out a little business-type card, held it in front of him, and read me the spiritual tenets concerning my divine right to remain silent in the face of reasonable questions and to have a free government lawyer.

"Who pays for these free lawyers?" I asked. "I mean who sees to it that their secretaries are on Blue Cross?"

"Luig," said Rock from his chair in the corner, "any kind of reaction you have now could be used against you." He seemed to want to say more. He glanced up at Dershon and Covaletzki, who both continued to stand, and then he chose to remain silent himself.

"Rocco, I appreciate the subtle warning. Out with it, boys. I've had a busy weekend. I've been framed before, arrested before, recently suspended, and there is nothing I resent more right now than having my precious time on earth wasted in Delaware. I am a man with a mission."

"Understanding your rights, will you answer our questions?" asked Morris Dershon through the thin hole in his face.

"Out with it," I said. "Spit it out. Identify the subject matter. What are you people here for?"

"We think you know something about the shooting of John Gandry, and we'd like your cooperation," said Morris Dershon.

"Outstanding. Is he dead?"

"He's in a coma," said DiGiacomo.

"Now see that," I said. "All this while you've been standing around acting stupid, and you really have a legitimate reason to be here. Is this the way you work a case, or were you extending me professional courtesy?"

"Lou," said DiGiacomo, "this is real serious."

"How'd it happen?" I asked.

"You tell us," growled the detective who had told me about my rights.

"What technique," I said. "Learn that from your chief?"

"Look here," said Morris Dershon with surprising firmness considering his lilting voice, "you were seen in Gandry's neighborhood Friday afternoon by a surveillance officer. You were observed walking right up to the front door and breaking his window with a brick. In fact, he was in the house when you went to his front door, and after you left he called the radio room to find out what you were doing there and whether you had a warrant. We have Gandry's call to the radio room on tape like any other call to the radio room, and that tape is evidence. I might point out that you had a motive to kill him because he made you out a fool in the way you bungled the Morris case and forced me to release Gandry, making the whole system look like shit. You are an extremely revenge-oriented person. Everyone knows why you really came back to the States. Furthermore, you knew about the attack on the Mastropolito boy, didn't you?"

"Well done, Bulldog. You got me. Yes I did. I knew all about the Mastropolito boy. Deputy Attorney General Honey Gold showed me the witness's statement. You can ask her. You can also ask her where I've been all weekend. You see, gentlemen, I've got what you could call an airtight alibi. You'll never take me alive."

"We just left her," said the nameless Detective Hulk. "What time did you leave her apartment on Saturday morning, July third, 1976, and what time did you meet her at the Howard Johnson?"

"Let me guess," I said. "Don't tell me. Gandry was shot sometime on the morning of the third after I left Honey's apartment and before I met her near the bridge. There goes my airtight alibi. Take me away. Can I plead lunacy?"

"Lou, they're serious," said Rocco.

"DiGiacomo, let Captain Dixon handle this," said Dershon sharply.

Captain Dixon looked pleased. He now had a name and a rank and he could handle it. "What time on Friday?" he repeated.

"We met at the Howard Johnson's at 11:10 A.M., as you well know, and I left Honey Gold's apartment around six-forty A.M., but I don't like you, Dixon. I'll bet you made Shy Whitney's skin crawl every time you walked into the Detective Division."

"He's sick," said Covaletzki.

Morris Dershon began talking to me in a soothing voice: "You know, Lou, we knew you were in New York with Honey. She phoned me for permission to take Monday and Tuesday off, and she told me you were going with her, but we didn't know where you were staying. Look, we don't like this any more than you do, but we've got certain information that has to be checked out. You understand, don't you?"

"Yea-yah," I said.

"Look here, we know about your emotional reaction to hearing the Supreme Court's death penalty decision," said Dershon. "You didn't even finish your eggs, and right after that on your way home from Honey's you heard on the radio that Johnny Mastropolito's body had been found in a shallow grave in the woods."

"Peppers and eggs," I said.

"That's right," said Dershon, getting palsy-walsy. "Peppers and eggs. Lou, you've been under a lot of emotional strain. We can appreciate the pressure you've been under. You had a very emotionally exhausting day on Friday — that was the day you read the Mastropolito witness interview, the same day your mentor, Shy Whitney, was buried, the same day you threw a symbolic brick at Gandry's window."

"The brick wasn't symbolic. It was a purpose pitch."

"Look at the difficult time you gave that Delaware state trooper," Dershon said. "We know you have got plenty of pent-up rage inside of you. We can feel it in you and we can relate to it. We don't blame you. We understand you. We can help you. You may not trust us, but I repeat, we can help you. Have you ever heard of extreme emotional distress or irresistible impulse? With a plea to either, you could be back in Brazil in short order."

"Copacabana, here I come," I said. "See the cop from Ipanema. How'd you like an irresistible impulse, Bulldog?"

"He's playing with you," said Covaletzki, but not in that slow, deliberate monotone of his. There was a hint of hysteria in his voice. "Let's stop wastin' time. We know about the panhandler you cut in New York. You fuckin' psycho. You half-killed the guy."

"Where were you this weekend?" I said looking at Covaletzki.

"Is that a threat?" Covaletzki thundered. "Are you fucking threatening me? Hah? Hah?"

Dershon walked over to Covaletzki the way a referee takes a boxer to a neutral corner. "Easy," he said several times. When Covaletzki was neutralized Dershon came back to me.

"Where exactly were you before 11:20 A.M. on Saturday?" asked Dershon.

"Ah, a direct question. Your technique's not bad. When I left Miss Gold that morning I stopped for something you people call self-service gasoline. Then I came back to the hotel to change and freshen up and then went to Wanamaker's to buy some clothes. When I got back I changed into my new clothes and took a crap. Then I drove to the Howard Johnson's by the bridge, arriving about 11:10. When was he shot and how?"

"With a .22 long rifle," said Rock. "Just like Shy."

"Don't try that again," said Dershon. "You purposely gave him caliber. Now if he says anything about a .22 it will have come from what you told him and not from guilty knowledge. DiGiacomo, you know what you are doing. I want you downstairs in the lobby."

"That's an order," said Covaletzki.

"Good-bye, Rocco," I said.

"I ain't movin'," he said.

"I hope you gentlemen can get organized long enough to finish up with me. When was he shot?"

"10:00 A.M. on Saturday morning," blurted Rock.

"That would put me leaving Wanamaker's."

"Did you buy anything? Do you have any receipts?" asked Dershon.

"Yes I did, and no I don't."

I got up from my bed so that I wouldn't have to be looking up to face these people who insisted on standing.

"Look, we want to give you the benefit of every doubt," said Dershon. "We'll even go through every piece of garbage in the hotel trash for your receipts."

"They already collected it," said Dixon. "It's dumped all over the landfill by now. They have a Sunday collection."

"Just like church," I said. "What happened to the tail on Gandry?"

"Gandry lost the tail by going in the woods," said Rock, talking quickly before anyone could cut him off.

"DiGiacomo, if you open your mouth one more time, I'm having you arrested for hindering prosecution, and I will personally prosecute you," said Dershon.

"And we know how good the Bulldog is. What else do you have on me?"

"You were the hunter and now the quarry has been bagged," Dershon spit out at me. "You were stalking Gandry on Friday afternoon at a time when you were suspended and had no police reason or business to be in that neighborhood. You were tracking him and you caught up with him Saturday morning, and now the best you can tell us is that you were in a department store shopping. Furthermore, when you showed up at the

Howard Johnson's, you had been smoking cigarettes. A small point, perhaps, but were you trying to cover any telltale odor of gunsmoke? You were also too tired to drive the whole way up. Honey drove north from Camden. I'll bet you had a very active and tiring morning after you left Honey's apartment. And we know all about your little speeches on law and order and the good old days, your heyday. You feel yourself fully responsible for what Gandry did to Mastropolito because it was your fault that I had to release him, and it's eating away at you. The chief tells me you were a crack shot. At the range and on the street. And you've killed before, Razzi. You have motive, opportunity, and means. We'll have more on you before this is over. I've a feeling Ms. Gold could tell us more, and she will once her eyes open up. You just think about my offer to settle this affair right now."

"What about Johnny Mastropolito's family?" I asked. "I can't be your only suspect."

"He had no family," said Dixon. "He lived at Miraculous Medal Hall."

"I'll tell you what," I said. "I'll solve the Gandry shooting for you if you help me find Figaro."

"He's sick," shouted Covaletzki from his neutral corner. "We should take him to the state hospital for a seventy-two-hour commitment. He's a dangerous fucking nut. He's dangerous. I tell you he's dangerous and you people better get him put away."

"Dangerous is as dangerous does," I said. "Where do you people think I got a .22 rifle? From Sears? I know better."

"We'll find that out," said Dixon, "don't think we won't."

"Okeydokey," I sighed. "If you think you can find it I want you to go out the door. And if you insist on applying your stimulating technique to Charlie Smotz's grandson's shooting, go knock on somebody else's door. Keep at it, and maybe Dixon here and his partner Jingles will make enough overtime to put patios on their houses. Get out. Thank God I know my rights, boys. There's no such thing as somebody being wanted for questioning anymore, remember? You can't question me. I demand a whatchamacallit. One of those free ones. Get me someone like Dershon."

I opened the door for them and they filed out. Dershon lagged behind and quietly told me how serious the whole thing was, but if I tried to go back to Brazil tonight, well, that was my business. Loud enough for Covaletzki to hear, I told Dershon that I still had "very pressing business in this area" and that as soon as I was finished I would "check back to see if there was anything I could do to aid him in his noble pursuit of the cowardly Gandry *hashashin*."

They were almost to the elevator when I called out: "Halt in the name of the law. I forgot to give you something." I walked out after them and pushed an envelope at Covaletzki that I had picked up from my night table. Covaletzki glared at me and curled his upper lip. He didn't reach for the envelope. Dershon took it from me. It was my retirement papers, signed, sealed, and now delivered. I turned away as he opened the envelope.

I faced Rock and said, "You have your doubts about me, don't you? Rock, you'll lose the gift to know the truth when you hear it if you have to tell lies to make cases."

He looked at me as though I still didn't understand the serious trouble I was in.

"Shy Whitney's murderers walk the earth, and breathe the air. They eat the flesh of animals, and tomatoes are killed to feed them," I said to Dershon. "Spend this kind of energy getting them for Mary."

"Listen, you little deviate," said Covaletzki, "we're gonna be back with fugitive warrants as soon's we get a confirmation from New York City. You can't go around stabbing people after you disarm them. You're not a judge, jury, and executioner. You can't take the law into your own hands like that."

"Want to meet me somewhere?" I asked, glaring at him. Instantly Rocco leaped between us. The elevator came and Dershon hustled Covaletzki into it.

"Aw, Lou," Rock said as he jumped in and the doors shut.

42

I dialed Honey's number and when she answered I said, "The course of true love never did run smooth. If they arrest me, are you going to prosecute the case? You should've done more 'indicating' tonight and a lot less telling."

After a long pause she said, "I'm sorry, I really am." There was another long pause and she said, "Especially for telling about the incident in New York. But the way they walked in here, Lou, I thought they already knew about it. I thought that's why they were here. They started right in asking me a lot of questions, and then Captain Dixon says, 'All right, Miss Gold, what happened when you were in New York?' and I thought they knew and I wanted to make sure they understood just how it was, how we were threatened. Oh, God. I'm not going to feel guilty about this. I'm not. We should never have left that man, just lying there."

"Maybe. What caused you to tell them about my reaction to the death-penalty decision? You got very personal with these strangers."

She began to cry. "Lou, they asked me questions. I answered them truthfully. The more I answered, the more they wanted to know; and then they told me about Gandry, and everything seemed to point to you. But I didn t tell them some things I could have . . . the strain you've been under, you know, your nervous stomach, the 'crazy cloud formations' rolling around your brain. Or the fact that you left Gandry's name off a list of people you were tired of seeing. They'd have said you left his name off because you knew he was dead. Oh Lou, I've been worried sick about you ever since they left. I'm really confused about you."

"How serious are they about arresting me?"

"Extremely. Mostly Covaletzki. They're not going to stop. They are probably going to arrest you soon, maybe after they check out your alibi, if you gave them one."

"Do you believe I did it?"

"I don't believe you did, but I'm not the right person to ask. 'Cause I don't want to believe you did. You're certainly capable of it, but if you didn't do it, who else did?"

"A kid like Gandry makes enemies he's not even aware of, but the only pigeon I have to offer is Carlton Cruset."

"I don't like that particularly. He's not the physical type. Although, he did go with you to Gandry's neighborhood, right?"

"Wrong. I went with him."

"They told me they questioned Cruset about how you were acting and what you were saying when you were with him at Gandry's. It didn't sound to me as if they gave him any consideration as a suspect. Why would he shoot Gandry, or have him shot for that matter?"

"Forget motives. It's too early. Maybe he'd do it to impress me. He's not a healthy man. He identifies with John Brown, the abolitionist martyr. I have no evidence against him, but a strong hunch, and I don't know how much time I have before they arrest me for something, either Gandry or Fifth Avenue. I got the impression Dershon wants me to sneak back to Brazil."

"If you tried it they'd have another piece of circumstantial evidence against you. Flight. Running away as a sign of guilty knowledge. They'd tail you and pick you up at the airport."

"Thanks for the tip, but I was staying anyway."

"I'm glad. I'm so terribly sorry, Lou. The whole thing was so sudden. When they first told me, the second they told me, I really felt you hadn't done it, and then everybody started putting the pieces together and then, I don't know, I got confused and caught up in it."

"Don't worry. I wouldn't have wanted you to lie. It'll work out for me. Mary Whitney says I'm overdue for good luck. I have some ideas. I'll get out of this."

"Can I help you?"

"You can't. It's against the rules. Good night, Honey."

"Lou, did they tell you a witness came forward on Shy?"

"No."

"He showed up at the police station on Friday saying he'd been out of town and didn't know anybody'd been shot. He said that an instant before he caught his train he looked down from the platform and saw a young black male directly below him on the street carrying what looked like a rifle. He picked Lloyd's photo out of a display of a hundred pictures. You never know, do you, Lou?"

"No, you don't, Honey. That's great news. It makes up for a lot."

"Good night, Lou. I wish you'd let me help."

"Maybe later. Good night, Honey."

I hung up. My hand was shaking as I dialed Marian's number. There was no hydroelectric plant in my bloodstream anymore. I breathed deeply to slow the shaking. Don't let anybody kid you. When you're the target, you shake. It's nature, and the shaking gets you moving. It makes the target harder to hit.

Still no answer. Then I remembered the phone messages. I put on a shirt and slacks, grabbed my room key, sprinted to the elevator, and took it down to the ground-floor ashtray. I put my hand into the refuse hole and retrieved all those crumpled messages. Each had the same return phone number and, bravo, it wasn't the Cruset number. I went up to my room and dialed the new number.

A young man answered.

"Put Marian on the phone, quickly," I snapped.

In short order Marian was on.

"It's your ex-husband. You've been calling me. What's up?"

"I . . . I read about John Gandry's shooting in this morning's paper. That really was something."

"Do you think I shot him?"

"Lou, you know I don't know about these things. I never understood your police work. I wouldn't blame you if you did. Sometimes these days it's the only answer."

"Who was that?"

"Dr. Joe Doney, Sarah's therapist, and mine, too, actually. He's in the other room. We can talk privately. I didn't know where to turn so I came here. Lou, Carlton's been acting stranger than ever. He just might be dangerous, and I don't know what to do. Policemen came today, and he told them you had thrown a brick at Gandry's window. When they left he went into a violent tirade about my being an impediment to his work. It was all I could do to get him to allow Sarah to stay at her girlfriend's house. After she left he screamed at me that he hadn't driven you to Gandry's house just to throw a brick and that you weren't the thoroughbred he thought you were, as if it were my fault. It was worse than any of his postcoital outbursts of rage. When he aimlessly bowls over anything and everything. Joe, Dr. Doney, calls them blitzkriegs. He's been so supportive through all the ups and downs."

"I'm sure he has. Where's Carlton now? There's no answer. I thought you had servants."

"They don't live in. I can only guess where Carlton is."

"Guess for me."

"I guess he's in his locked room like a caged animal. He does that often, Lou. He won't answer the phone and he won't come out of that room. He's the only one with a key. It's a nightmare. This is the worst I've seen him . . . he causes such psychological damage to us. I wish there was some way out. He has us caged up . . . it's dreadful of me to speak like this, but I can never forgive him for turning Sarah against us both."

"I can imagine. You and Sarah can't go on living like this. Meet me at Blayne's Tavern parking lot and bring your front door key."

"There's the burglar alarm."

"Then meet me at your front door. Come alone. Cut your engine and headlights at the gate. Climb out your car window and walk up to the house on the grass, so as not to make noise."

"You're not going to do anything foolish tonight, are you?"

"Tell Dr. Joe you'll be right back, that you and I and Carlton are going to have a little talk to air out our feelings. The doctor will like that, won't he?"

"Yes," she said, "I suppose. As long as it doesn't go beyond talk."

"Just be there." I hung up on her. She had wanted to play me off against him as early as that first night at dinner in the Green Room. She'd be there. I put on my white linen suit, which was back from room service, and my burgundy accessories and went down to the lobby and out the revolving door and directly across Eleventh Street to the outdoor unattended parking lot that held my Granada. An unmarked car with Captain Dixon and Jingles in it was parked a block to my left, on Eleventh. I walked up to my car. My peripheral vision saw them duck, but in no time they were peeking. No confidence.

I put the key in the door of my car, opened it, checked the glove compartment, found the minicassette recorder Honey had loaned me and slipped it into my right side pocket, lifted the backseat cushion out of position, fiddled behind it, and then put it back into position. I then shut and locked the car door and walked back across Eleventh and into the hotel and watched.

When Dixon pulled the unmarked car up to the parking lot, Jingles got out with a wire coat hanger and headed for the Granada.

"What's that big creep doing with that coat hanger over in the parking lot?" I asked the doorman. "Breaking into cars? You better go outside and straighten out that big lug."

The doorman grabbed an in-house telephone. Within seconds John Judson from security responded rapidly across the lobby toward the front door, putting on his tan blazer as he moved. He either didn't notice me or didn't acknowledge me if he did. He went through the revolving glass door and drew his .38 and held it down at his side.

Jingles turned around to face Judson, leaving my car door open and the interior light of my Granada shining on his back. I couldn't hear what Judson said, but my guess is he said, "Freeze," because he held his gun out in front of him with both hands, aiming it at K-5 Jingles.

Soon they all recognized one another, and Judson holstered his gun and went up to Jingles, verbally abusing him and gesturing at him. Dixon stayed in the car, leaving his partner out on the limb. I was counting on DuPont Company policy being against an open-door policy on guests' cars, police business or no, and I counted right.

Jingles stretched out his arms apologetically, shrugged his shoulders, rearranged my backseat, locked and shut my car, and got in his. Dixon drove the legal one-way on Eleventh to Market. He didn't try to back up a block to his old spot, and he didn't try to drive the wrong way. After all, he'd just gotten caught with his partner's hand in the cookie jar, and the tendency when something like that happens is to play everything else straight to a fault. I knew he'd have to circle the block to take up position again.

The instant I saw them commit to a right turn on Market, I ran at top speed through the revolving door. I passed a startled Judson who, by now, recognized me. I crossed the street to my car.

My aim was true on the door keyhole. I got in and had the key in the ignition smoothly. I started up and pulled out of the parking lot and onto Eleventh. I made the same turn they had on Market and then again on Tenth, but when I got to Shipley, I made a left and went straight to Eighth. There I made a right and headed for plantation country.

43

I cut my lights the last hundred feet and stopped at the stone gateposts alongside Marian's Mercedes wagon. Just as I'd instructed Marian, I climbed out the Granada window feet first so as not to show light or make car-door noise that Carlton might hear.

The front door was open a crack, and she eased it out wider and appeared in the doorway. She was dressed for a party, but with a downcast gaze more appropriate for a sentencing.

She whispered, "His cars are here. I'm sure he's in there. I turned the burglar alarm off. Lou, you really shouldn't be here. Not like this. I'll be all right in my own room. I've a lock on the door. You shouldn't involve yourself in our problems. Sally and I are not worth it. You've got to be selfish. Lou, you've got to think of yourself. I can't imagine what might happen if you try to talk to Carlton tonight."

"I can imagine what might happen; I might talk to him. I think he's gotten me into the soup, but don't you worry, just let me in. Are there any guns in his private bedroom, besides the .45 he carries?"

"Guns? There are three antiques in the southeast den. I don't know if they function, but God knows what he has in his room." She stepped outside toward me and started to close the door on us. "Don't frighten me with talk of guns." Just in time she stopped the door from closing with her backhand. "I've been in his room twice. No one has seen much of it. Not even the housekeeper. He cleans it himself."

"Where is it?"

"Lou, I don't want to be involved in whatever you're doing. I never thought about his having guns, or anything like that. This whole thing is beginning to frighten me. I told Dr. Doney that I'd try to calm you down and send you home. Trying to talk to Carlton tonight could be dangerous to . . . to both of you. You probably ought to go. I'm sure Sarah and I will manage . . . somehow. You musn't think of us . . . not after all these years."

I gripped her hard by the shoulders and looked directly into her eyes. "They're going to arrest me for the Gandry shooting, and I think I can show them that your husband did it. He'll be in jail for a long time if I can. Now that wouldn't be too bad, would it?"

She hesitated a second, bewildered, until a trace of hope brought a glint to her eyes. "Lou," she whispered. "Be careful. And remember later, I warned you. I did try to stop you."

"You'll be safe in your car. Wait for me. If you see Carlton walk out alone, take off and get help."

"Oh, God. What am I doing? This isn't turning out right." She began to break down as if to cry, but didn't. Instead, she turned and trotted away.

"Which room is his?" I called after her in a loud whisper, but she kept going. I tiptoed into the foyer and up the marble steps to the second floor, trying to guess my way to Carlton's room. If Marian had been more cooperative and less dramatic, it would have been a whole lot easier. I hoped she didn't get the bright idea to come up. She used to hate to be left out of things.

At the top I saw a hall leading off to the right and left. The wood floor was bare. I tried to sense whether my drunken subconscious the other night had picked up the direction of his footsteps in the second-floor hallway while I was downstairs talking to Marian. Had I heard his footsteps directly over us, or were they over the library? I wished I were Rex the Wonder Dog. I took three steps to the right, but it didn't feel good. There was a faint odor of Marian to it, or else I was imagining it. Still, it felt like her side of the upstairs. Hers and Sarah's. I turned and headed to the left. It felt manly. The odds were fifty-fifty anyway.

Four ordinary doors on each side of the manly hallway were closed. At the extreme end was a fifth door, a four-foot-wide heavy and ominous door that looked hand-carved even at a distance in the dark.

I reached the big door and gently fingered the ornate brass handle. Nothing. Locked. My night vision was coming, and I could make out a video camera mounted high on the wall above the door, the kind they use for security in banks. I looked above the other doors; none of them had cameras.

I tiptoed to the door on the left nearest the big door and pressed my ear to it. It had a feeling of hollowness, that there was no life behind that door. The handle gave. I opened it slowly, peeked in, and when my eyes fully adjusted I saw that it was most likely a guest room and that there was nobody in it. I went back to the big door and pressed my head to it, but the carved ornamentation wouldn't allow me to get my ear flat against anything. I heard and sensed nothing but my own breath magnified by my intense concentration. I got on my hands and knees and sniffed at the crack under the door jamb. It had a slightly different odor from the guest room. It smelled lived in. There was a trace of food. I got up and took out my wallet. I removed my laminated Brazilian driver's license and, with an occasional eye on the video camera, I quietly slid the card slowly through the jamb. As soon as I pushed the card in, I could feel that I was dealing with a dead bolt and that I needed a lockpick. Not only didn't I have anything that resembled a lockpick, but I hadn't used burglar tools in years.

I slipped into the guest room, softly shut the door behind me, and looked around. On the night table in a silver ashtray I saw a little silver box of matches with Marian Cruset's monogram on the cover. I picked it up. I went to one of the closets in the room, and there were seven wire hangers with paper wrapped around them from the dry cleaner's. I lifted them one by one, carefully, the way a child plays pick-up sticks.

I opened my door and went up to the big door, knelt on the hard floor, and with the matches lit the paper on one of the hangers and slid it under the door. I glanced at the video camera. I lit another and slid it under. I lit and slid three more. I could smell the fumes from the burning paper. I lit the last two and slid them under. I heard movement. Someone was getting out of bed, and my heart pounded with each creak of the box spring. Footsteps on the carpet gingerly approached the door from the other side. They were the long strides of a tall man. He stopped short at the door. He turned on the light. My heart sank. He hadn't gone for the bait. He wasn't going to rush out through that door fearing fire, in a panic, vulnerable.

I heard the unmistakable sound of an automatic pistol being cocked.

"Carlton," I called under the door jamb. "It's Lou Razzi. I'm in trouble. You've got to let me in. You've got to hide me."

A very bright light went on in the hallway. In the corner above the door the TV camera swung sharply around and focused down on me. A tiny red light came on and glowed under the lens. Carlton unlocked the door. He took a few steps back from the door as it opened and said, "Come in."

I got off my knees and walked in. I closed and locked the door behind me. Carlton was facing me, with his .45 pointed at my chest. He had a steady hand. I was standing on charred hangers, with my back up against the door.

"They're getting all set to arrest me for shooting Gandry," I said, "and I didn't do it, but I think I know who did and I need your help. You said to call on you if I ever needed you. Can I come all the way in?"

Carlton waved me in with the gun. The room was ice-cold. Over white pajamas he wore a blue velour robe with gray trim. His skin was ashen. He was unshaven. A tray of used chicken bones lay on the Oriental carpet near the bed. He was hiding out.

I stared briefly at the .45. He took his finger off the trigger and put it outside the trigger guard. I looked up and saw a very sudden weakness in his eyes, a flinch. I took two steps to him, put my left hand gently on his pistol hand, and said, "Put it down, Carlton. You don't need that sort of thing with me."

I stepped back from him, letting go of his gun hand. He softly clicked his lips, without anywhere near the precision I was used to, and lazily put the safety on and put the gun in his bathrobe pocket, with the handle sticking out at a forty-five-degree angle.

"What is all this about?" he asked. "What do you expect from me? I may be a man of influence, but I cannot quash an official inquiry."

In two steps I was on him again. Sinking my weight into my left leg, I threw an overhand right to his chin. I hit him right on the switch, and he went down just the way he was supposed to. I picked the .45 out of his bathrobe pocket, undid the safety, and pointed the barrel at him.

"Get on your feet, you amateur. You've made big trouble for me, and that trouble is making it easy for my enemies in

Delaware. But I will say this for you, Carlton old boy, you've got more guts than I ever figured you for."

I safetied the gun and put it into my left side pocket, since the right side held the minicassette recorder. I went over and sat in an antique Chippendale chair in a corner of the room away from the big door. I knew he would be in no shape in the knees to run and that the distance between us would start to make him feel secure — until I pulled the rug again. He felt on the floor for his aviator glasses with the yellow tint and put them back on. He got to his feet very slowly.

"What are you doing here?" he asked. "You've got no right to be in my bedroom. This is private property."

"Now would you look at who's got rights? What's so sanctified about your bedroom? Are you unbalanced about your privacy? Are you the kind of guy who's afraid to take a wee-wee in front of men? When you were a kid in gym class, did you cover up real good in the locker room? What's private property really mean to you?" He slowly inched to his canopied bed and stood facing me, holding on to one of the posts for support. His glazed eyes told me that Carlton couldn't take a punch.

"My personal life is hardly your concern. Did you commit common burglary, or did Marian let you in the front door so that you could act in one of her sordid little melodramas? Do you two plan to kill me and live on my money?" He handled that private-property gibberish well. He was unquestionably the most intelligent subject I'd ever tackled.

"I came up the stairs without an invitation. You, especially, ought to know that you're not safe in your own castle. There are many things I want to talk to you about, Carlton. Look directly into my eyes. That's a boy. Now keep them there. I am not interested in Marian, and I know you believe that. I can see that in your eyes. I am interested in you and in me and in Gandry. Does your jaw hurt?"

"No," he said too quickly.

"Carlton, you're fibbing, but we'll overlook that because it's a minor fib and because you are a remarkable man. You have disassembled the Gandry monster for me and for the world, and for that I am truly grateful. However, I must confess that my gratitude has been dampened by recent events. You see, I am now, as you know, under investigation for what may turn out to be murder. I hope for your sake I am not arrested. That would be a drag for me. Jail took things out of me once, and I worked very hard in Brazil to put them back in. I'll never go to jail again. It makes one lose confidence, jail does. Don't let your eyes stray from mine, Carlton."

Carlton sagged farther into the bedpost. Perhaps he had so many things to pay attention to he couldn't possibly pay attention to his stability. Or maybe it was just merely physical from the punch. I decided to take a chance and dive in.

"Carlton, you are trying to get that face of yours under control, aren't you? It's just dying to break loose. You're making a Herculean effort to keep a poker face. That's one of the absolute first signs of guilt. Your lips are pressed firmly, not smiling, not frowning . . . noncommittal. Your teeth are clenched, but not so tight as to be from genuine emotion. Your eyes stare straight ahead pleadingly and you blink consciously on a periodic basis. You are trying to look innocent. You are hiding human emotion behind a mask. Please don't feel you have to go through facial routines on my account. Carlton, it takes a lot of courage to do what you did to a notorious young man under police surveillance. You have more than atoned for your cowardice during Sarah's rape. Don't be startled. Never mind how I know these things."

"I don't know what you are talking about." He clicked. He was agitated.

"Wrong, Carlton. I said Sarah's rape. That's not the kind of reaction you give to strong words like that unless you do know what I'm talking about."

"I know that Gandry is comatose," he said calmly, regaining composure, "if that's what you mean, and I knew he was under surveillance." This could be an all-nighter, I thought.

"Carlton, look at me." I needed to assert control once and for all. "I have a surprise for you. I resigned from the department tonight. I am a civilian. I am unrestrained. I am inextinguishable. I am power personified. And I warn you, if you make me go through the strenuous labor of searching and interrogating and interrogating and searching, I will definitely, definitely," I shouted, "turn you in. I will turn in whatever I find and whatever I wring out of you, and it will all be usable." I softened. "If, however, you honestly and fully level with me at once and give me a statement on tape like Mrs. Smotz, I will keep your confession and use it only if I'm brought to trial for Gandry's shooting. Well, what is it? Do I go to work on you and then tie you up and give your private property a toss and then go to work on you again, or do you level with me right now? I'm a professional, Carlton. Since the beginning of recorded history there have been only so many secret places to hide weapons. I'll find yours," I shouted, "and whatever else I find will go to the authorities, unless you play ball right now. I vow on my mother's grave that as long as you level with me at once, I will use your confession only if they try to pin it on me. My terms are reasonable. The Bible says, 'And ye shall know the truth, and the truth shall make you free.' I want you to make me free, Carlton." I took the .45 out of my pocket for effect.

He appeared to be pondering the implications.

"Suppose you shot Gandry," I pressed. "Suppose, for argument's sake, you did it. Think out loud, Carlton, what are the implications?"

"Suppose I did it," he said deliberately, measuring every word before it passed his lips. "It makes sense that you should have my confession to protect yourself — that is, if I did what you think I've done — but what protection do I have, would I have, that you would use it only if you were brought to answer for the charge?"

"Cruset, you don't want to consider the implications. You want to negotiate. My terms are nonnegotiable. You are wasting my time. I think you ought to take your clothes off." I unsafetied the .45. "Right now." I barked the order.

He let his robe and his pajamas slip to the floor, and he stepped out of them naked, except for a very old tattoo of an American flag on his left upper arm, a forty-eight-star flag. His hands hung loosely over his genitals.

"Hands up, Cruset."

He put his hands up.

"Now, turn around and consider carefully the gamble that you are taking if you fail to level with me the first time around." He turned around and faced the wall. I stepped up behind him and put the muzzle of the gun into his rectum. He reacted to the .45 as if it were a deadly ice cube. "Within two hours I will have dismantled every wall in this room, every floorboard, every part of the ceiling. Everything. And if I find nothing I will start on the next room. By tomorrow at this time you will confess to anything. And it will be too late to save yourself."

His knees buckled. "Please," he said. "Please . . . trust me. I'll give you a statement . . . on videotape, if you prefer." He nodded in the direction of his Sony Betamax equipment on a dresser.

I went to the machine and pressed "play/record." It began to work. I opened the massive door and checked the hallway for Marian. No sign. I stood him in the path of the camera.

"Tell the camera what you did to John Gandry," I said.

"I shot him," he said and clicked for emphasis. He grasped his bruised chin with the fingers of his right hand and moved the jaw from side to side for emphasis.

"You'd better tell me more," I said.

"I fired from the roof of the Shelton School as he walked through the woods. I presumed the police tail would be some distance behind him in the woods. I used a .22 long rifle with a silencer and aimed for his heart."

"Why?"

"I had heard the news about the poor little boy he'd killed, and I knew he'd kill other little boys." He rubbed his jaw again.

"Where's the rifle?"

"I threw it in the Brandywine."

"Come on back in," I said and shut the door behind him.

I pressed "stop" and then "rewind" and played the tape back, including the part with me kneeling in the hallway. I pressed "eject." The tape came out to me and I put it in my side pocket, taking out the unused cassette recorder to make room for it. I ejected the blank audio cassette tape and tossed it and the now-empty audio recorder onto the bed so that Carlton would have confidence that whatever he said wasn't being taped. I pulled his head by his gray hair down to my height and jabbed his navel with the gun until pain showed on his face.

"Do you think me so naive? So stupid? You'll call the police as soon as I leave. I saw you making a great display of massaging your jaw on camera. You'll say I punched you on the jaw. Threatened you with a gun. Coerced you. And you agreed to say anything on tape just to get rid of me. You gave me no real details on that tape. You told me what anyone with your police connections would know by now. And to think I offered you your freedom. Now Carlton, you are going to wish you were dead, because you are going to jail. Got any rope or do I have to use electrical cord?"

"Wait. It's true. What you say is true," Carlton said, with his neck stretched down and his head tilting, his hands still high in the air, severe terror in his eyes.

"It's too late for talk now, Carlton. I offered you a sacred trust, but you just proved yourself to be unworthy."

"Wait, please wait. I'll give you the rifle I used on Gandry. Trust me. I have other weapons to show you, laser scopes, silencers. Let me show you."

"Show me," I snapped. I let go of his hair and pushed his head back. I removed the muzzle from his belly. "Walk me to the rifle you used on Gandry."

He went to a closet and opened it. One of two lightbulbs hanging from the same overhead fixture automatically lit. The other did not. The closet was a cedar-lined walk-in, loaded with clothes and shoes. The unlit remaining bulb had a pull chain. Carlton slowly shuffled to the pull chain, his hands still over his head, and pulled it. That bulb lit. The back wall of the closet slid up to the ceiling like a garage door. It exposed a room the size of the first closet. An overhead light was on in that room. Its other walls were sheets of stainless steel. It had no windows, no door, and, at one time, must have been part of the closet. The room contained five three-drawer letter-size stainless-steel file cabinets, each drawer with a three-by-five label on it. The cabinets dominated the room. We walked in, Carlton first and me poking the gun into his kidneys.

"How do we shut this wall down behind us?" I asked.

"We can't. It only works from the closet bulb. I lock the closet door behind me when I come in here," he said over his shoulder.

"Lie down," I ordered, "with your hands tucked under your belly." He did so in the floor space that was left in the room.

There were seven rifles, each with a telescopic sight, in a rack on the wall opposite the files. One of them was a .22 rifle with a silencer attached to the muzzle. Not something you see every day.

I tried all the file drawers. They were good and locked.

On top of the fifth file cabinet was a shortwave radio. I smashed it four times with the butt of the .45. The antenna wire came in through a small round hole in the wall, and I yanked it out. I stepped over Carlton to the rifles and picked the .22 off the rack. I cocked it. It was unloaded and had recently been cleaned.

"This room must have seemed impregnable for you to bring the murder weapon back home. Did you kill the carpenter who built this place so no one but you would know it was here, and will you kill me, too, the first chance you get?"

"Trust me. Join me. Work with me. We could accomplish miraculous things together."

"Carlton, where are the keys for these files?"

Carlton opened his mouth as if to speak, hesitated, and closed his mouth defiantly. I put the .22 rifle back in the rack, turned to Carlton, and kicked him in the ribs. "Come on, Carlton."

He reflexively slid his right arm up so his hand could touch his bruised ribs and still stay tucked under his body, and then I stepped on his elbow.

"As you can tell, Carlton, I am blue in the face," I said, raising my voice. "Not just with you. With everybody. From now on, whenever I ask you a question you answer it, or it's the last polite question I ask. Do you understand?"

"Implicitly."

"Solid. Cough up the keys." I spit the words at him.

"In a pair of red socks that are rolled up in the top drawer of my dresser."

"Super. Now what is in these files? Target One through Target Eight. Data on your other kills? Start with this one, the first, start with the file labeled Target One."

"Aren't you going to get the key and read them?"

"Perhaps you don't understand. You're supposed to make this easy for me. Now start with Target One."

"It's the Judge Sampley file."

"Well?"

"My confederates and I followed him for eighteen days and nights until he was positively rip-roaring DUI. We simply called in his location, description, and license plate. We called it in anonymously, claiming he had run us off the road. The state police had no choice but to arrest him. Someone also happened to call the media. Oh, he was drunk most of those other eighteen nights, but not rip-roaring the way we wanted him. It forced his resignation."

"A liberal?"

"Positively red. Blood red. Abortion red. You've heard of *Husband vs. Wife*."

"Target Two."

"Nothing special. A fire of unknown origin at a methamphetamine lab that the police suspected but couldn't get enough probable cause to search. The fire department did the searching for them. All legal. Eight busts and each one stuck."

"Three."

"An attempted rape of a coed. The suspect wore a stocking mask. They had picked him up within minutes right nearby. The girl in the dormitory couldn't be positive it was him. When they brought him back to her, all she could identify was his clothing. It was him all right. He had a terrible record of sex crimes."

"You kill him?"

"No. No need to. He was blind in one eye. We simply cut one eyehole in a nylon stocking and left it in the weeds behind the dorm. D-WOC publicized a large reward for the whereabouts of a stocking mask or any other information about the rape. A librarian walking her dog found it two days after the rape. The single eyehole in the stocking mask made the difference. Your Honey Gold prosecuted that case. She called him the Man in the One-Eyed Mask in her summation. I would have made some reference to Homer's Cyclops."

"What's Target Eight? Your most recent?"

"Gandry," he exhaled.

"Seven"

"Harrison Lloyd."

"The surprise witness?"

"Yes. He's one of us."

"What about the rest? Any more shootings?"

"No. No. The others are similar to the Lloyd case. We provided witnesses and evidence. Gandry was a special and irregular decision I felt constrained to make."

"How can you ever be sure you've got the right guy to bear false witness against?"

"We look before we leap. We purchase classified information from the inside and we study it carefully. There is never any doubt."

"The other file drawers have no labels. How come?"

"Not done. Not even selected. Let me up. Surely, you must

trust me now. I have told you things that no one outside our group knows. Come on, man, our trust must begin somewhere."

"I'm afraid not tonight."

"What do you mean?"

"You didn't level with me at once, Carlton. That was the only deal I offered and you lost it. You lost it when you lied and said you threw the rifle into the Brandywine. You only get one strike in this league. I threw you a curve and you bailed out of the box. I knew you wouldn't be truthful in your first time at bat. Subjects always hold something back in the beginning."

He looked directly into my eyes for the first time and saw only compassion in them. It scared him. He began to tremble and then whimper, and tears rolled down his long cheekbones and across his nose and dropped to the floor.

"Professor Cruset," I said gently, "I will do all I can to help you."

"'This country,'" he said, looking up at me from the floor, "'with its institutions, belongs to the people who inhabit it. Whenever they shall grow weary of the existing government, they can exercise their constitutional right of amending it or their revolutionary right to dismember or overthrow it.' Do you know who said that?"

"Don't feed me a straight line," I said. "I'm deadly serious about what I have to do."

"Abraham Lincoln," he said. "The United States Supreme Court must be dismembered before it runs our ship of state aground. Impeachment is a . . . impeachment . . ."

"Professor, wait here in the box. If it gets stuffy, put your lips to the hole where I ripped out the antenna. Don't torture yourself. The torturing will be over for you soon. Believe me, you'll feel a sense of relief now that the craziness has stopped. Maybe you'll get some peace in your life from now on."

I left with the collection of rifles, threw them on the bed, and went back into the closet and fooled with the switches until the sliding door came down and sealed him in.

"You're not going to leave me to die." I heard his muffled shout, barely audible through the wall.

"Professor," I shouted back, "I'm going down to make a phone call, and then I'll be right back with policemen to arrest you for Gandry's shooting and the Target plots and to search this house. Breaking you the way I did has been no pleasure, but I promise to help you. I won't be gone long."

I went to his dresser and found the rolled-up red socks and unrolled them. I took out the key to the Target files and put it in my pocket. At the bottom of the drawer was bond paper. I pulled it out. The original "Target Manifesto." I put that in my pocket too. I grabbed the .22 rifle from the bed and walked down the stairs. Marian was waiting in a chair at the foot of the marble steps. She must have had confidence in me.

"What did you do to him?" she asked without getting up. "Did you arrest him?"

"Not exactly." I walked past her to the phone and dialed Honey.

"It's Lou. Did I wake you?"

"I haven't been sleeping, Lou, I've been worrying about you. They're livid at you for slipping their tail. I tried to reach you. I've got good news. The New York PD can't locate the mugger. He went to a clinic, and after they set his arm and stitched him up, he snuck out. He probably gave a phony name."

"I guess I left him with a lasting impression," I said. "Even if they do find him I've got something to bargain with. I have Gandry's shooter, Professor Carlton Cruset, locked in a stainless-steel box, and I've got eight other things that he did."

"Holy shmoley. I just knew that's where you went, but I didn't tell them, Lou. I didn't tell them."

I smiled. She didn't tell them.

Marian got up suddenly and walked over to the phone. "Jesus Christ, Lou," she said loudly. "To whom are you talking?"

"Where are you now?" asked Honey. "Who's with you?"

I cupped the receiver and said firmly to Marian: "Sit down in the Chippendale chair and listen to what I tell Deputy Attorney General Honey Gold and then you'll know what's going on around your house. I'm afraid you're in for some scandal, my dear. You're about to have another husband go to jail, or at least to the booby hatch."

I uncupped the receiver and said to Honey: "When the morons came to the hotel to question me, I resigned from the department. With my brand-new wings on, I flew to Cruset's house and gained entrance into his private room by burning coat hangers under his bedroom door."

"Huh?" said Honey. "Coat hangers?"

"That's right, but it doesn't matter. I busted in, and I busted him on the jaw. He confessed to shooting Gandry. I have that on video tape. I have the rifle, too. I also recovered files on some new-style vigilante activity. It was in a secret room that I have him locked in now. The man's definitely ahead of his time. I'm still at his house, and the voice you heard is that of his legal heir, Marian Kenney Razzi Cruset."

"You are incredible," Honey said. "And the best part is I think it may all be legal."

"I'm getting the hang of it. Do you make house calls?"

"What do you mean?"

"Get the donkeys together and come on over to Cruset's. Bring cuffs and bring a search party. This house needs a good toss from top to bottom. These files are —"

"Don't tell me any more. I'm not sure we ought to know everything right now. Let me call Dershon."

We hung up. I waited twenty minutes in silence as Marian relaxed. She seemed to be contemplating the upside of her brand-new wings.

The phone rang and I answered it.

"This is Dershon. No arguments. No discussions. Before we set one foot in Carlton Cruset's room and open his files without a search warrant, you had better meet us in Chief Covaletzki's office. Can Professor Cruset get out if you leave him alone in the house for an hour?"

"Probably not."

"That's a chance we'll have to take. We can't go in without a search warrant. Get in here quickly and bring that videotape and the rifle. The sooner we can review it, the sooner we can get a search warrant, and we'll want your signature on the affidavit as a civilian. He'll have the best legal talent in the land behind him. He's not going to be using some kid out of law school. On this one we are going to cross every *t* and dot every *i*."

"You really swing for the fences, don't you? A regular Babe Ruth. Caution goes right to the wind with you."

"Frankly, Razzi, with your known mental state and penchant for violence, we may still not have sufficient probable cause for a search and seizure, even after we review your so-called taped confession."

"Mr. Razzi, Bulldog. I am an American citizen, a civilian, and you are a public servant in need of my cooperation."

"Fair enough."

"Fair enough, who?"

"Fair enough, Mr. Razzi."

"I like your style, kid."

44

The only video machine they had at the station was a VHS format that wouldn't handle Carlton's Betamax tape. At two in the morning, at Marian's request, Dr. Joe Doney showed up with his personal Betamax player. He left after satisfying himself of Marian's "condition." Her help earned Marian the right to watch the tape with the rest of us, but after the viewing she had to leave the chief's office. On her way out she cast frost at Honey, who ignored her.

"You are right, Mr. Civilian Razzi. We owe you an apology," said Morris Dershon.

"I accept."

"I never doubted you, Lou," said DiGiacomo, clapping his hands loudly. "I just didn't want you makin' no dumb mistakes is all. I was being like your lawyer. You know how words get twisted. Let's get the presses rolling on the search warrant. Hah? What?"

Dixon slid a sheet of paper in the typewriter and began typing the captions.

"Not so fast," said Covaletzki. "Let's let the lawyers handle this. Mr. Chief Deputy, is it your opinion that we have enough good probable cause?"

"I don't see why not," said Dershon.

"You don't? I'm no lawyer, but I'm just wondering here,"

said Covaletzki as he clasped his hands on his walnut-veneer desk and leaned forward in his chair. "We can't run a comparison on any slug that we test-fire from the .22 because the pieces taken out of Gandry are down in Washington at the FBI lab and, besides, it fragmented pretty good inside of him. I think it might have been carved out, like a dumdum. I'm not sure about that, but I think Augrine said something about that. So I don't know that there's ever gonna be any way to scientifically tie this .22 down as the murder weapon. Now the way I see it, that means the whole search warrant depends on this here videotape, and I've got some problems with the tape. Like I say, I'm no lawyer, but it just seems to me maybe we ought to take another look at the tape again."

"Kindly be specific," said Dershon. "This is one case none of us can afford to make a mistake on. I don't mind being thorough, but I don't want to waste time on any fishing expeditions."

"Like I say, I'm no lawyer, but I mean first of all the man is buck-ass naked, and we know from our own personal knowledge and indications that he was struck about the face at least one time. Hell, you can see it on the tape. See, what I'm getting at is voluntariness. Are these words on this tape Professor Cruset's own voluntary words?"

"I see," said Dershon.

"You see?" said Honey furiously. "For Christ's sake, we're discussing probable cause for a search. We're not discussing whether we can win a jury trial. We've got more than enough for a search warrant."

"I'd be careful." Covaletzki shook his head. "The whole thing could be read wrong, like maybe Cruset's getting set up by Razzi and his ex-wife, what with Marian Cruset being right along there with Razzi every step of the way, wearing that low-cut dress."

"Look," Honey said to Dershon, ignoring Covaletzki, "Cruset said on tape that the shot was fired from the Shelton High School roof and that his rifle had a silencer, and Mr. Razzi, who just solved your shooting for you, in case you forgot, didn't know either of those facts."

"Unless he did the shooting," said Covaletzki.

I grabbed the bottom of Covaletzki's cheap desk and tipped the whole thing onto him in a thunderous crash caused mostly by the glass top sliding off and shattering. Covaletzki's chair flew back with him in it, and he was instantly on his feet with his butt against the wall, reaching for his gun. Dixon grabbed me before the desk landed. DiGiacomo grabbed Covaletzki's elbow before his hand could touch his .38.

Covaletzki pointed at me with his free hand and shouted, "See what I mean. He's dangerous. Everything he seized is illegal. The tape. The search. The rifle. Everything."

"No, it is not," said Dershon soothingly. "Let's everybody calm down. Let's everybody have a mentholated cigarette and get ourselves together."

"Lock him up, Dixon," Covaletzki yelled, still pointing. "I want him locked up for offensive touching and criminal mischief, and menacing, and terroristic threatening. Cuff him. The fuckin' lunatic. Cuff him."

"Wait a minute," said Dershon. "I said calm down. Let's calm down, shall we? Here, have a Newport. I don't care what you two do to each other after tonight, but tonight we are assembling probable cause for warrants on Carlton Cruset, and Civilian Razzi is going to sign the affidavit for the warrant application."

"It's a waste of time," said Covaletzki. "The whole thing is illegal."

"No, it is definitively not illegal," said Dershon. "I agree with Ms. Gold."

"Oh yes, it is illegal. The man is still a police officer. He can't do anything he done tonight."

"Make sense, Covaletzki. Razzi resigned. I saw his resignation papers myself. I handed them to you in the elevator."

"That resignation was void. Nix. Snuffo. You're a lawyer, you ought to know that."

Everything got quiet. All eyes on Covaletzki. I laughed.

"Void?" asked Dershon softly. "Snuffo?"

"It's not my fault," said Covaletzki, now pointing at Dershon. "You're the lawyer. You should know the law."

"DiGiacomo, Dixon, and Majeski — kindly leave this room and close the door tightly behind you," said Dershon as he began to pace. "We're in a need-to-know situation. Honey, Chief, Lou — please take a seat." When the others left with see-no-evil expressions on their faces and we all sat down, he lit a cigarette and continued: "Chief, are you telling us that you did, or are you telling us that you did not, accept Mr. Razzi's resignation last night at the hotel?"

"A man on departmental charges cannot resign without the chief's expressed consent, and I did not give him no expressed consent. You cannot have a man putting in for a pension any time he wants if he's got pending charges on him that could cost him his pension. How could you ever take a guy's pension that way?"

"Perhaps I haven't made myself clear. Let me try again. In your heart and mind, when Mr. Razzi handed the papers to me and I handed them to you, in your heart and mind you gave him permission to resign. Is that not so, Chief Covaletzki?"

"It's not that simple."

"Yes, it is that simple. It is just as exquisitely simple as that. This is a political no-win case for me. Strike that. Let me put it another way. No one, repeat, no one, is ever going to accuse

Morris Dershon of helping a major contributor to his party beat a felony rap, in fact an attempted murder rap. Let us not mention what he has done to the integrity of the entire criminal justice system in this state. Let us simply focus on the fact that we are dealing with a murderer. In case you haven't forgotten, Chief Covaletzki, murderers are still considered dangerous to the community at large."

"Regardless of their party affiliation," I pointed out.

"It's not that simple," said Covaletzki in a low voice. "I sent this whacko Razzi a letter right after we got back from the hotel. I typed it myself and put it in the mail. That's what I was doing in here while youse were downstairs."

"So?" asked Dershon, singing the syllable.

"It's postmarked. It'll show that I turned down his resignation request."

"So? We shall get it in tomorrow's mail, or I should say this morning's mail, and we shall burn it, with Mr. Razzi's permission, of course, which I don't believe will be unreasonably withheld."

"I put carbon copies in the mail."

"So?"

"To the city solicitor."

"So? We shall obtain the copies from the city mailroom after the morning's delivery. Heaven help me."

"That's a federal offense," said Covaletzki.

"And you will commit it because you wrote the insipid letter."

"I sent a copy to Tom Moygar at the *News Journal*."

"Holy shit!" screamed Dershon as he kicked the underside of Covaletzki's upturned desk, splintering the thin bottom wood.

"He's the one been covering Razzi for the paper," said Covaletzki.

"And you wanted further public embarrassment for Mr. Razzi. No wonder he hates your guts."

"Wait a minute," said Honey. "Let's not panic. We have a chance to create some new law on this. Lou was operating under a good-faith assumption that he was no longer on the force and that he could investigate without the restraints of the exclusionary rule."

"Your point is made, Honey," said Dershon. "But we are not writing a law-review article. These issues were difficult enough when we were laboring under the assumption that he was a cop who had resigned and was acting on his own authority. I shall figure something out, but it will not be to create new law. I just need a modicum of cooperation."

"Can't Marian give us the right to search the house without a warrant?" I asked. "It's her house, too."

"It is not her secret room and they are not her file cabinets," said Dershon. "Besides, searching is not the answer anymore. Not since friend Covaletzki permanently stained your initial search and interrogation by putting you back on the department roster. We already have the rifle illegally, and now we cannot ever use it in court. We have an illegal confession that is unusable and a man in a closet who is right now, as we stand here, illegally our prisoner. It is much too risky to attempt to rehabilitate the Gandry arrest or any of the other vigilante activities. What we need is a new crime, a brand-new conspiracy. Razzi, you've got to go back. You're the only man who could pull it off at this point, and I'm afraid Cruset is far more dangerous today than he was yesterday. What's that they say about wounding your enemies?"

"What do you have in mind? Should I bring a bottle of Smirnoff s and some cleaning fluid with me? Should I tell Carlton to drop in on Gandry and finish him off with a dry cleaner cocktail straight up? That's Cruset's best hospital trick."

"Don't tell him to do anything. That would be entrapment," said Dershon. "Simply tell him you've changed your mind. You've decided not to turn him in. Tell him you want to join him. Ask him what his next move is. Be careful not to openly suggest a conspiracy to him. Hint, but get him to utter the actual words. Make it be his plan. Then stick to him like a dirty shirt until he commits an overt act in furtherance of the conspiracy. Any act. Just getting in his car and starting it up is good enough. As long as the conspiracy is new."

"What conspiracy?" I asked.

"Any new criminal conspiracy. Gandry's good, or Target Nine, whatever it would normally be."

"I still wear blue," I said. "In case you've forgotten, I still have a bell around my neck. I'm still a cop."

"I like that," said Dershon. "Very nice image. The Blue Plague. It strikes only policemen. Well, we needn't be overly concerned. This is an undercover operation, not a search and seizure. You can wear blue for this one."

"However," said Honey, "what if Cruset doesn't fall for it? You'll still want Lou to pick up Carlton's files. We've got to find out how he gets his inside information. I think that's as important as anything. Lou shouldn't leave without those files, and he shouldn't touch those files if he's got this Blue Plague we're talking about."

"Are we on 'Candid Camera'?" I asked. "I keep thinking Dorothy Collins is going to pop up with a microphone and tell me you people have been pulling my leg."

"Honey's right," said Dershon. "We need a fallback position. Chief, begin composing a typewritten acceptance of Razzi's resignation, put the date prominently on it, and put in it that he is to get his pension and that your previous letter is to be disregarded in its entirety. Address it to him for hand-delivery right now. Make it clear in the letter that you have had a change of heart due to Mr. Razzi's recent good-faith efforts to aid law enforcement and your sincere hope that he return to Brazil. Do you have that, Chief, recent good-faith efforts and your sincere hope?"

"I got it."

"This is hairy," said Honey. "It's beginning to sound like dirty tricks and traps."

"Honey, leave the room," said Dershon. "For your own protection."

"Not on your life," said Honey.

"I think maybe you'd better, Honey," I said. "I don't know that I'm going to do this, but I want to hear him out, and he won't let it all hang out in front of you."

She said, "For you, I'll leave the room," and she did.

"Very well," said Dershon. "That leaves us, and us it will have to be. No one outside this room can ever know what we do here today. Do you have a Kel Kit, Chief?"

"Sure."

"Get it."

"What's that?" I asked.

"Civilian Razzi, you will wear a Kel Kit transmitter in an elastic body bandage against your belly. It will transmit to a monitor hooked up to a reel-to-reel recorder in Chief Covaletzki's vehicle."

"Don't make me laugh," I said. "The chief as my backup?"

"We have no choice. And he's not backup. You don't need backup for Cruset. The chief will just be there to man the tape recorder. He will be less than five hundred feet from you, listening to your progress and recording it at the same time. If you obtain a new conspiracy, we shall have a permanent record of it and all will be above board, so to speak. However, if you fail to elicit a new conspiracy, then a new game plan will go into effect. Merely signal to Covaletzki by working the words *Blue Plague* into your conversation. The chief will then close down his operation, erase what he has on his tape, and go home. You will then begin the alternate plan, the civilian plan."

"Which is?" I asked.

"As every cop knows, there is a clock in the city clerk's office that stamps the date and time on any piece of paper placed under it. It will occur to you after you leave here that the chief's letter ought to be stamped so that all the world will know that from that precise moment on you are a private citizen. Naturally, whatever you do you are doing on your own and for your own reasons, and there cannot be even the slightest hint that you acted as our agent, that you wore a department Kel Kit, or that Chief Covaletzki followed you, or that we had this entire conversation. We shall say that we told you your initial search and confession were illegal. To show our good faith and appreciation, we let you resign with a pension, hoping you would immediately go back to Brazil. We decided not to do anything further with your information until we could test-fire the rifle you brought us and find out if the FBI had a sufficient bullet fragment for comparison purposes, and even then we knew we couldn't use the rifle as evidence. We didn't know what to think, and we hadn't totally excluded you as a suspect. For all we knew, it was your rifle. We then called Marian Cruset in, advising her to free Professor Cruset — I'm saying that's what we *will* do, and we'll keep her here for two hours while I debrief her. That, Civilian Razzi, will be the extent of our knowledge. Apparently you, on your own, when you left us, decided to clock in Covaletzki's little letter and go back into the house to handle this matter, the same way you handled that whole thing with Gandry and Mrs. Smotz. You did leave the door unlocked, didn't you?"

"Yes, I did."

"If we are pressed, we shall freely admit that we wondered what sort of old-flame connection you had with Mrs. Cruset and whether your zealousness in pursuit of Cruset was in fact motivated by that connection. Whatever your motivation, we shall reluctantly applaud you when you return with the goods on Cruset for shooting Gandry, the Target files, and another confession.

"This civilian plan is risky. It may never result in the obtaining of admissible evidence, but it is decidedly better than your returning empty-handed. We shall never be able to use the rifle or the original confession, but the fact that you are now a civilian may cure you of the Blue Plague, such that whatever you get on this trip may be usable, and may not be 'fruit of the poisonous tree.' But who can say? It's a chance we'll have to take, if it comes to that. I implore you, however, to do your best to obtain a new conspiracy to kill Gandry. It is so much safer for us all. You cannot imagine."

"The cure for this plague," I said, "sounds worse than the disease. It would probably be unfair to blame your law school, so I'll just blame your parents. You weren't brought up right. You're the one sending me back out there, as your agent, whether I'm a cop or not. I'll never say I thought any of this up when I didn't. I won't tell stupid lies for you."

"You won't have to. We'll plea-bargain the case before it reaches a suppression hearing, but if we can't, you still won't need to testify. You can be temporarily in Brazil, even if only for a swim at Ipanema that lasts long enough to miss the suppression hearing. Covaletzki and I will do the testifying in accordance with the official version, and no matter what you think of me I shall feel no more guilt than a waiter who doesn't report all of his tips. You see, Civilian Razzi, these days there are so many rules that we are all guilty of something all of the time. We live in governmental original sin."

"Do you go along with this, Covaletzki?" I asked.

"Sure. It's a good idea. We gotta do the right thing here. So we bend the rules just a little bit. There's no harm done. We're only trying to get the truth out in the open. He might've framed some innocent people with his bullshit, just like what was done to you. You and me ought to be able to bury the hatchet long enough to get this job done, and he's right, you're the only one could do it now. Here's the wire transmitter. Help me put the reel-to-reel on the passenger seat. I'll give you a head start, and then I'll follow you."

"First give him the letter," said Dershon, "and while he's downstairs at the city clerk's, you and I shall run a test on the transmitter and check the batteries on the reel-to-reel, and then we shall set it up. Do this for us, Lou. Think of your daughter living with that man."

"You've got yourself a deal," I said. "On the way to the clerk's I'll say good night to Honey. She's probably pissed we kicked her out. You gentlemen are responsible for a lot of problems between us."

45

"You were very cruel to me," said Carlton as he sat on the edge of his bed, clutching his robe tight around him. "I thought I'd lose my mind in my secret room."

"Then you know how I felt in jail for two years," I said. "But you're free now. Doesn't it feel good?"

He sighed. "So now you want to help our cause. I just don't know if I've got any fight left." He closed his eyes wearily, hung his head, and sighed again as a horn beeped once in the distance. "Gandry was intended as practice, a learning experience to prepare me for the ultimate, Target Nine, but instead it wore me out."

"What are you saying? Wore you out? You have fight left. Take a deep breath. This is no time to let me down. I finally realize that you did Gandry, in part, for me. You knew how responsible I felt for little Johnny Mastropolito's death, and God bless your heart, Professor, you tried to do the right thing by me. I feel like an ingrate. I was selfish. The only thing I cared about was my personal safety, the fear of going to jail. Professor, it's a terrible fear, but I've recovered and so will you. We'll do Target Nine together. Like John Brown at Harpers Ferry."

"We got a problem, Professor," said Covaletzki as he stepped into the room pointing his .357 at me. "Move an inch from that chair, Razzi, and you're history. I know what you done to that trooper and to that guy up in New York. You ain't gettin' ten feet near me."

"That soft soap about Cruset framing innocent people came out of your mouth like rotten pork," I said. "It didn't fool me, but now I get the whole picture. You're Cruset's inside man. You've been feeding him information, haven't you?"

"You guessed it, shit-for-brains."

"I'm sure he pays well."

"I don't do it just for the money, but you wouldn't understand that."

I laughed. "You've had your hand out for money all your life. It's a habit with you. Like some people gamble, you skim."

"He's wearing a wire, Professor," he said. "He met with Dershon and them, and he came out here to get more on you. I volunteered to be his backup so's I could get you out of this thing. We gotta do something with him."

Professor Cruset sat in a daze like a prisoner of war.

"He's not telling you the whole truth," I said. "Before this is over he'll have to kill you, too. If he thought he could trust you to keep his name out of this, he wouldn't be in this room in the first place. He can't let you get arrested, get a lawyer, and look to make deals to save yourself. He'll kill me all right, but he'll make it look like you did it. Watch him ask if you've got any guns left lying around. Once he does me, he'll get you out for a ride, maybe to search for a place to bury me, then he'll kill you and bury us both. If you're lucky he'll kill you before you start digging the grave. He'll even pack a bag for you to make it look like you ran away after you killed me. By the time they find your body, if they ever do, no one will care how you bought it. And your Target files, what do you know, they'll disappear with you. Professor, he no more believes he needs your help in killing me than I do, but if you did help him kill me, he still could never trust you. You're too screwy."

Covaletzki's gun moved a half inch in the direction of Carlton.

"See, Professor," I said, "look how his gun moved ever so slightly. He can't trust you. He's going to do us both, only this time he's going to frame you instead of me. He's good at framing people, aren't you?"

"Yeah, I'm good at it. Look at you, dummy. I'm sorry, Professor, but he's got a point. I could never trust you. I got no choice. Believe me, this ain't somethin' I wanna do. Not to you anyway."

Professor Cruset looked old, very old and very pathetic. His mouth twitched, closing and opening as if he were nursing on his mother.

"That's enough, Covaletzki," I said, "don't torture him, and don't forget my wire." I lifted my shirt and showed him.

"Don't make me laugh." He waved the gun back at me. "It only transmits to the monitor in my car, and I turned the thing off before I got out. You must think I'm as dumb as you. You can't be serious with that shit."

"I'm as serious as a heart attack. I've been under the impression that everything we've been saying was being heard and recorded, that somebody even switched on your police radio and broadcast this conversation to cops all over the county. I can almost see their faces now."

"Your mind's gone, motherfucker, and you're goin' with it." He pulled a beat-up .25 automatic out of his pants pocket and smiled that pinch-lipped smile of his.

"The murder weapon," I said. "Beep the horn again, Honey. This is getting serious."

Covaletzki's car horn honked outside, and the color drained from his face as he realized just how serious it was.

46

My reward was to ride with Covaletzki back to the station. He cried most of the way. Through his sobs, and in between telling me he must have been out of his mind and that he had kids in college and that everything since he was born had been a struggle for him, he explained the frame: "Janasek paid off the Chester PD Vice once a month, and they laid off the old Body & Soul. Then the head of their Vice took care of us through Hanrahan. It was goin' on for a long time before I even got involved. Hanrahan worked it out with Janasek years back when Hanrahan ran Vice. Anyway, we laid off Janasek's Hotel in Delaware. The gamblin'. That's all. Then us guys on Vice got a taste on payday. Includin' DiGiacomo. Ask him yourself. He was in Vice three years. The fuck. He got his full cut, and he got his dick wet at the Body & Soul whenever he got a hard-on. Just like everybody else. Take my word for it. That's all the fuck there was to it. You can see it. Can't you? You started blabbin' to Janasek about the Body and Soul and about DiGiacomo leavin' Vice and becomin' your partner — Janasek got worried the Wilmington dicks were gonna start shakin' him down, too. Pretty soon everybody on the department's gonna have their hand out and he can't be supportin' everybody. So he gives me a bunch of shit and wants to know what he's payin' for, and I call Hanrahan. Hanrahan knew you weren't on the take and so he assumes you were on to his deal with the Chester PD. So he figures he's gotta nail you first before you nail him. A total misunderstanding. Everybody thought you was talkin' about the Body & Soul Lounge when you was talkin' about the old movie. Everybody panicked. Honest to God. That's it."

I believed him. It was just that stupid. Still, it really did make me feel free to hear his words after all those years. And you know, even he looked better after he told me. We both relaxed a lot, like the war was over. I can still hear the sound of his voice, word for word, and I can still close my eyes and feel the effect it had on me.

The whole frame was so quick and so mindless, so apparently motiveless, that Rocco didn't figure it out in '61. He just convinced himself that I grabbed a little money for myself and stuck it in my locker. I guess when you're on the take you have a tendency to believe it of everybody. But what Rocco considered his real crime of silence against me was that when Figaro's story surfaced in '76 and Rocco learned that I'd been framed, he said nothing to me about the regular paydays from Janasek. With Rocco it was understandable. He thought slowly. He always relied on a partner to do his thinking, his catcher to call his pitches. Rocco viewed his secret as not very useful information because he figured I'd never get to Figaro, so why expose himself for no reason? Besides, he had no idea that Covaletzki was involved. And he wasn't alone on that score. All my old friends thought it was just Hanrahan and Figaro. Rocco cried like crazy when I confronted him. He admitted the truth with a great sigh of relief, a palpable unburdening. I put my arm around Rocco and told him to forget it, that he couldn't know how his silent piece of the puzzle would have helped me get the picture sooner. I had to hear the real McCoy from Covaletzki, anyway, and that took what it took. Rocco took his pension with no further repercussions — thanks to Honey's going to bat for him with the city administration — and he and Rocco, Jr., started a small construction company.

Elmo Covaletzki, it seems, ran true to form for his entire career. As Hanrahan said on January 9, 1961: "Covaletzki here works a private-pay job every chance he gets. It's a sign of ambition." And then some. Janasek paid him. Professor Cruset paid him, and who knows how many other private paydays he had.

One tidy headline in the *News Journal* on the morning of November 11, 1976, tells the rest of the story about Covaletzki holding a gun on me and Dershon monkeying with the rules: CHIEF: TEN IN THE CAN; CHIEF DEPUTY: CANNED. I paid my driving-under-the-influence fine, but that didn't make the paper.

Every Brazilian opal mogul should have a Wilmington office. One never knows when the DuPont Company might close and Delaware need a new industry. So I opened up in Wilmington, and I keep tabs on the growing Lopes family by "interurbano America" and by having become a frequent flyer. The operation in Brazil is so smooth and successful that Lopes himself picks me up at the airport in Belém. Especially when I bring my American lawyer, Honey Esquire, now in private practice.

Somehow Figaro got wind of everything and one fine day he called me at the Wilmington office. He offered to meet with me for an hour some place in public in broad daylight for $10,000 in small bills, in advance. I told him I already owned the story he had for sale, but for him to do keep in touch.

Sarah is a tough subject to talk about. The day after Covaletzki's arrest and Carlton's exposure, and with Marian's help and Honey's help, I got Sarah to agree to see a psychiatrist that Honey knew, one who specializes in the needs of rape victims.

For the first time Sarah told the three of us about having had severe anxiety attacks and recurrent nightmares since shortly after the rape. It was quite a moment. Here, I had just brought about the downfall of the only father Sarah had ever known, yet incredibly she was opening up to me. The freedom to break silence, to confess things, to open up, to talk, had an immediate healing effect on her. In the past she had waxed eloquent about this basic human need to speak the truth, yet she had been herself denied the right to practice it for far too long. One night a few weeks later in Montreal, she told us that the worst influence on her life was not the rape but the fear of death during the rape, the fear of any moment becoming cold, stiff, and lifeless forever. As everlastingly harmful as was the rape, compared to the imminence of death, the rape was like the wallet you give to a robber to keep him from killing you. At least that's what she believes it was in her case. She continues in therapy. She's faced up to the fact that Carlton's crime of silence — keeping the rape a secret to "protect" Sarah and to foreclose any questioning of his own masculinity — has done her more harm than good. Because treatment was delayed, the scars are uglier and the wounds incompletely healed. But she also knows that her adoptive father acted, in part, out of ignorance, and she keeps in touch with him. Her sexuality and her feelings toward men are tangled, but not irretrievably so. There are no easy answers for my daughter, but little by little I see a sense of humor coming out like a recessive gene. So I know the therapy is working. God bless. And God bless her for trusting me and God bless Marian for encouraging it.

While we were up in Montreal later that summer with Sarah watching Nadia Comaneci set the world on fire, Honey asked me why I had used her and not Rocco to nail down my Target Nine — my getting of a brand-new usable conspiracy against Covaletzki. Why I had approached her outside the chief's office on my way to the city clerk, made her my backup, and bombarded her with orders: "Tail Covaletzki to Cruset's. If he leaves his car and goes into the house, get into his car any way you can. Smash the window if you have to. Turn on the battery-operated reel-to-reel and tune us back in from a Kel Kit they're going to put on me. Call for help on his radio and then leave the mike on to broadcast our conversation. Beep the horn once to signal to me that everything is done. Then sit tight and listen. If it gets hairy, scram." Well, I explained my threefold reasoning: (a) "it would make a more interesting story if a woman did it," (b) she "deserved a chance" to atone for her betrayal, and (c) Covaletzki would be less likely to notice her little yellow Subaru following him than Rocco's blue Plymouth. She wasn't satisfied with my answer and kept on me until I finally broke. "Honey," I confessed, "I didn't have a whole lot of time to explain what I needed, and if and where and how. I needed a smart cookie in a hurry, a speed listener, my very own Flushing, New York, hot momma with big brains."

Because of the information contained in the Target files, ironically, the attorney general had to release several convicted people before their time. They got what the courthouse regulars called a Cruset pardon. Who knows, maybe they were all innocent to begin with. Because of the illegal way I had gathered Target files and the fact that Carlton refused to testify against any of them, the attorney general could not prosecute the false witnesses.

Target Seven, Harrison Lloyd, was never arrested for the unspeakable murder of Shy Whitney, but he's still doing time for everything else. Maybe lucky for him. Target Eight, John Gandry, never came out of his coma and died in the hospital. We never did get a new conspiracy or any usable evidence against the professor, so he too escaped prosecution. At the height of all the "sordid" media exposure, Marian divorced him. He settled nicely on her, liquidated his assets and moved alone to — guess where — Harpers Ferry, West Virginia, the bloody battleground of his hero John Brown the abolitionist and the home of Professor Andrew Bliss, Carlton's fictional *hashashin*. So far he appears to have retired quietly without ever getting to his Target Nine, "whatever it would normally be," in the words of Dershon.

Honey told me that an old college friend of hers took a security job at the U.S. Supreme Court. On her first day they handed her a gun, a name tag, and a recent candid photograph of Professor Carlton Cruset.

I said, "Oh my God, I hope the old boy's not still pissed off."

Honey said, "If I were in your shoes, buster, I wouldn't be losing any sleep over his Target Nine. I'd be worried about his Target Ten."

"Hmm," I said. "Just how effective do you think you'll be at throwing your body across mine to shield me when the shooting starts?"

"I honestly don't know, Lou, but you have the right to remain silent while I practice. If you can."